ISAAC ASIMOV PRESENTS
THE BEST SCIENCE FICTION FIRSTS

Also by the editors

Isaac Asimov Presents the Best Fantasy of the 19th Century

*Isaac Asimov Presents the Best Horror and Supernatural
of the 19th Century*

Isaac Asimov Presents the Best Science Fiction of the 19th Century

ISAAC ASIMOV

PRESENTS THE BEST
SCIENCE FICTION FIRSTS

Edited by Isaac Asimov,
Charles G. Waugh,
and Martin H. Greenberg

BEAUFORT BOOKS, INC.
New York / Toronto

*No character in this book is intended to
represent any actual person; all the incidents
of the stories are entirely fictional in nature.*

*Library of Congress Cataloging in Publication Data
Main entry under title:*

Isaac Asimov presents the best science fiction firsts.

*1. Science fiction, American.   I. Asimov, Isaac, 1920–
II. Waugh, Charles.   III. Greenberg, Martin Harry.
IV. Title: Best science fiction firsts.*
PS648.S3I77   1984   *813'0876'08*   *83-21405*
ISBN 0-8253-0184-X

*"Minus Planet," by John D. Clark, Ph.D., copyright © 1937 by
Street & Smith Publications, Inc. Reprinted by permission of the author.*

*"Yesterday House," by Fritz Leiber, copyright © 1952 by Galaxy
Publishing Corporation. Reprinted by permission of Robert P. Mills,
Ltd.*

*"Neutron Star," by Larry Niven, copyright © 1966 by Galaxy Publish-
ing Corporation. Reprinted by permission of Kirby McCauley, Ltd.*

*"The Faithful," by Lester del Rey, copyright © 1938 by Street & Smith
Publications, Inc. Reprinted by permission of the author and his agents,
the Scott Meredith Literary Agency, Inc., 845 Third Ave, New York 10022.*

*"The Voyage that Lasted 600 Years," by Don Wilcox, copyright ©
1940 by Ziff-Davis Publishing Co. Reprinted by arrangement with
Forrest J. Ackerman as Holding Agent; Heir or Estate please contact
Ackerman Agency at 2495 Glendower Ave., Hollywood, CA 90027.*

*"A Logic Named Joe," by Murray Leinster, copyright © 1946 by Street
& Smith Publications Inc. Reprinted by permission of the agents for the
author's estate, the Scott Meredith Literary Agency, Inc., 845 Third
Avenue, New York, NY 10022.*

*"The Test," by Richard Matheson, copyright © 1954; copyright
renewed © 1982 by Richard Matheson. Reprinted by permission of Don
Congdon Associates, Inc.*

*"Reason," by Isaac Asimov, copyright © 1941 by Street & Smith
Publications, Inc. Copyright renewed © 1969 by Isaac Asimov.
Reprinted by permission of the author.*

*Published in the United States by Beaufort Books, Inc., New York.
Published simultaneously in Canada by General Publishing Co. Limited*

Printed in the U.S.A.   First Edition
10 9 8 7 6 5 4 3 2 1

CONTENTS

Introduction:
TO BE THE FIRST

Isaac Asimov

There is glory in being the first to do something admirable—the first to climb Mt. Everest, the first to run a four-minute mile, the first to go around the world by ship, or by airplane, or by rocket.

It may be that others can then repeat the task and do it with just as much bravery or skill, but to be hundred and fifty-second, or even twenty-second, or even *second* is somehow meaningless. In the races of the world, there are only two divisions: first and also-ran.

The result is a tendency to sub-classify in order to multiply the firsts—not merely to feed the vanity of the doers but to increase the satisfaction of the watchers. There is such a thing as a first man in orbit, but also a first American in orbit, a first woman in orbit. The time will undoubtedly come when we will have a first married couple in orbit, a first teenager in orbit, a first person from West Virginia in orbit and so on. If you want to see this thing carried to an extreme, consider the baseball record book, where you can find out which third-baseman hit the most doubles in a single season in home games on cloudy days.

When we think of firsts, we usually think of physical feats, but it seems to me that what separates human beings from other living things is not a matter of physical attributes but mental ones. It is a much more human feat to be the first to get an unusual idea and to place it before humanity.

For instance, who was the first to get the idea of a lost civilization. It seems to us now that that is a very easy idea to have, even a hackneyed one—but that's only because enough people have now talked about such things to weary us with the whole notion. But suppose you lived in a primitive society in which you knew only what you saw and remembered

1

and were told by older people. The universe would be bounded within a few dozen square miles and three or four generations, and why should it ever occur to you that there might be other people beyond the horizon and before the haze of memory.

It isn't easy to put one's self into that position, but perhaps you can get a notion of the difficulty of being a cogitative first if, right now, you try to imagine in detail some plausible idea that no one else has ever had.

I won't wait for you, but will go on to say that the first person, as far as we know, who had the lost-civilization idea for the first time was Plato, the Greek philosopher. In the fourth century B.C., he wrote two dialogues in which he described the story of Atlantis.

I say *as far as we know*. How can we be sure that Plato was not building on the ideas of predecessors? He himself describes the story as having been told to Solon, an Athenian statesman who lived two centuries earlier than he, by Egyptian priests. The Egyptians may well have had records of the destruction of the island of Thera by a volcanic eruption, and the fatal weakening of the Minoan civilization thereby, eleven centuries before the time of Plato. Plato, then, perhaps did not have a new idea but was merely presenting an old fact in attractive literary guise.

How can we know?

We know that Yuri Gagarin was the first person to orbit the Earth in a spaceship, and we know that Neil Armstrong was the first person whose footwear made physical contact with the moon's surface, but ideas and concepts are a little harder to pin down.

It is very tempting to say that the first person who conceived of a voyage to the Moon was Lucian of Samosata who, in the second century, wrote a tale in which he describes such a voyage. What we are really saying, however, is that Lucian was the first person to write a story based on such an idea. Even that is perhaps not as good as it sounds. He was the first person to write such a story, copies of which have survived to our time. Can we be sure that earlier stories were not written; that they have not survived? Can we be sure that millions of people have not looked at the Moon and imagined being carried there by birds or angels or demons; that they did not have the literary skill to write about it?

Well, then, let us confine ourselves to writers and not pretend to be readers of human minds. And since writers whose profession it is to think up new ideas, or to try to do so, are usually science fiction writers, let us confine ourselves to them. For instance—

Newton, in 1687, worked out the laws of motion, including the third law—that of action and reaction—which is the principle that serves to accelerate a rocket. By that time, scientists had known for some forty years that air did not fill the Universe but was restricted to a thin layer about the Earth, and that the space between the Earth and Moon was almost entirely vacuum. That enormously complicated the notion of travelling from the Earth to the Moon and, in fact, Newton showed that the only method of doing so (known in his time) was to make use of the rocket principle. (Even in our own time, this remains the only known way of reaching the Moon.)

Well, then, who was the first science fiction writer who seized upon this Newtonian picture of the Universe and who mentioned rockets in connection with a trip to the Moon. The answer is Cyrano de Bergerac (yes, he really lived, nose and all) and the odd thing is that he talked about rockets as a way of reaching the Moon in a book he wrote in 1650, almost forty years before Newton presented his great theories. Does this mean that Cyrano should get some of the credit showered upon Newton? No! Cyrano was merely speculating idly while Newton advanced his ideas with mathematical and scientific rigor.

If this is one of the most amazing examples of science fictional prescience, almost as amazing are the ideas that science fiction writers fail to get. For instance, during the first part of the twentieth century, innumerable science fiction stories were written about trips to the moon, before such a trip became a reality. During that time, too, innumerable science fiction stories dealt with television before it was a reality. As far as I know, however, not a single science fiction story prior to 1969 combined the notions and described a landing on the Moon that was carried out with hundreds of millions of people on Earth watching the process by television. Yet that is what happened in 1969. (I am told, however, that the combination of notions did take place in the comic strip "Alley Oop," in a sequence that was drawn prior to 1969, which is all the more reason, I think, that professional science fiction writers ought to be chagrined.)

Can we make a collection of "first ideas," then? Yes, if we set up reasonable limits.

In the first place, we have to eliminate the mere concept. People having imagined invisible beings throughout history and, undoubtedly, far back into prehistoric times, but suppose we consider only surviving written stories about invisible beings?

3

What's more, we want to eliminate fanciful myths and legends, but restrict ourselves to modern science fiction, as written since 1800.

Furthermore, considerations of space make it impossible to include novels, while presenting a portion of a novel designed merely to display a new idea is likely to make for frustrating reading. Therefore, let us confine ourselves to modern science fiction short stories.

In that case, we now present you with twelve first-rate science fiction short stories, each of which represents the first appearance of an interesting idea. Read and enjoy.

(Note: Even within the narrow limits we have set, it is possible that, in one or more cases, we missed an earlier science fiction short story dealing with the idea in question. Do let us hear from you if you know of such a case.)

ANTIMATTER

The construction of antimatter is the reverse of ordinary matter. For example the neutrally charged antineutron has an oppositely oriented magnetic movement and the positron is a positively charged equivalent to the negatively charged electron. First proposed by physicist Paul Dirac in 1928, the concept was supported by the discovery of the positron in 1932. Antiprotons and antineutrons were subsequently observed in particle accelerators in 1955.

Most believe antimatter constitutes an extremely small proportion of the universe, though some have speculated about the existence of antimatter galaxies. However, the phenomenon captured the imagination of many science fiction writers possibly because exploding radiation occurs when antimatter touches matter.

The first antimatter story appears to be "Minus Planet" (*Astounding Stories*, April 1937). Its author, John D. Clark, was a professional chemist and rocket scientist until retirement. One of only two science fiction stories he published, it remains an entirely readable and important work even though most of its science is now dated.

Subsequent antimatter stories include those by A. E. van Vogt, James Blish, Fredric Brown, and Larry Niven as well as novels such as Charles Harness's *The Ring of Ritornel* (1968) and Ian Watson's *The Jonah Kit* (1975).

For obvious reasons, a popular theme seems to be the not-to-be-consummated romance between a matter man and an antimatter woman (or vice versa). A good example is A. Bertram Chandler's "Chance Encounter" (included in *Starships*, Fawcett-Crest, 1983) which introduces his famous series character John Grimes.

5

MINUS PLANET

John D. Clark, Ph.D. (1937)

I

*N*ow that it's all over, and we have escaped the more serious of the possible consequences, we wonder why we were so slow to see what was happening. For it might have been foreseen. We knew that the position of man in the universe was precarious enough, and that the very existence of matter itself wasn't much more stable. That is—we knew it, but we didn't realize it. There *is* a difference, and that difference was almost enough to eliminate not only man but the Earth itself from celestial history.

The warnings were plain enough. They lasted for years. Biologists had noticed that the evolution of animal and plant life in the northern hemisphere was steadily accelerating due, probably, to the gradual and completely inexplicable increase in the intensity of the cosmic rays from the direction of Polaris.

These rays increased the number of mutations in the germ plasm of all living matter exposed to them. New varieties of plants, freak animals, queer monsters born to normal men and women, were coming into the world at a steadily increasing rate. There were advantages, of course. Many of the new varieties of plants and animals were extremely useful, and there were geniuses as well as monsters born to commonplace human beings. But, on the whole, the inhabitants of the planet didn't like the situation. The scientists liked it even less than did anybody else. You see, they couldn't explain it—and when a scientist can't explain something, he is likely to be annoyed. It makes him look so foolish.

7

It was on January 15, 2156, that the astrophysicist, Dr. James Carter, had the first glimmer of light—literally. He was working on the new five-hundred-inch reflector of the Mt. McKinley observatory at the time, and noticed a darkening of his photographic plate from the spectrometer focused on Polaris in the northern sky. He repeated his observation, and got the same result; a uniform darkening over the whole spectral range.

"As though," he said to his assistant, "the whole damned spectrum were light struck! And I never knew any source of light that would give a continuous spectrum from infrared to cosmic rays, with the cosmics the strongest. There doesn't seem to be any line structure at all—just as though there were a hot body out there heated to a few billion degrees centigrade!"

The assistant, Dr. Michael Poggenpohl, usually known as Doc Mike, wrinkled his diminutive nose, and scratched his flaming head. "That," he remarked, "doesn't make sense! A body that hot on the outside wouldn't stay that way. And where did it come from, anyway, Jimmy?"

Jimmy uncoiled his six foot three of giraffelike build from his usual thinking position (in which he rested comfortably on the back of his neck), lighted a cigarette, and grunted. The noise was not gracious, but neither was his mood nor the expression on his somewhat battered face.

"Right now, I want some information on where this alleged source of light is. Will you make arrangements for the observatories on Mars and Venus to take simultaneous observations with us on the northern sky? No, I don't want a spectrum. I *have* a spectrum, and it has me baffled. I merely want a simple photographic observation. Everything this object, whatever it is, is sending out, seems to affect the plate. And I want to know *where* it is. The question of *what* it is, can wait. Move on now, little one, and pretend that you're earning the money the commissariat of science is paying you!"

Mike held his nose insultingly, and moved to obey. "And how about the jack," he asked sweetly, "that they're foolish enough to waste on you?"

"It's not waste, old fruit. Geniuses have to be supported. I'm the genius!"

"I've been wondering what it was. I thought you must be somebody's uncle. O.K., I'll get the messages off right away. The light-beam operator ought to be able to get in touch with Mars directly, but Venus is on the other side of the Sun right now, and he'll have to relay to him.''

"Don't bother me with trifles! Go away and let me think in peace!"

"You mean loaf," said Mike, and departed.

But Jimmy didn't loaf when the other man had gone. He reached for a dozen reference books, a slide rule, and a wad of paper, and immediately became oblivious to all about him. He remained in that state for some hours, and only returned to the real world when Mike reappeared with the televised plates from the other observatories. They all showed the same thing: a small, brilliant point against the background of the northern constellations.

It had evidently been overlooked previously, since it was almost invisible to the eye, even through the largest telescope, and appeared only on the photographic plate, which was sensitive to the invisible ultraviolet, gamma, and cosmic radiation which accounted for the major part of its energy. The plates were sent via pneumatic tube to the calculating room, with a request that the distance of the unknown body be determined, if possible, from the observations of the three planets. The two scientists sat down to think it over.

"Mike, what do you know about matter, anyway? What's it composed of?"

"What's the matter? I thought *you* were the genius. And why ask a kindergarten question at this time of day, anyway?"

"Go on, go on. I'm asking the questions. What's matter made of?"

"Well, if you must know, it seems to be made of assorted particles of electricity. An atom consists of a heavy, positive nucleus, with a lot of light, negative electrons floating around it. To be precise, the nucleus consists of, say, 'z' protons and 'n' neutrons. They weigh almost the same, and the protons have unit positive charges, while the neutrons are neutral. The whole nucleus has a positive charge, then, of plus 'z'. (Ordinary hydrogen hasn't any neutrons—just a single lone proton for a nucleus.) Then, of course, there are 'z' negative electrons floating around outside to neutralize the whole affair. You ought to know, though! You developed the method of splitting the nucleus on a commercial scale to get the energy out of it!"

"Yes, yes, I know. But what is a proton made of?"

"That? Oh, it seems to be a neutron closely tied up with a

positron—a *positive* electron that doesn't weigh much of anything.''

''Then, candidate, what are the fundamental units of matter?''

''What is this, anyhow? Another damned Ph.D. exam? The *fundamental* particles would be the neutron, with most of the mass and no charge, and the positron and electron, with positive and negative charge respectively, and no mass to speak of. And so what?''

''Very good, Rollo. And now, what is light?''

''T'hell with light! I can think of lots better things to discuss.'' He flicked the communicator switch, and the round face of the commissary clerk looked out at him from the view plate. ''Send up two—no—four liters of beer! And make sure it's cold!''

Carter grinned like a ghoul, and slid farther down on his neck. ''Make that six liters, will you? But this is serious. What happens when a positron meets an electron?''

''All right,'' Doc Mike said wearily. ''You get a photon of light coming out of where the two met. Can be most any frequency—usually very high, cosmic or gamma. I wish he'd hurry with that beer! And what's this all about, anyhow?''

''Wait and see—and get ready for a trip. I need the information on those plates, though, and several sets of observations some days apart. Here's the beer!''

II

Two weeks later two frightened scientists looked at each other over the final results from the calculating room. The figures were before them. The unknown, which continued to radiate faintly but continuously in its peculiar fashion, was some ten thousand million miles from the Earth, and was coming closer. And unless the gods of mathematics had completely forsaken them, within two years it would hit the Earth, or come so close to it that the latter would be as thoroughly wrecked as though it had sustained a direct hit.

The body was not large—no larger than the Moon—but its manner of radiation was unique. High-frequency light comes from a hot body. And a body that small *couldn't* be that hot; it would have cooled off long ago. And if it *were* that hot, the intensity of the radiation received by the Earth would have been much greater—greater, in fact, than that received from the Sun, in spite of the small size of the unknown and its great distance from the Earth. It just didn't make sense. And it didn't make sense to the other astronomers of the solar system. Nothing had appeared in the popular press, nor was it likely to. An iron-clad censorship had been clamped down. The danger was serious enough, and panic would make it worse.

Carter spoke. "We're going out to take a look, Mike. Or I am, anyway. Would you like to come along?"

"Uh-huh. You need somebody to take care of you. When do we leave?"

"In half an hour. My ship is ready to go. It has a lot of new gadgets on it, too. This should be a good chance to try them out. Let's go."

Just half an hour later the rocket blasted free from the snow-covered space port near the observatory. It was an improved experimental model of those used at the time, all of which depended upon the principle discovered and developed by Carter himself, which had made space travel something more than an insane gamble.

Hydrogen gas was fed into the converter, where terrific static and magnetic fields converted it into helium. Immense energy, developed from the loss of mass, appeared in the process, which energy imparted a tremendous velocity to the flaming helium gas which escaped through the rocket jets at the stern of the ship. An acceleration up to ten times that of gravity could be maintained, but five gravities was the usual limit for any length of time. More than that, and the passengers lost consciousness. Five was uncomfortable enough, but men in good training could stand it, if they didn't attempt to move from their padded and pivoted chairs.

The trip was uneventful. A week later the rocket was circling cautiously around the unknown body. It was about the size of the Moon, but little could be seen of its surface, which appeared to be under a continuous bombardment with some immensely high explosive. The flashes from the explosions, consisting mainly of cosmic, gammas, and UV's, were evidently the source of the light which had puzzled the observers. Carter and Poggenpohl crouched behind their lead-glass screens and watched.

"Looks like a fluorescent screen being bombarded by electrons, Jimmy. Somewhat larger scale, though. More bombardment on the forward side, too."

"Yes, there is. It looks as though it were sweeping a path through space as it approaches the Earth. Man that gun, will you, please, and fire a solid shot at it when we go around the rear of it again?''

"O.K. Don't see what you're driving at, though. Do you expect a bell to ring, like in a shooting gallery? I'll signal when I fire, and aim directly at the center when we're exactly behind it.''

The minute went by, then, "Ready—fired! Watch for it!''

There was no need to watch. Twenty minutes later, when the hundred-pound piece of steel hit the surface of the wandering planet, there was a tremendous flash, dwarfing those which had been observed.

Carter appeared to be pleased, or at least satisfied, and called to the other. "All right, Mike. I'm going to cut the rockets and let the ship take up an orbit around this peculiar object. You take the measurements of distance to the surface and time the orbit, and I'll measure its diameter. Considering the fate of that piece of steel you sent out of the gun, I don't think we'll land this time. It might be unhealthy.''

There followed a period of several hours, during which the only sound was the click of the calculating machine, and Mike's gasp as he saw the final result. "Good Lord, Jimmy! This cockeyed animal isn't any bigger than the Moon, and she weighs as much as Jupiter! Are we nuts—or is it?''

Jimmy laughed as he cut in the rockets and swung the ship around for home. "The latter, Mike! *It's* demented—completely. We're no crazier than usual. Gather around and I'll explain.''

"It's about time! Now, *what* have you got up your sleeve, anyway?''

"You remember, when we first saw this thing, I put you through a quiz on matter? I had a hunch then, and I've proved it. You described the sort of matter with which we are familiar. Look here. You said that matter was made up of neutrons and positrons, in the last analysis, in the nuclei, and of electrons on the outside. Well, there is another sort of matter possible. What is to prevent an *electron* from combining closely with a neutron, and forming a *negative* proton? The possibility was mentioned way back in 1934, and I think the old boy even gave his hypothetical particle a name—an 'antron,' I think he called it. Now take some of these antrons, and some extra neutrons, and make a nucleus out of them, and then release enough positrons on the outside to balance the

12

antrons. And one has an atom with a *negative* atomic number, since the atomic number of an atom, of course, is the number of positive charges on the nucleus.

"And now one makes a whole universe with these minus elements. And one makes oneself out of them, too, and lives in the place, and can't tell the difference between it and a regular universe. All the physical laws will be the same—but just wait until part of your new universe hits part of a regular universe! Then there'll be the devil to pay and no pitch hot! Figure it out. What do you think will happen?"

"Uh—let's see. First the outer electrons in our matter will neutralize the outer positrons in the reverse matter—and there'll be a hell of a lot of light or other radiation—UV, gamma, cosmic and what not. Then the nuclei will get together. Nothing will happen to either set of neutrons. But the positrons on the protons will neutralize the electrons on the antrons, and there'll be another burst of radiation and a lot of neutrons left over. So the net result will be a mob of neutrons and a flock of radiation. What do you think? Is that thing out there"—he gestured toward the anomalous planet they were leaving behind—"out of a reverse universe?"

"I think so. It has all the symptoms. Long, long ago, how long ago, Heaven only knows, it escaped from some nebula in outer space—some nebula that's built in reverse—and headed this way. And here it is. The glowing and flashing surface is the result of its contact with cosmic dust—the little particles of matter that drift around through all space. And every time it picks some up there's a flash; all the charged particles are neutralized and head away from it as light. And it has added a few more neutrons to its collection. They probably sift down to the center of gravity of the thing. That's why it's so infernally heavy."

"Then, teacher"—Mike was having an idea—"it was probably a rather ordinary planet when it started out on its travels. Barring being built backward, that is! I'd make a guess that it was about half the mass of Jupiter when it started, and, I suppose, had about half the volume. But every time it picked up some normal matter it both shrunk and got heavier. The mass of the positrons and electrons lost would be too small to lose sleep over, and, on the average, it would pick up one neutron for every one of its own freed from a nucleus.

"So it's 'most used up now—an awful flock of neutrons left, and just a little bit of normal reverse matter. The neutrons will have most of

13

the mass, and the reverse matter will take up almost all of the space. Neutrons don't take up any volume to speak of.''

"Right. So now it has twice the mass it started with, approximately, and a minute fraction of its original volume. When the rest of the reverse matter is finally neutralized it will be a little heavier, and so small that it'll be completely invisible. Maybe there'll be a few cubic centimeters of neutrons, or some absurd amount like that, with all that mass. But we'd better hurry! It won't be very amusing if that neutralizing is done with some of the Earth's surface! Hold tight—here comes some acceleration!''

III

Ten days later Carter and Poggenpohl presented their report to the commissariat of science of the United States of America, and two days later they attended an emergency meeting of the heads of the departments of science of the governments of the world. Carter was speaking.

"So you see, gentlemen, what the situation is. You all understand the theory of the phenomenon, and you know that the observatories of the world and of the other two inhabited planets have checked our own telescopic observations. In addition, there is the phenomenon we observed when the six-inch projectile hit this—this—''

"Call it 'Gus,' '' whispered Mike disrespectfully.

Jimmy glared at him, and continued, ''—this—minus planet. I am aware of no alternative theory to explain the behavior of this anomalous body, and most of you appear to be inclined to adhere to the one Dr. Poggenpohl and I have presented.'' He looked around the table and saw nothing but a succession of reluctant nods.

"Then, the question is, what to do about it? If it were normal matter it would be bad enough. But then, it might be possible to install huge rocket tubes on the intruder and drive it out of its course sufficiently to miss the Earth by a safe margin. But what can we do with this thing, when, if we touch it, we shall be annihilated? And if we don't touch it, we shall be annihilated anyhow. At least the Earth, and those who can't escape to the other planets will be annihilated, and that means ninety-nine per cent of the population. For you know that our combined rocket fleets aren't enough to move one per cent of the Earth's population in the time we have available. And even if we could move them—the other planets are only barely inhabitable by man, and certainly could not support all of us.''

''There's one thing we must do,'' remarked the science commissary of the Russians, ''and that is to keep this situation a secret, for the present at least. For if we don't, there will be such a rush for the few rockets we have that half the world's population will be killed in a few days in the panic. And the rockets themselves will be smashed. We won't be able to do anything at all with them.''

''There's no doubt at all on that point,'' said the delegate from the Federated States of Europe. ''I take it that the meeting is unanimous on that point?'' There was another chorus of nods, but this time more enthusiastic. ''But has anybody any idea of how to move this—minus planet—out of the course it's following?''

There was a sodden silence, and then Mike rose slowly to his feet, his red hair bristling with what looked like an idea. ''Gentlemen, there's one other way to move our little country cousin out of his course. Hit him with something heavy that's moving fast enough to do the job.''

''But what will happen to that thing, whatever it is? Won't it be annihilated?''

''Not so you could notice it, when it comes to the effect. All the electrons and positrons will be gone, and it won't be normal matter any more, but the neutrons will be left, and they will have the momentum they started with.''

''Very well, Herr Poggenpohl, but what can we hit it with that will be big enough to make any difference? All the space ships in the solar system, firing all their biggest guns for a year, wouldn't be enough to do anything to its course! After all, it weighs as much as Jupiter!''

''There's one projectile available that would be big enough to make quite a perceptible dent in its path: the Moon! We can spare it. All it does is produce the tides. Mount rocket tubes on the Moon, pry it up out of the solar system, and sock the intruder so that its course will be changed and it will fall into the Sun! We can do that if we hit it while it's still far enough away from the system.''

The council gasped at the suggestion, and there was a chorus of excited protests, which slowly died, as the sheer magnitude of the plan gripped the imaginations of the assembled scientists. Nobody thought of putting the question to a formal vote, and in twenty minutes the meeting had been changed, automatically, into an executive council, which was in an excited argument about ways and means, in which calculating machines, reference books, celestial mechanics, the quantum theory, and polylingual profanity played a prominent part.

Carter pounded on the table and shouted until he managed to attract the attention of the disputants. "Gentlemen," he said, "I suggest that we present our plans to the various governments, in order to obtain their cooperation in the execution of our project. And I also suggest that publicity can do no harm now, since we have an apparently practicable remedy for the difficulty. The amateur astronomers will let the cat out of the bag very soon, anyway, if we don't make some statement. And finally, may I suggest that we request the President of the United States to make a television broadcast, explaining the situation to the public, asking their cooperation, and assuring them that the said situation is, as it were, well in hand?"

The assembled scientists stared blankly at him, nodded absent-mindedly, and returned to their discussion, more violently than before. Carter grinned at Mike, lighted a cigarette, and wandered out of the room, in search of a communicator in some place that was quiet enough so that he could make his message to the President heard above the din.

The President revealed the danger to the world in one of his famous fireside broadcasts, concluding with a request that every one remain quietly at his normal duties, unless called upon to cooperate in some way with the scientists who were working at what appeared to be a practicable method of saving the planet.

The heads of the other governments of the world made similar broadcasts.

As might be expected, most of the population of the Earth paid no attention to the broadcasts, being quite unable to realize the situation. The Earth had never been destroyed, therefore it could not be destroyed, and the scientists were crazy as usual. That attitude was typical of the major part of the inhabitants of the globe—the great, average masses.

But there were two other attitudes apparent. On the one side there were those intelligent enough to understand the danger and the measures that were being taken against it. They were the scientists, engineers, and technicians of the world, and the well-educated part of the other classes of the population.

On the other side were the unbalanced, the fanatics, and the extremely ignorant, who were the tools of the first two. They rioted, for no apparent reason, but merely because they were frightened, they tried to make up in two years for the dullness of their lives, not realizing that the dullness of those lives was largely due to the dullness of their intellects. Some of them—and they were less trouble than the others—merely got drunk and remained that way. A few of them actively obstructed the work that had to be done.

One of them, one Obidiah Miller, who had been, it was rumored, a circuit rider in the Tennessee Mountains, was the most virulent. He was an ignorant man, but he possessed a native shrewdness which, combined with his surprising oratorical powers and his religious fanaticism, had a tremendous effect on the more ignorant and weak-minded portions of the population.

Fanatics are always followed by fools, of which there is an inexhaustible supply. When the danger appeared, the intelligent parts of the populace decided that the reasonable thing to do was to cooperate with the scientists who were trying to cope with it. The fanatics proclaimed, and the fools believed, that the approaching calamity was the judgment of God on an impious world. Especially did they protest that the Moon should not be moved. First, because it couldn't be moved; second, because the Lord hadn't intended it to move; and third, because, since God had evidently intended that the minus planet should destroy the Earth for its wickedness, it would be an act of impiety even to attempt to avert the collision.

"Would ye seek, brethren, to attempt to stave off the Day of Judgment, as foretold in the Holy Scriptures? Would ye seek"—his hill-billy accent rolled out over the sheep-faced crowd—"to avert the day when the righteous shall be raised to the right hand of God, and the wicked shall be cast down to Hell? Will ye let the wicked meddlers into matters that are best left alone attempt to stave off the almighty hand of God? Wreck the space ports! Smash the rockets! Kill the idolators!"

There was an answering rumble from the crowd, as Mike and Jimmy slipped away from its outskirts. "The 'idolators,' " Mike remarked, as they sidled into a building, "sounds like us. I would recommend, with all due respect to the gentleman's religious convictions, that steps be taken. With an ax, for choice, before he starts gumming the works."

"There appears to be something in what you say. Personally, I have no desire to become a martyr to science before it's absolutely necessary. Let's get the chief of the Federal police on the wire, and have him gather our friend in and send his congregations home. And some guards with machine guns and things around the space ports might not be amiss. We haven't any time to be bothered by fools!''

In the next few days there was an epidemic of raids on the pseudo-religious protest meetings, and there was a great gathering-in of the more rabid of the fanatics, including Obidiah Miller, who was planted, gently but firmly, in a lunatic asylum. Guards were placed around the space ports, and assigned to the more important of the scientists who were employed on the gigantic task. There were a few attempts at sabotage and assassination, but all of them failed.

The work was pressed. The astronomical observatory on the Moon was dismantled and carried to the Earth piecemeal, as were many of the valuable fittings of the space port there. Since the development of atomic power, this port was not as necessary as it had been in the old days of combustion rockets. Then, the huge atomic drills, operated by men in space suits, started the excavation of the deep shafts that were to act as rocket tubes. Some fifty of them were drilled, most of them parallel, but a few at divergent angles, to act as the steering mechanism of the huge space ship into which Luna was being converted. At the bases of these shafts the reaction chambers were excavated, and lined with refractory material. The automatic fuel-supply system was installed, whereby millions of tons of the very material of the satellite itself were carried to the reaction chambers.

There, the lighter elements, oxygen, silicon, aluminum, etc., were to be converted into iron vapor, which was to be driven out of the rocket tubes by the atomic energy released in the process. Iron itself, though common on the Moon, was not suitable as a fuel, since, in respect to *atomic* changes, it is the most stable of all the elements. The whole fuel system was automatically controlled, with all controls in duplicate.

The controlling mechanism, which consisted, in effect, of fifty throttles—one for each rocket tube—was arranged to be controlled by remote radio control from a space ship, which would convoy the huge projectile to its destination. All the rocket tubes, of course, were on one hemisphere of the Moon, since there would be no need of stopping it in its course, once it had been started.

Thousands of men were needed for the construction work—of all types from manual laborers to astrophysicists. And all of them were working at high pressure. Work never stopped for months at a time. Accidents were many—an atomic drill is not the safest instrument in the universe, and working in a space suit is always dangerous.

As a result, the work took a steady toll of lives, and there was a steady inflow of new labor onto the job. But the work went on in spite of accidents. It had to. When a man was killed, if there was anything at all left of him, the body was tossed to one side and another man took his place. The record of the construction would be an epic in itself—one which there is no space to record here.

The plan of operation was simple—in theory. The Moon was to be gradually dragged away from the Earth—gradually, to avoid inducing huge tides and devastating Earthquakes, then driven north "above" the solar system, out of the plane of the ecliptic. It was to be driven into the minus planet at such an angle and at such a velocity that the latter would be deflected away from the Earth, and the residual mass of neutrons would fall directly into the Sun, where they would do no harm. It was calculated that the normal matter of the Moon would a little more than neutralize the negative matter of the minus planet, so that the residue that finally reached the Sun would consist of a small planetoid of normal matter surrounding an extremely massive core of neutrons.

IV

It was July 6, 2157. Carter and Poggenpohl were rechecking the calculations of the course the Moon would have to take on its last voyage. Finally, they finished with the last decimal and leaned back. "And that, my boy, is how it shall be done!" Jimmy threw his pencil at the calculating machine and inserted his face into a liter of beer.

"All you have to do is push the button and save the world. We'll have to do some reckoning, though, on the initial escape from the Earth. Otherwise, if we're a little brusque about it, the tides will put New York under fifty feet of water, and the mayor might possibly be annoyed with us. How far behind schedule are those primates of engineers, who are supposed to be building the rocket tubes on that soon-to-be ex-companion of our more romantic moments?"

"They ain't. Bill Douglas was here last night, and he said that they

19

would be ready to go in two weeks. And we have three to spare. He's a week ahead of schedule. There's just a little more wiring to do. And we don't have to do any calculating on tidal effects, either. I did it myself a month ago. It won't be as tough as it looks—a gradual acceleration of the Moon's velocity in its orbit, and a gradual, simultaneous acceleration away from the Earth. I planned those rocket tubes, too, so that they won't shower the Earth with vaporized iron. They won't point this way until they're a long way from here. You stick to my firing chart, and you'll get away with it. And I figured what the tides would be, too, so you don't have to worry about that. I done it with my little calculator!''

''I say—I thought *I* was the genius around here! I'll have to have the brass hats increase your salary fifteen, or possibly twenty, cents a week!''

''You don't have to worry about that, either!'' Mike grinned like a gargoyle. ''I've already attended to it. I caught the commissary of science in a good mood the other day and hit him for five hundred dollars more per week. Got it, too. In fact, it's already spent. You're invited to come and help drink some of it tonight.''

''Accepted without qualification. How about those tides, though? How bad will they be?''

''Not so bad. About three meters maximum above mean high water along the coast. They've almost finished building concrete sea walls around the cities and the important communications along the coast, and they're evacuating the other coastal lowlands. But *you* wouldn't know about that. You've been too busy with that trick integraph of yours to know whether you're alive or—''

A buzz of the communicator interrupted Mike. He flicked the switch, and the agitated face of the chief of the Federal police appeared on the screen. ''Dr. Poggenpohl! That nut, Obidiah Miller, escaped from the loony bin last night! We haven't been able to track him down. Probably get him in a couple of days, but watch yourself in the meantime, and warn Dr. Carter. I'll send over a couple more guards. No sense in taking any chances now.''

''Thanks, chief. I'll warn Dr. Carter. But there isn't much our little friend can do right now. The job's almost done. Thanks for the warning, though.'' He flicked off the switch. ''Oh, hell, nothing we can do about it! I only hope he stays away from here. I *don't* like nuts. They get in my hair. And by the way, there's another guy who is cursing us up one side and down the other. The power commissary is quite wrathy.

"We're taking the Moon away from him, and he can't produce any tidal power any more. He'll have to rip up all his plants and convert them into atomic-power outfits. He doesn't love us. He wants to write off the original investment on the old plants, so that his department can make a good showing. And they didn't have any upkeep to speak of, and the power was free and required no brains whatever to produce. So, as I remarked, he does not love us. In fact, I think that he'd like to boil us in oil or do something else equally lingering and humorous to us."

"Oh, well. Invite him to the party. Perhaps, if we get him tight enough he won't mind it so much."

V

It was August 1, 2157. The last of the construction crews had been removed from the Moon; all the movable equipment had been returned to the Earth, and everything was ready for the start. The control space ship was waiting for Carter and Poggenpohl, who were to guide the Moon on its last journey. In twenty hours, at exactly 16:27, GMT, August 2, 2157, the first rocket was to be fired.

Mike had strolled out to the ship, where he was intent on inspecting his quarters, when there was a frantic ringing of alarm bells, and a white-faced field attendant raced across the field. "Dr. Poggenpohl! Stop! There's trouble on the Moon! Just got word. A—" He stopped suddenly as Jimmy ran up alongside of him.

"There's going to be hell, Mike! That damned nut Miller's gummed things. When he got loose he got himself included in one of the last construction crews on the Moon, and when they left for Earth he hid and stayed there. And he's wrecked the remote-control apparatus completely!"

"How do you know?"

"He had to brag about it. He called me up on the communicator three minutes ago and told me what he'd done. Just wanted to rub it in. He's a martyr, of course. Perfectly willing to die with the Earth if he can keep everybody else from living. And there isn't any time to fix the control; we have to start in twenty hours, come hell or high water. And *they'll* both come if we don't. Wait until I catch that messiah! I'll roast his liver over a slow fire!"

21

"What are you going to do about it, Jimmy? That damned minus planet will rip us out by the roots if we don't do something fast!"

"I'm going to the Moon and run the thing by hand. Tell them to get the experimental rocket ready."

"The hell you say! You'll get yourself annihilated! And how are you going to do it, anyway?"

"Oh, there's an auxiliary control for the tubes on the Moon itself, off to one side of the rocket area. Rather on the edge, between the rocket hemisphere and the forward or blank hemisphere. I can control it from there—if I can get there before our friend Obidiah thinks of smashing it, too."

"Maybe so, but you'll get yourself killed just the same. How are you going to get out from under when the two hit?"

"I'll have the rocket parked alongside," said Jimmy, "and dive into it when I have Luna lined up for a direct hit. I've a pretty good chance—maybe one in ten, or so. I'll go alone, of course. There's no sense in anybody else's taking the chance."

"That's what you think!" Mike's red hair bristled even more belligerently than usual, and he glared up at the other's face. "I'm going along. You can't handle that brute alone for a week—you're just nuts! And if you can draw to an inside straight, so can I!

"Hey!" he shouted across the field. "Provision the experimental rocket for two men for four weeks! And make it fast! I'll tear your liver out if I have to wait twenty minutes! Jimmy, get your gun! We'll have to settle with Obidiah."

Nobody's liver was torn out. Fifteen minutes later the little rocket roared clear of the field with the two men inside. Ten hours later they were in their space suits, bounding in long, ungainly leaps across the Lunar landing field toward the control room. In the helmet radio, Jimmy could hear Mike cursing fluently in three languages. "Lord," he thought, "if that ape has smashed things already—then we *shall* be in a jam!"

They reached the control cubicle, and peered in the ports. The control board was invisible from there. They crept into the air lock. As the inner door swung silently open they saw a gaunt figure in a space suit raising a huge spanner over the main controls.

.   Jimmy's gun roared. The figure pitched forward between the levers, and the spanner clanged to the floor. "This is no time for chivalry, Mike. Throw that thing out the air lock, will you, while I see if the controls are all right? The fool must have just remembered the direct controls. It's lucky that we arrived when we did!"

It was August 2, 2157, 16:24 GMT. The rocket had been moored by huge steel cables, with a quick-release arrangement, against the door of the control room. Three minutes to go.

Both men were in the padded and pivoted chairs before the control board. "We, who are about to die," Jimmy said casually, "salute you. Is everything ready?" He swung the safety-release lever over, activating the control buttons. "Will you tell them that I died in the odor of sanctity?"

"No," said Mike, "I will not. Your odor is not of sanctity. It reminds me more of beer. You may fire when you are ready, Gridley!"

Jimmy glued his eyes to the firing chart, and his fingers to the first bank of buttons. Twenty seconds to go. Mike shivered a little, and tried to disguise the shiver with a yawn. He started counting seconds.

"Ten—nine—eight—seven—six—five—four—three—two—one—fire!"

There was a shattering, ground-transmitted roar. The Moon under their feet trembled, and through the ports silhouetted against a hellish glare, they saw the construction scaffolding fall to the ground. The roaring increased. It was like a continuous explosion. Mike tore his handkerchief into bits, stuffed pieces into his ears, and did the same for Jimmy, who was too busy with the controls to do anything for himself.

The roar increased and the flares waxed to an absolutely unendurable brightness, and there was a feeling of acceleration, as though the floor beneath their feet were tilting. Mike covered the ports against the glare, and sat down again. He lighted two cigarettes, one of which he placed in Jimmy's mouth.

The wall against which the rocket was moored had become the floor. The Moon was traveling faster than it had for millions of years, and was gradually drawing away from the Earth. They had no instruments with which to observe the latter, but Mike could imagine the growing tides, the tremblers, and the spectacle in the sky. "I hope they make movies from the Earth," he remarked to nobody in particular. "I'd like to see them if we ever get out of this."

He broke open some food and water, ate, and took the controls while Carter ate, and then, plugging his ears more thoroughly, lay down on an air mattress and went placidly to sleep, after setting an alarm to wake him, with an electric shock, after six hours. Any alarm depending on sound for its effect would be completely useless.

When he awoke and took the controls, the Earth was far behind, and the minus planet was a brilliant spot on the view plate, a little left of dead center. It was coming closer all the time. The roaring of the jets continued unabated. The whole hemisphere of the Moon "below" them, when he ventured to look, was one white glare, with the incandescent iron vapor shooting hundreds of miles into space.

August 12, 2157, 3:28 GMT: The last watch was in progress. Jimmy was at the controls. Both of them were in their space suits, and the doors of the control-room air lock, which now appeared, because of the acceleration, to be below them, were wide open directly over the open, outer door of the air lock of the rocket, into which a rope dangled from a stanchion beside the control board.

The minus planet was visible through the port in the opposite wall—now the roof—filling most of the sky, and rapidly growing larger. The acceleration was still at maximum, as the greatest possible velocity at the time of the collision was not only desirable but necessary. The seconds sped, and yet dragged, as the minus planet grew.

3:30: Jimmy held up two fingers. Two minutes more! He waved Mike toward the air lock. The latter looked around the room to see if he had forgotten anything, and then slid "down" into the rocket's air lock and grabbed the control that would free the moorings.

3:31: The minus planet was bigger—much bigger. It filled most of the sky. Mike gazed anxiously up at Jimmy.

3:32: Jimmy leaped from the controls and slid down into the air lock. He tossed out the rope as Mike released the moorings and slammed the outer door of the lock. There was the sudden baffling sensation of weightlessness, as all acceleration left the ship, which was now falling freely after the Moon, toward the intruder. There was a *whoosh* as they opened the inner door, not waiting for the pressure to equalize, and pulled themselves by the guide rails toward the control cabin. The gyroscopes were already turning over at full speed, and the rocket tubes had been warmed up.

3:34: Mike slammed himself into the control seat, swung the stick which controlled the motors turning the ship around the stabilizing gyroscopes, and, heading her out to one side of the impending collision, jammed on the maximum safe acceleration of five gravities. Jimmy had managed to reach a chair, and was attempting to pull off his space suit, but the acceleration forced his arms down by his sides, and almost pulled him through the seat of the chair. Mike shoved the acceleration up another notch, and switched on all the view plates.

4:45: The acceleration was still on at six gravities, but neither of the men were interested in it. Their eyes were glued to the view plate, which bore on the impending collision. It was a matter of seconds. Already the Moon was breaking up, and most of the rocket tubes had gone out. Then—

There was a blinding flash on the view plate, and it went black, burned out by the tremendous impact of the radiation. Mike cut the acceleration to zero, and fainted. But Jimmy didn't know it. He was unconscious.

About an hour later they came to—bruised, battered, and burned by the radiation which had filtered through the supposedly ray-proof walls of the ship. They switched on an acceleration of half a gravity, so that they could navigate comfortably in the rocket, and swung her ninety degrees around the gyros, so that they could see the remains of the intruder through the side ports. The view plates were useless. There was a small, incandescent planetoid falling toward the Sun. Mike turned a spectrometer on it, gazed a minute, and then grinned all over his blistered face. "It looks like we've done it! There isn't a damned bit of minus matter left on the thing. It glows like a normal hot body—like a young Sun about the size of Ceres."

Jimmy tried to grin back, and couldn't. His face hurt too much. "Right-oh! The Moon neutralized the last of it, with some left over. There's nothing there now except neutrons and some white hot iron, silicon, and whatever else the Moon was made of. It's terrifically heavy, and it's hotter than the seven hinges of hell, but it's nothing to fear. It will fall into the Sun in a month or so. But *you* look like the way I feel, and that's like the latter end of a misspent life. You'd better strip. I'll get the antiburn goo from the medicine chest, and we can butter ourselves up. Then, we can let the ship coast a while while we get some sleep. And finally, if there's enough of her left to navigate, we can wend our way homeward. But sleep is what I want most right now—"

Two weeks later, two tanned and filthy astrophysicists stepped out

25

of the air lock of a burned and blistered rocket onto the tarmac of the space port at Washington, stopped short, and gazed with horror at the galaxy of gold graid and blazing stuffed shirts that approached them. They glanced from side to side with the expression of hunted animals, and then, with the mien of early Christian martyrs, stepped forward to undergo the horrors of an official reception by the combined governments of the solar system.

CLONE

Scientific attempts to create artificial life go back at least as far as Mary Shelley's *Frankenstein* (1818). Advances in science during the twentieth century produced intense speculation on this subject, including such approaches as matter duplication (William F. Temple's *Four-Sided Triangle*, 1949), genetic manipulation (James Blish's *The Seedling Stars*, 1956), and parthenogenesis (Poul Anderson's *Virgin Planet*, 1959).

The method currently in vogue is cloning, a process suggested by the famous British biologist, J. B. S. Haldane. It involves replicating an individual by taking the nucleus (read chromosomal pattern) from a normal cell and implanting it in an egg cell whose nucleus has been removed. Stimulating the combined cell to begin division, the embryo is then implanted in a womb or possibly grown in an artificial womb. The resulting child would be an identical twin to—though X number of years younger than—the nucleus donor.

Contrary to the way clones have sometimes been portrayed in movies or books, they would not be born as adults physically (unless confined to an artificial womb for sixteen or seventeen years), nor would they possess the memories or skills of their donors. There is no reason to believe they would possess special abilities such as telepathy or that they would even grow up to be particularly like their donors, unless provided with a similar environment.

"Yesterday House" (*Galaxy Science Fiction*, August 1952) may be the first scientifically based story of cloning—although one could argue parthenogenesis was being described. Its distinguished author, Fritz Leiber, is a recipient of the Grandmaster Award of the Science Fiction Writers of America, and a winner of both Hugo and Nebula awards.

YESTERDAY HOUSE

Fritz Leiber (1952)

I

*T*he narrow cove was quiet as the face of an expectant child, yet so near the ruffled Atlantic that the last push of wind carried the *Annie O.* its full length. The man in gray flannels and sweatshirt let the sail come crumpling down and huried past its white folds at a gait made comically awkward by his cramped muscles. Slowly the rocky ledge came nearer. Slowly the blue *V* inscribed on the cove's surface by the sloop's prow died. Sloop and ledge kissed so gently that he hardly had to reach out his hand.

He scrambled ashore, dipping a sneaker in the icy water, and threw the line around a boulder. Unkinking himself, he looked back through the cove's high and rocky mouth at the gray-green scattering of islands and the faint dark line that was the coast of Maine. He almost laughed in satisfaction at having disregarded vague warnings and done the thing every man yearns to do once in his lifetime—gone to the farthest island out.

He must have looked longer than he realized, because by the time he dropped his gaze the cove was again as glassy as if the *Annie O.* had always been there. And the splotches made by his sneaker on the rock had faded in the hot sun. There was something very unusual about the quietness of this place. As if time, elsewhere hurrying frantically, paused here to rest. As if all changes were erased on this one bit of earth.

The man's lean, melancholy face crinkled into a grin at the banal fancy. He turned his back on his new friend, the little green sloop, without one thought for his nets and specimen bottles, and set out to

29

explore. The ground rose steeply at first and the oaks were close, but after a little way things went downhill and the leaves thinned and he came out on more rocks—and realized that he hadn't quite gone to the farthest one out.

Joined to this island by a rocky spine, which at the present low tide would have been dry but for the spray, was another green, high island that the first had masked from him all the while he had been sailing. He felt a thrill of discovery, just as he'd wondered back in the woods whether his might not be the first human feet to kick through the underbrush. After all, there were thousands of these islands.

Then he was dropping down the rocks, his lanky limbs now moving smoothly enough.

To the landward side of the spine, the water was fairly still. It even began with another deep cove, in which he glimpsed the spiny spheres of sea urchins. But from seaward the waves chopped in, sprinkling his trousers to the knees and making him wince pleasurably at the thought of what vast wings of spray and towers of solid water must crash up from here in a storm.

He crossed the rocks at a trot, ran up a short grassy slope, raced through a fringe of trees—and came straight up against an eight-foot fence of heavy mesh topped with barbed wire and backed at a short distance with high, heavy shrubbery.

Without pausing for surprise—in fact, in his holiday mood, using surprise as a goad—he jumped for the branch of an oak whose trunk touched the fence, scorning the easier lower branch on the other side of the tree. Then he drew himself up, worked his way to some higher branches that crossed the fence, and dropped down inside.

Suddenly cautious, he gently parted the shrubbery and, before the first surprise could really sink in, had another.

A closely mown lawn dotted with more shrubbery ran up to a snug white Cape Cod cottage. The single strand of a radio aerial stretched the length of the roof. Parked on a neat gravel driveway that crossed just in front of the cottage was a short, square-lined touring car that he recognized from remembered pictures as an ancient Essex. The whole scene had about it the same odd quietness as the cove.

Then, with the air of a clockwork toy coming to life, the white door opened and an elderly woman came out, dressed in a long, lace-edged dress and wide, lacy hat. She climbed into the driver's seat of the Essex, sitting there very stiff and tall. The motor began to chug bravely, gravel skittered, and the car rolled off between the trees.

The door of the house opened again and a slim girl emerged. She wore a white silk dress that fell straight from a square neckline to hip-height waistline, making the skirt seem very short. Her dark hair was bound with a white bandeau so that it curved close to her cheeks. A dark necklace dangled against the white of the dress. A newspaper was tucked under her arm.

She crossed the driveway and tossed the paper down on a rattan table between three rattan chairs and stood watching a squirrel zigzag across the lawn.

The man stepped through the wall of shrubbery, called, "Hello!" and walked toward her.

She whirled around and stared at him as still as if her heart had stopped beating. Then she darted behind the table and waited for him there. Granting the surprise of his appearance, her alarm seemed not so much excessive as eerie. As if, the man thought, he were not an ordinary stranger, but a visitor from another planet.

Approaching closer, he saw that she was trembling and that her breath was coming in rapid, irregular gasps. Yet the slim, sweet, patrician face that stared into his had an underlying expression of expectancy that reminded him of the cove. She couldn't have been more than eighteen.

He stopped short of the table. Before he could speak, she stammered out, "Are you he?"

"What do you mean?" he asked, smiling puzzledly.

"The one who sends me the little boxes."

"I was out sailing and I happened to land in the far cove. I didn't dream that anyone lived on this island, or even came here."

"No one ever does come here," she replied. Her manner had changed, becoming at once more wary and less agitated, though still eerily curious.

"It startled me tremendously to find this place," he blundered on. "Especially the road and the car. Why, this island can't be more than a quarter of a mile wide."

"The road goes down to the wharf," she explained, "and up to the top of the island, where my aunts have a treehouse."

He tore his mind away from the picture of a woman dressed like

Queen Mary clambering up a tree. "Was that your aunt I saw driving off?"

"One of them. The other's taken the motorboat in for supplies." She looked at him doubtfully. "I'm not sure they'll like it if they find someone here."

"There are just the three of you?" he cut in quickly, looking down the empty road that vanished among the oaks.

She nodded.

"I suppose you go in to the mainland with your aunts quite often?"

She shook her head.

"It must get pretty dull for you."

"Not very," she said, smiling. "My aunts bring me the papers and other things. Even movies. We've got a projector. My favorite stars are Antonio Morino and Alice Terry. I like her better even than Clara Bow."

He looked at her hard for a moment. "I suppose you read a lot?"

She nodded. "Fitzgerald's my favorite author." She started around the table, hesitated, suddenly grew shy. "Would you like some lemonade?"

He'd noticed the dewed silver pitcher, but only now realized his thirst. Yet when she handed him a glass, he held it untasted and said awkwardly, "I haven't introduced myself. I'm Jack Barr."

She stared at his outstretched right hand, slowly extended her own toward it, shook it up and down exactly once, then quickly dropped it.

He chuckled and gulped some lemonade. "I'm a biology student. Been working at Wood's Hole the first part of the summer. But now I'm here to do research in marine ecology—that's sort of sea-life patterns— of the inshore islands. Under the direction of Professor Kesserich. You know about him, of course?"

She shook her head.

"Probably the greatest living biologist," he was proud to inform her. "Human physiology as well. Tremendous geneticist. In a class with Carlson and Jacques Loeb. Martin Kesserich—he lives over there at town. I'm staying with him. You ought to have heard of him." He grinned. "Matter of fact, I'd never have met you if it hadn't been for Mrs. Kesserich."

The girl looked puzzled.

Jack explained, "The old boy's been off to Europe on some conferences, won't be back for a couple days more. But I was to get started anyhow. When I went out this morning Mrs. Kesserich—she's a drab sort of person—said to me, 'Don't try to sail to the farther islands.' So, of course, I had to. By the way, you still haven't told me your name.''

"Mary Alice Pope," she said, speaking slowly and with an odd wonder, as if she were saying it for the first time.

"You're pretty shy, aren't you?"

"How would I know?"

The question stopped Jack. He couldn't think of anything to say to this strangely attractive girl dressed almost like a flapper.

"Will you sit down?" she asked him gravely.

The rattan chair sighed under his weight. He made another effort to talk. "I'll bet you'll be glad when summer's over."

"Why?"

"So you'll be able to go back to the mainland."

"But I never go to the mainland."

"You mean you stay out here all winter?" he asked incredulously, his mind filled with a vision of snow and frozen spray and great gray waves.

"Oh, yes. We get all our supplies on hand before winter. My aunts are very capable. They don't always wear long lace dresses. And now I help them."

"But that's impossible!" he said with sudden sympathetic anger. "You can't be shut off this way from people your own age!"

"You're the first one I ever met." She hesitated. "I never saw a boy or a man before, except in movies."

"You're joking!"

"No, it's true."

"But why are they doing it to you?" he demanded, leaning forward. "Why are they inflicting this loneliness on you, Mary?"

She seemed to have gained poise from his loss of it. "I don't know why. I'm to find out soon. But actually I'm not lonely. May I tell you a secret?" She touched his hand, this time with only the faintest trembling. "Every night the loneliness gathers in around me—you're right about that. But then every morning new life comes to me in a little box."

"What's that?" he said sharply.

"Sometimes there's a poem in the box, sometimes a book, or pictures, or flowers, or a ring, but always a note. Next to the notes I like

33

the poems best. My favorite is the one by Matthew Arnold that ends . . .''

> Ah, love, let us be true
> To one another! for the world, which seems
> To lie before us like a land of dreams,
> So various, so beautiful, so new,
> Hath really neither joy, nor love, nor light,
> Nor certitude—

''Wait a minute,'' he interrupted. ''Who sends you these boxes?''

''I don't know.''

''But how are the notes signed?''

''They're wonderful notes,'' she said. ''So wise, so gay, so tender, you'd imagine them being written by John Barrymore or Lindbergh.''

''Yes, but how are they signed?''

She hesitated. ''Never anything but 'Your Lover.' ''

''And so when you first saw me, you thought—'' He began, then stopped because she was blushing.

''How long have you been getting them?''

''Ever since I can remember. I have two closets of the boxes. The new ones are either by my bed when I wake or at my place at breakfast.''

''But how does this—person get these boxes to you out here? Does he give them to your aunts and do they put them there?''

''I'm not sure.''

''But how can they get them in winter?''

''I don't know.''

''Look here,'' he said, pouring himself more lemonade, ''how long is it since you've been to the mainland?''

''Almost eighteen years. My aunts tell me I was born there in the middle of the war.''

''What war?'' he asked startledly, spilling some lemonade.

''The World War, of course. What's the matter?''

Jack Barr was staring down at the spilled lemonade and feeling a kind of terror he'd never experienced in his waking life. Nothing around him had changed. He could still feel the same hot sun on his shoulders, the same icy glass in his hand, scent the same lemon-acid odor in his nostrils. He could still hear the faint *chop-chop* of the waves.

And yet everything had changed, gone dark and dizzy as a landscape glimpsed just before a faint. All the little false notes had come to a sudden focus. For the lemonade had spilled on the headline of the newspaper the girl had tossed down, and the headline read:

HITLER IN NEW DEFIANCE

Under the big black banner of that head swam smaller ones:

FOES OF MACHADO RIOT IN HAVANA
BIG NRA PARADE PLANNED
BALBO SPEAKS IN NEW YORK

Suddenly he felt a surge of relief. He had noticed that the paper was yellow and brittle-edged.

"Why are you so interested in old newspapers?" he asked.

"I wouldn't call day-before-yesterday's paper old," the girl objected, pointing at the dateline: July 20, 1933.

"You're trying to joke," Jack told her.

"No, I'm not."

"But it's 1953."

"Now it's you who are joking."

"But the paper's yellow."

"The paper's always yellow."

He laughed uneasily. "Well, if you actually think it's 1933, perhaps you're to be envied," he said, with a sardonic humor he didn't quite feel. "Then you can't know anything about the Second World War, or television, or the V-2s, or bikini bathing suits, or the atomic bomb, or—"

"Stop!" She had sprung up and retreated around her chair, white-faced. "I don't like what you're saying."

"But—"

"No, please! Jokes that may be quite harmless on the mainland sound different here."

"I'm really not joking," he said after a moment.

She grew quite frantic at that. "I can show you all last week's papers! I can show you magazines and other things. I can prove it!"

She started toward the house. He followed. He felt his heart begin to pound.

35

At the white door she paused, looking worriedly down the road. Jack thought he could hear the faint *chug* of a motorboat. She pushed open the door and he followed her inside. The small-windowed room was dark after the sunlight. Jack got an impression of solid old furniture, a fireplace with brass andirons.

"Flash!" croaked a gritty voice. "After their disastrous break day before yesterday, stocks are recovering. Leading issues . . ."

Jack realized that he had started and had involuntarily put his arm around the girl's shoulders. At the same time he noticed that the voice was coming from the curved brown trumpet of an old-fashioned radio loudspeaker.

The girl didn't pull away from him. He turned toward her. Although her gray eyes were on him, her attention had gone elsewhere.

"I can hear the car. They're coming back. They won't like it that you're here."

"All right, they won't like it."

Her agitation grew. "No, you must go."

"I'll come back tomorrow," he heard himself saying.

"Flash! It looks as if the World Economic Conference may soon adjourn, mouthing jeers at old Uncle Sam who is generally referred to as Uncle Shylock."

Jack felt a numbness on his neck. The room seemed to be darkening, the girl growing stranger still.

"You must go before they see you."

"Flash! Wiley Post has just completed his solo circuit of the globe, after a record-breaking flight of seven days, eighteen hours and forty-five minutes. Asked how he felt after the energy-draining feat, Post quipped . . ."

He was halfway across the lawn before he realized the terror into which the grating radio voice had thrown him.

He leaped for the branch overhanging the fence, vaulted up with the risky help of a foot on the barbed top. A surprised squirrel, lacking time to make its escape up the trunk, sprang to the ground ahead of him. With terrible suddenness, two steel-jawed semicircles clanked together just over the squirrel's head. Jack landed with one foot to either side of the sprung trap, while the squirrel darted off with a squeak.

Jack plunged down the slope to the rocky spine and ran across it, spray from the rising waves spattering him to the waist. Panting now, he stumbled up into the oaks and undergrowth of the first island, fought his way through it, finally reached the silent cove. He loosed the line of the *Annie O.*, dragged it as near to the cove's mouth as he could, plunged knee-deep in freezing water to give it a final shove, scrambled aboard, snatched up the boathook and punched at the rocks.

As soon as the *Annie O.* was nosing out of the cove into the cross waves, he yanked up the sail. The freshening wind filled it and sent the sloop heeling over, with inches of white water over the lee rail, and plunging ahead.

For a long while, Jack was satisfied to think of nothing but the wind and the waves and the sail and speed and danger, to have all his attention taken up balancing one against the other, so that he wouldn't have to ask himself what year it was and whether time was an illusion, and wonder about flappers and hidden traps.

When he finally looked back at the island, he was amazed to see how tiny it had grown, as distant as the mainland.

Then he saw a gray motorboat astern. He watched it as it slowly overtook him. It was built like a lifeboat, with a sturdy low cabin in the bow and wheel amidship. Whoever was at the wheel had long gray hair that whipped in the wind. The longer he looked, the surer he was that it was a woman wearing a lace dress. Something that stuck up inches over the cabin flashed darkly beside her. Only when she lifted it to the roof of the cabin did it occur to him that it might be a rifle.

But just then the motorboat swung around in a turn that sent waves drenching over it, and headed back toward the island. He watched it for a minute in wonder, then his attention was jolted by an angry hail.

Three fishing smacks, also headed toward town, were about to cross his bow. He came around into the wind and waited with shaking sail, watching a man in a lumpy sweater shake a fist at him. Then he turned and gratefully followed the dark, wide, fanlike sterns and age-yellowed sails.

II

The exterior of Martin Kesserich's home—a weathered white cube with narrow, sharp-paned windows, topped by a cupola—was nothing like its lavish interior.

In much the same way, Mrs. Kesserich clashed with the darkly gleaming furniture, Persian rugs and bronze vases around her. Her shapeless black form, poised awkwardly on the edge of a huge sofa, made Jack think of a cow that had strayed into the drawing room. He wondered again how a man like Kesserich had come to marry such a creature.

Yet when she lifted up her little eyes from the shadows, he had the uneasy feeling that she knew a great deal about him. The eyes were still those of a domestic animal, but of a wise one that has been watching the house a long, long while from the barnyard.

He asked abruptly, "Do you know anything of a girl around here named Mary Alice Pope?"

The silence lasted so long that he began to think she'd gone into some bovine trance. Then, without a word, she got up and went over to a tall cabinet. Feeling on a ledge behind it for a key, she opened a panel, opened a cardboard box inside it, took something from the box and handed him a photograph. He held it up to the failing light and sucked in his breath with surprise.

It was a picture of the girl he'd met that afternoon. Same flat-bosomed dress—flowered rather than white—no bandeau, same beads. Same proud, demure expression, perhaps a bit happier.

"That is Mary Alice Pope," Mrs. Kesserich said in a strangely flat voice. "She was Martin's fiancee. She was killed in a railway accident in 1933."

The small sound of the cabinet door closing brought Jack back to reality. He realized that he no longer had the photograph. Against the gloom by the cabinet, Mrs. Kesserich's white face looked at him with what seemed a malicious eagerness.

"Sit down," she said, "and I'll tell you about it."

Without a thought as to why she hadn't asked him a single question—he was much too dazed for that—he obeyed. Mrs. Kesserich resumed her position on the edge of the sofa.

"You must understand, Mr. Barr, that Mary Alice Pope was the one love of Martin's life. He is a man of very deep and strong feelings, yet as you probably know, anything but kindly or demonstrative. Even when he first came here from Hungary with his older sisters Hani and Hilda, there was a cloak of loneliness about him—or rather about the three of them.

"Hani and Hilda were athletic outdoor women, yet fiercely

proud—I don't imagine they ever spoke to anyone in America except as to a servant—and with a seething distaste for all men except Martin. They showered all their devotion on him. So of course, though Martin didn't realize it, they were consumed with jealousy when he fell in love with Mary Alice Pope. They'd thought that since he'd reached forty without marrying, he was safe.

"Mary Alice came from a purebred, or as a biologist would say, inbred British stock. She was very young, but very sweet, and up to a point very wise. She sensed Hani and Hilda's feelings right away and did everything she could to win them over. For instance, though she was afraid of horses, she took up horseback riding, because that was Hani and Hilda's favorite pastime. Naturally, Martin knew nothing of her fear, and naturally his sisters knew about it from the first. But—and here is where Mary's wisdom fell short—her brave gesture did not pacify them; it only increased their hatred.

"Except for his research, Martin was blind to everything but his love. It was a beautiful and yet frightening passion, an insane cherishing as narrow and intense as his sisters' hatred."

With a start, Jack remembered that it was Mrs. Kesserich telling him all this.

She went on, "Martin's love directed his every move. He was building a home for himself and Mary, and in his mind he was building a wonderful future for them as well—not vaguely, if you know Martin, but year by year, month by month. This winter, he'd plan, they would visit Buenos Aires, next summer they would sail down the inland passage and he would teach Mary Hungarian for their trip to Budapest the year after, where he would occupy a chair at the university for a few months . . . and so on. Finally the time for their marriage drew near. Martin had been away. His research was keeping him very busy—"

Jack broke in with, "Wasn't that about the time he did his definitive work on growth and fertilization?"

Mrs. Kesserich nodded with solemn appreciation in the gathering darkness. "But now he was coming home, his work done. It was early evening, very chilly, but Hani and Hilda felt they had to ride down to the station to meet their brother. And although she dreaded it, Mary rode with them, for she knew how delighted he would be at her cantering to the puffing train and his running up to lift her down from the saddle to welcome him home.

39

"Of course there was Martin's luggage to be considered, so the station wagon had to be sent down for that." She looked defiantly at Jack. "I drove the station wagon. I was Martin's laboratory assistant."

She paused. "It was almost dark, but there was still a white cold line of sky to the west. Hani and Hilda, with Mary between them, were waiting on their horses at the top of the hill that led down to the station. The train had whistled and its headlight was graying the gravel of the crossing.

"Suddenly Mary's horse squealed and plunged down the hill. Hani and Hilda followed—to try to catch her, they said—but they didn't manage that, only kept her horse from veering off. Mary never screamed, but as her horse reared on the tracks, I saw her face in the headlight's glare.

"Martin must have guessed, or at least feared what had happened, for he was out of the train and running along the track before it stopped. In fact, he was the first to kneel down beside Mary—I mean, what had been Mary—and was holding her all bloody and shattered in his arms."

A door slammed. There were steps in the hall. Mrs. Kesserich stiffened and was silent. Jack turned.

The blur of a face hung in the doorway to the hall—a seemingly young, sensitive, suavely handsome face with aristocratic jaw. Then there was a click and the lights flared up and Jack saw the close-cropped gray hair and the lines around the eyes and nostrils, while the sensitive mouth grew sardonic. Yet the handsomeness stayed, and somehow the youth, too, or at least a tremendous inner vibrancy.

"Hello, Barr," Martin Kesserich said, ignoring his wife.

The great biologist had come home.

III

"Oh, yes, and Jamieson had a feeble paper on what he called individualization in marine worms. Barr, have you ever thought much about the larger aspects of the problem of individuality?"

Jack jumped slightly. He had let his thoughts wander very far.

"Not especially, sir," he mumbled.

The house was still. A few minutes after the professor's arrival Mrs. Kesserich had gone off with an anxious glance at Jack. He knew why and wished he could reassure her that he would not mention their conversation to the professor.

Kesserich had spent perhaps a half hour briefing him on the more important papers delivered at the conferences. Then, almost as if it were a teacher's trick to show up a pupil's inattention, he had suddenly posed this question about individuality.

"You know what I mean, of course," Kesserich pressed. "The factors that make you you, and me me."

"Heredity and environment," Jack parroted like a freshman.

Kesserich nodded. "Suppose—this is just speculation—that we could control heredity and environment. Then we could recreate the same individual at will."

Jack felt a shiver go through him. "To get exactly the same pattern of hereditary traits. That'd be far beyond us."

"What about identical twins?" Kesserich pointed out. "And then there's parthenogenesis to be considered. One might produce a duplicate of the mother without the intervention of the male." Although his voice had grown more idly speculative, Kesserich seemed to Jack to be smiling secretly. "There are many examples in the lower animal forms, to say nothing of the technique by which Loeb caused a sea urchin to reproduce with no more stimulus than a salt solution."

Jack felt the hair rising on his neck. "Even then you wouldn't get exactly the same pattern of hereditary traints."

"Not if the parent were of very pure stock? Not if there were some special technique for selecting ova that would reproduce all the mother's traits?"

"But environment would change things," Jack objected. "The duplicate would be bound to develop differently."

"Is environment so important? Newman tells about a pair of identical twins separated from birth, unaware of each other's existence. They met by accident when they were twenty-one. Each was a telephone repairman. Each had a wife the same age. Each had a baby son. And each had a fox terrier called 'Trixie.' That's without trying to make environments similar. But suppose you did try. Suppose you saw to it that each of them had exactly the same experiences at the same times. . . ."

For a moment it seemed to Jack that the room was dimming and wavering, becoming a dark pool in which the only motionless thing was Kesserich's sphinxlike face.

"Well, we've escaped quite far enough from Jamieson's marine worms," the biologist said, all brisk again. He said it as if Jack were the one who had led the conversation down wild and unprofitable channels.

"Let's get on to your project. I want to talk it over now, because I won't have any time for it tomorrow."

Jack looked at him blankly.

"Tomorrow I must attend to a very important matter," the biologist explained.

IV

Morning sunlight brightened the colors of the wax flowers under glass on the high bureau that always seemed to emit the faint odor of old hair combings. Jack pulled back the diamond-patterned quilt and blinked the sleep from his eyes. He expected his mind to be busy wondering about Kesserich and his wife—things said and half said last night—but found instead that his thoughts swung instantly to Mary Alice Pope, as if to a farthest island in a world of people.

Downstairs, the house was empty. After a long look at the cabinet—he felt behind it, but the key was gone—he hurried down to the waterfront. He stopped only for a bowl of chowder and, as an afterthought, to buy half a dozen newspapers.

The sea was bright, the brisk wind just right for the *Annie O*. There was eagerness in the way it smacked the sail and in the creak of the mast. And when he reached the cove, it was no longer still, but nervous with faint ripples, as if time had finally begun to stir.

After the same struggle with the underbrush, he came out on the rocky spine and passed the cove of the sea urchins. The spiny creatures struck an uncomfortable chord in his memory.

This time he climbed the second island cautiously, scraping the innocent-seeming ground ahead of him intently with a boathook he'd brought along for the purpose. He was only a few yards from the fence when he saw Mary Alice Pope standing behind it.

He hadn't realized that his heart would begin to pound or that, at the same time, a shiver of almost supernatural dread would go through him.

The girl eyed him with an uneasy hostility and immediately began to speak in a hushed, hurried voice. "You must go away at once and never come back. You're a wicked man, but I don't want you to be hurt. I've been watching for you all morning."

He tossed the newspapers over the fence. "You don't have to read them now," he told her. "Just look at the datelines and a few of the headlines."

When she finally lifted her eyes to his again, she was trembling. She tried unsuccessfully to speak.

"Listen to me," he said. "You've been the victim of a scheme to make you believe you were born around 1916 instead of 1933, and that it's 1933 now instead of 1953. I'm not sure why it's been done, though I think I know who you really are."

"But," the girl faltered, "my aunts tell me it's 1933."

"They would."

"And there are the papers . . . the magazines . . . the radio."

"The papers are old ones. The radio's faked—some sort of recording. I could show you if I could get at it."

"*These* papers might be faked," she said, pointing to where she'd let them drop on the ground.

"They're new," he said. "Only old papers get yellow."

"But why would they do it to me? *Why?*"

"Come with me to the mainland, Mary. That'll set you straight quicker than anything."

"I couldn't," she said, drawing back. "He's coming tonight."

"He?"

"The man who sends me the boxes . . . and my life."

Jack shivered. When he spoke, his voice was rough and quick. "A life that's completely a lie, that's cut you off from the world. Come with me, Mary."

She looked up at him wonderingly. For perhaps ten seconds the silence held and the spell of her eerie sweetness deepened.

"I love you, Mary," Jack said softly.

She took a step back.

"Really, Mary, I do."

She shook her head. "I don't know what's true. Go away."

"Mary," he pleaded, "read the papers I've given you. Think things through. I'll wait for you here."

"You can't. My aunts would find you."

"Then I'll go away and come back. About sunset. Will you give me an answer?"

She looked at him. Suddenly she whirled around. He, too, heard the *chuff* of the Essex. "They'll find us," she said. "And if they find you, I don't know what they'll do. Quick, run!" And she darted off herself, only to turn back to scramble for the papers.

"But will you give me an answer?" he pressed.

She looked frantically up from the papers. "I don't know. You mustn't risk coming back."

"I will, no matter what you say."

"I can't promise. Please go."

"Just one question," he begged. "What are your aunts' names?"

"Hani and Hilda," she told him, and then she was gone. The hedge shook where she'd darted through.

Jack hesitated, then started for the cove. He thought for a moment of staying on the island, but decided against it. He could probably conceal himself successfully, but whoever found his boat would have him at a disadvantage. Besides, there were things he must try to find out on the mainland.

As he entered the oaks, his spine tightened for a moment, as if someone were watching him. He hurried to the rippling cove, wasted no time getting the *Annie O.* underway. With the wind still in the west, he knew it would be a hard sail. He'd need half a dozen tacks to reach the mainland.

When he was about a quarter of a mile out from the cove, there was a sharp *smack* beside him. He jerked around, heard a distant *crack* and saw a foot-long splinter of fresh wood dangling from the edge of the sloop's cockpit, about a foot from his head.

He felt his skin tighten. He was the bull's-eye of a great watery target. All the air between him and the island was tainted with menace.

Water splashed a yard from the side. There was another distant *crack*. He lay on his back in the cockpit, steering by the sail, taking advantage of what little cover there was.

There were several more *cracks*. After the second, there was a hole in the sail.

Finally Jack looked back. The island was more than a mile astern. He anxiously scanned the sea ahead for craft. There were none. Then he settled down to nurse more speed from the sloop and wait for the motorboat.

But it didn't come out to follow him.

V

Same as yesterday, Mrs. Kesserich was sitting on the edge of the couch in the living room, yet from the first Jack was aware of a great change. Something had filled the domestic animal with grief and fury.

"Where's Dr. Kesserich?" he asked.

"Not here!"

"Mrs. Kesserich," he said, dropping down beside her, "you were telling me something yesterday when we were interrupted."

She looked at him. "You *have* found the girl?" she almost shouted.

"Yes," Jack was surprised into answering.

A look of slyness came into Mrs. Kesserich's bovine face. "Then I'll tell you everything. I can now."

"When Martin found Mary dying, he didn't go to pieces. You know how controlled he can be when he chooses. He lifted Mary's body as if the crowd and the railway men weren't there, and carried it to the station wagon. Hani and Hilda were sitting on their horses nearby. He gave them one look. It was as if he had said, 'Murderers!'

"He told me to drive home as fast as I dared, but when I got there, he stayed sitting by Mary in the back. I knew he must have given up what hope he had for her life, or else she was dead already. I looked at him. In the domelight, his face had the most deadly and proud expression I've ever seen on a man. I worshiped him, you know, though he had never shown me one ounce of feeling. So I was completely unprepared for the naked appeal in his voice.

"Yet all he said at first was, 'Will you do something for me?' I told him, 'Surely,' and as we carried Mary in, he told me the rest. He wanted me to be the mother of Mary's child."

Jack stared at her blankly.

Mrs. Kesserich nodded. "He wanted to remove an ovum from Mary's body and nurture it in mine, so that Mary, in a way, could live on."

"But that's impossible!" Jack objected. "The technique is being tried on cattle, I know, so that a prize heifer can have several calves a year, all nurtured in 'scrub heifers,' as they're called. But no one's ever dreamed of trying it on human beings!"

Mrs. Kesserich looked at him contemptuously. "Martin had mastered the technique twenty years ago. He was willing to take the chance. And so was I—partly because he fired my scientific imagination and reverence, but mostly because he said he would marry me. He barred the doors. We worked swiftly. As far as anyone was concerned, Martin, in a wild fit of grief, had locked himself up for several hours to mourn over the body of his fiancée.

"Within a month we were married, and I finally gave birth to the child."

Jack shook his head. "You gave birth to your own child."

She smiled bitterly. "No, it was Mary's. Martin did not keep his whole bargain with me—I was nothing more than his 'scrub wife' in every way."

"You *think* you gave birth to Mary's child."

Mrs. Kesserich turned on Jack in anger. "I've been wounded by him, day in and day out, for years, but I've never failed to recognize his genius. Besides, you've seen the girl, haven't you?"

Jack had to nod. What confounded him most was that, granting the near-impossible physiological feat Mrs. Kesserich had described, the girl should look so much like the mother. Mother and daughters don't look that much alike; only identical twins did. With a thrill of fear, he remembered Kesserich's casual words: ". . .parthenogenesis. . .pure stock . . .special techniques . . ."

"Very well," he forced himself to say, "granting that the child was Mary's and Martin's—"

"No! Mary's alone!"

Jack suppressed a shudder. He continued quickly. "What became of the child?"

Mrs. Kesserich lowered her head. "The day it was born, it was taken away from me. After that, I never saw Hilda and Hani, either."

"You mean," Jack asked, "that Martin sent them away to bring up the child?"

Mrs. Kesserich turned away. "Yes."

Jack asked incredulously, "He trusted the child with the two people he suspected of having caused the mother's death?"

"Once when I was his assistant," Mrs. Kesserich said softly, "I carelessly broke some laboratory glassware. He kept me up all night building a new setup, though I'm rather poor at working with glass and usually get burned. Bringing up the child was his sisters' punishment."

"And they went to that house on the farthest island? I suppose it was the house he'd been building for Mary and himself."

"Yes."

"And they were to bring up the child as his daughter?"

Mrs. Kesserich started up, but when she spoke it was as if she had to force out each word. "As his wife—as soon as she was grown."

"How can you know that?" Jack asked shakily.

The rising wind rattled the windowpane.

"Because today—eighteen years after—Martin broke all of his promise to me. He told me he was leaving me."

VI

White waves shooting up like dancing ghosts in the moon-sketched, spray-swept dark were Jack's first beacon of the island and brought a sense of physical danger, breaking the trancelike yet frantic mood he had felt ever since he had spoken with Mrs. Kesserich.

Coming around farther into the wind, he scudded past the end of the island into the choppy sea on the landward side. A little later he let down the reefed sail in the cove of the sea urchins, where the water was barely moving, although the air was shaken by the pounding of the surf on the spine between the two islands.

After making fast, he paused a moment for a scrap of cloud to pass the moon. The thought of the spiny creatures in the black fathoms under the *Annie O.* sent an odd quiver of terror through him.

The moon came out and he started across the glistening rocks of the spine. But he had forgotten the rising tide. Midway, a wave clamped around his ankles, tried to carry him off, almost made him drop the heavy object he was carrying. Sprawling and drenched, he clung to the rough rock until the surge was past.

Making it finally up to the fence, he snipped a wide gate with the wire-cutters.

The windows of the house were alight. Hardly aware of his shivering, he crossed the lawn, slipping from one clump of shrubbery to another, until he reached one just across the drive from the doorway. At that moment he heard the approaching *chuff* of the Essex, the door of the cottage opened, and Mary Alice Pope stepped out, closely followed by Hani or Hilda.

Jack shrank close to the shrubbery. Mary looked pale and blank-faced, as if she had retreated within herself. He was acutely conscious of the inadequacy of his screen as the ghostly headlights of the Essex began to probe through the leaves.

But then he sensed that something more was about to happen than just the car arriving. It was a change in the expression of the face behind

Mary that gave him the cue—a widening and sideways flickering of the cold eyes, the puckered lips thinning into a cruel smile.

The Essex shifted into second and, without any warning, accelerated. Simultaneously, the woman behind Mary gave her a violent shove. But at almost exactly the same instant, Jack ran. He caught Mary as she sprawled toward the gravel, and lunged ahead without checking. The Essex bore down upon them, a square-snouted, roaring monster. It swerved viciously, missed them by inches, threw up gravel in a skid, and rocked to a stop, stalled.

The first, incredulous voice that broke the pulsing silence, Jack recognized as Martin Kesserich's. It came from the car, which was slewed around so that it almost faced Jack and Mary.

"Hani, you tried to kill her! You and Hilda tried to kill her again!"

The woman slumped over the wheel slowly lifted her head. In the indistinct light, she looked the twin of the woman behind Jack and Mary.

"Did you really think we wouldn't?" she asked in a voice that spat with passion. "Did you actually believe that Hilda and I would serve this eighteen years' penance just to watch you go off with her?" She began to laugh wildly. "You've never understood your sisters at all!"

Suddenly she broke off and stiffly stepped down from the car. Lifting her skirts a little, she strode past Jack and Mary.

Martin Kesserich followed her. In passing, he said, "Thanks, Barr." It occurred to Jack that Kesserich made no more question of his appearance on the island than of his presence in the laboratory. Like Mrs. Kesserich, the great biologist took him for granted.

Kesserich stopped a few feet short of Hani and Hilda. Without shrinking from him, the sisters drew closer together. They looked like two gaunt hawks.

"But you waited eighteen years," he said. "You could have killed her at any time, yet you chose to throw away so much of your lives just to have this moment."

"How do you know we didn't like waiting eighteen years?" Hani answered him. "Why shouldn't we want to make as strong an impression on you as anyone? And as for throwing our lives away, that was your doing. Oh, Martin, you'll never know anything about how your sisters feel!"

He raised his hands baffledly. "Even assuming that you hate me"—at the word "hate" both Hani and Hilda laughed softly—"and that you were prepared to strike at both my love and my work, still, that you should have waited . . ."

Hani and Hilda said nothing.

Kesserich shrugged. "Very well," he said in a voice that had lost all its tension. "You've wasted a third of a lifetime looking forward to an irrational revenge. And you've failed. That should be sufficient punishment."

Very slowly, he turned around and for the first time looked at Mary. His face was clearly revealed by the twin beams from the stalled car.

Jack grew cold. He fought against accepting the feelings of wonder, of poignant triumph, of love, of renewed youth he saw entering the face in the headlights. But most of all he fought against the sense that Martin Kesserich was successfully drawing them all back into the past, to 1933 and another accident. There was a distant hoot and Jack shook. For a moment he had thought it a railway whistle and not a ship's horn.

The biologist said tenderly, "Come, Mary."

Jack's trembling arm tightened a trifle on Mary's waist. He could feel *her* trembling.

"Come, Mary," Kesserich repeated.

Still she didn't reply.

Jack wet his lips. "Mary isn't going with you, Professor," he said.

"Quiet, Barr," Kesserich ordered absently. "Mary, it is necessary that you and I leave the island at once. Please come."

"But Mary isn't coming," Jack repeated.

Kesserich looked at him for the first time. "I'm grateful to you for the unusual sense of loyalty—or whatever motive it may have been— that led you to follow me out here tonight. And of course I'm profoundly grateful to you for saving Mary's life. But I must ask you not to interfere further in a matter which you can't possibly understand."

He turned to Mary. "I know how shocked and frightened you must feel. Living two lives and then having to face two deaths—it must be more terrible than anyone can realize. I expected this meeting to take place under very different circumstances. I wanted to explain everything to you very naturally and gently, like the messages I've sent you every day of your second life. Unfortunately, that can't be.

"You and I must leave the island right now."

Mary stared at him, then turned wonderingly toward Jack, who felt his heart begin to pound warmly.

49

"You still don't understand what I'm trying to tell you, Professor," he said, boldly now. "Mary is not going with you. You've deceived her all her life. You've taken a fantastic amount of pains to bring her up under the delusion that she is Mary Alice Pope, who died in—"

"She *is* Mary Alice Pope," Kesserich thundered at him. He advanced toward them swiftly. "Mary, darling, you're confused, but you must realize who you are and who I am and the relationship between us."

"Keep away," Jack warned, swinging Mary half behind him. "Mary doesn't love you. She can't marry you, at any rate. How could she, when you're her father?"

"Barr!"

"Keep off!" Jack shot out the flat of his hand and Kesserich went staggering backward. "I've talked with your wife—your wife on the mainland. She told me the whole thing."

Kesserich seemed about to rush forward again, then controlled himself. "You've got everything wrong. You hardly deserve to be told, but under the circumstances I have no choice. Mary is not my daughter. To be precise, she has no father at all. Do you remember the work that Jacques Loeb did with sea urchins?"

Jack frowned angrily. "You mean what we were talking about last night?"

"Exactly. Loeb was able to cause the egg of a sea urchin to develop normally without union with a male germ cell. I have done the same thing with a human being. This girl is Mary Alice Pope. She has exactly the same heredity. She has had exactly the same life, so far as it could be reconstructed. She's heard and read the same things at exactly the same times. There have been old newspapers, the books, even the old recorded radio programs. Hani and Hilda have had their daily instructions, to the letter. She's retraced the same time trail."

"Rot!" Jack interrupted. "I don't for a moment believe what you say about her birth. She's Mary's daughter—or the daughter of your wife on the mainland. And as for retracing the same time trail, that's senile self-delusion. Mary Alice Pope had a normal life. This girl has been brought up in cruel imprisonment by two insane, vindictive old women. In your own frustrated desire, you've pretended to yourself that you've recreated the girl you lost. You haven't. You couldn't. Nobody could—the great Martin Kesserich or anyone else!"

Kesserich, his features working, shifted his point of attack. "Who are you, Mary?"

"Don't answer him," Jack said. "He's trying to confuse you."

"Who are you?" Kesserich insisted.

"Mary Alice Pope," she said rapidly in a breathy whisper before Jack could speak again.

"And when were you born?" Kesserich pressed on.

"You've been tricked all your life about that," Jack warned.

"But already the girl was saying, "In nineteen hundred and sixteen.""

"And who am I then?" Kesserich demanded eagerly. "Who am I?"

The girl swayed. She brushed her head with her hand.

"It's so strange," she said, with a dreamy, almost laughing throb in her voice that turned Jack's heart cold. "I'm sure I've never seen you before in my life, and yet it's as if I'd known you forever. As if you were closer to me than—"

"Stop it!" Jack shouted at Kesserich. "Mary loves me. She loves me because I've shown her the lie her life has been, and because she's coming away with me now. Aren't you, Mary?"

He swung her around so that her blank face was inches from his own. "It's me you love, isn't it, Mary?"

She blinked doubtfully.

At that moment Kesserich charged at them, went sprawling as Jack's fist shot out. Jack swept up Mary and ran with her across the lawn. Behind him he heard an agonized cry—Kesserich's—and cruel, mounting laughter from Hani and Hilda.

Once through the ragged doorway in the fence, he made his way more slowly, gasping. Out of the shelter of the trees, the wind tore at them and the ocean roared. Moonlight glistened, now on the spine of black wet rocks, now on the foaming surf.

Jack realized that the girl in his arms was speaking rapidly, disjointedly, but he couldn't quite make out the sense of the words and then they were lost in the crash of the surf. She struggled, but he told himself that it was only because she was afraid of the menacing waters.

He pushed recklessly into the breaking surf, raced gasping across the middle of the spine as the rocks uncovered, sprang to the higher ones as the next wave crashed behind, showering them with spray. His chest burning with exertion, he carried the girl the few remaining yards to where the *Annie O.* was tossing. A sudden great gust of wind almost did what the waves had failed to do, but he kept his footing and lowered the girl into the boat, then jumped in after.

She stared at him wildly. "What's that?"

He, too, had caught the faint shout. Looking back along the spine just as the moon came clear again, he saw white spray rise and fall—and then the figure of Kesserich stumbling through it.

"Mary, wait for me!"

The figure was halfway across when it lurched, started forward again, then was jerked back as if something had caught its ankle. Out of the darkness, the next wave sent a line of white at it neck-high.

Jack hesitated, but another great gust of wind tore at the half-raised sail, and it was all he could do to keep the sloop from capsizing and head her into the wind again.

Mary was tugging at his shoulder. "You must help him," she was saying. "He's caught in the rocks."

He heard a voice crying, screaming crazily above the surf:

Ah, love, let us be true
To one another! for the world—

The sloop rocked. Jack had it finally headed into the wind. He looked around for Mary.

She had jumped out and was hurrying back, scrambling across the rocks toward the dark, struggling figure that even as he watched was once more engulfed in the surf.

Letting go the lines, Jack sprang toward the stern of the sloop.

But just then another giant blow came, struck the sail like a great fist of air, and sent the boom slashing at the back of his head.

His last recollection was being toppled out onto the rocks and wondering how he could cling to them while unconscious.

VII

The little cove was once again as quiet as time's heart. Once again the *Annie O.* was a sloop embedded in a mirror. Once again the rocks were warm underfoot.

Jack Barr lifted his fiercely aching head and looked at the distant line of the mainland, as tiny and yet as clear as something viewed through the wrong end of a telescope. He was very tired. Searching the island, in his present shaky condition, had taken all the strength out of him.

He looked at the peacefully rippling sea outside the cove and thought of what a churning pot it had been during the storm. He thought wonderingly of his rescue—a man wedged unconscious between two rock teeth, kept somehow from being washed away by the merest chance.

He thought of Mrs. Kesserich sitting alone in her house, scanning the newspapers that had nothing to tell.

He thought of the empty island behind him and the vanished motorboat.

He wondered if the sea had pulled down Martin Kesserich and Mary Alice Pope. He wondered if only Hani and Hilda had sailed away.

He winced, remembering what he had done to Martin and Mary by his blundering infatuation. In his way, he told himself, he had been as bad as the two old women.

He thought of death, and of time, and of love that defies them.

He stepped limpingly into the *Annie O.* to set sail—and realized that philosophy is only for the unhappy.

Mary was asleep in the stern.

COLLAPSED STARS

In 1916 Karl Schwarzschild, a German astronomer, advanced the idea that dying stars would collapse into incredibly small and dense spheres of matter due to gravity. Later work indicates that stars like our sun become white dwarfs. Those stars roughly one-and-one-half times larger stand a good chance of becoming supernovas, then collapsing into neutron stars—so called because the matter is so dense that it can exist only as neutrons. Finally, those stars over three times larger collapse into black holes so dense that light can not escape from it. (*The Collapsing Universe*, 1977, by Isaac Asimov offers further discussion of these phenomena.)

Frank K. Kelly's "Star Ship Invincible" (*Astounding Stories*, January 1935) seems to make the first fictional reference to black holes: "In the distance, receding, he saw a web of darkness deeper than infinity; a black hole in the void so dark that it was a purple scar blotting out the stars behind it." Kelly even suggests it may lead to another universe or another part of our own. But he conceives of it more as an intersteller bog or sink hole.

Larry Niven's "Neutron Star" (*Worlds of If*, October, 1966) first uses this concept as a story, while Robert Silverberg's "To the Dark Star" (1968) may be the first story using the concept of a black hole as a collapsed star.* Novels dealing with these phenomena include Joe Haldeman's *The Forever War* (1974) and Frederik Pohl's *Gateway* (1977).

*Frederic Brown's "Gateway to Darkness" (1949) introduces a weapon capable of collapsing matter (in this case a planetoid) into neutronic matter, but doesn't relate the concept to that of collapsing stars.

Jerry Pournelle's *Black Holes* (1979) is an anthology on the subject.

Larry Niven is the author or coauthor of more than a dozen novels, the winner of five Hugo Awards, and one of science fiction's leading hard-science writers.

NEUTRON STAR

Larry Niven (1966)

*T*he Skydiver *dropped out of hyperspace an even million miles above* the neutron star. I needed a minute to place myself against the stellar background, and another to find the distortion Sonya Laskin had mentioned before she died. It was to my left, an area the apparent size of the Earth's moon. I swung the ship around to face it.

Curdled stars, muddled stars, stars that had been stirred with a spoon.

The neutron star was in the center, of course, though I couldn't see it and hadn't expected to. It was only eleven miles across, and cool. A billion years had passed since BVS-1 burned by fusion fire. Millions of years, at least, since the cataclysmic two weeks during which BVS-1 was an X-ray star, burning at a temperature of five billion degrees Kelvin. Now it showed only by its mass.

The ship began to turn by itself. I felt the pressure of the fusion drive. Without help from me my faithful metal watchdog was putting me in a hyperbolic orbit that would take me within one mile of the neutron star's surface. Twenty-four hours to fall, twenty-four hours to rise . . . and during that time something would try to kill me. As something had killed the Laskins.

The same type of autopilot, with the same program, had chosen the Laskins' orbit. It had not caused their ship to collide with the star. I could trust the autopilot. I could even change its program.

I really ought to.

How did I get myself into this hole?

The drive went off after ten minutes of maneuvering. My orbit was established, in more ways than one. I knew what would happen if I tried to back out now.

All I'd done was walk into a drugstore to get a new battery for my lighter!

Right in the middle of the store, surrounded by three floors of sales counters, was the new 2603 Sinclair intrasystem yacht. I'd come for a battery, but I stayed to admire. It was a beautiful job, small and sleek and streamlined and blatantly different from anything that'd ever been built. I wouldn't have flown it for anything but I had to admit it was pretty. I ducked my head through the door to look at the control panel. You never saw so many dials. When I pulled my head out, all the customers were looking in the same direction. The place had gone startlingly quiet.

I can't blame them for staring. A number of aliens were in the store, mainly shopping for souvenirs, but they were staring too. A puppeteer is unique. Imagine a headless, three-legged centaur wearing two Cecil the Seasick Sea Serpent puppets on its arms, and you'll have something like the right picture. But the arms are weaving necks, and the puppets are real heads, flat and brainless, with wide flexible lips. The brain is under a bony hump set between the bases of the necks. This puppeteer wore only its own coat of brown hair, with a mane that extended all the way up its spine to form a thick mat over the brain. I'm told that the way they wear the mane indicates their status in society, but to me it could have been anything from a dock worker to a jeweler to the president of General Products.

I watched with the rest as it came across the floor, not because I'd never seen a puppeteer but because there is something beautiful about the dainty way they move on those slender legs and tiny hooves. I watched it come straight toward me, closer and closer. It stopped a foot away, looked me over, and said, "You are Beowulf Shaeffer, former chief pilot for Nakamura Lines."

Its voice was a beautiful contralto with not a trace of accent. A puppeteer's mouths are not only the most flexible speech organs around, but also the most sensitive hands. The tongues are forked and pointed; the wide, thick lips have little fingerlike knobs along the rims. Imagine a watchmaker with a sense of taste in his fingertips. . . .

I cleared my throat. "That's right."

It considered me from two directions. "You would be interested in a high-paying job?"

58

"I'd be fascinated by a high-paying job."

"I am our equivalent of the regional president of General Products. Please come with me, and we will discuss this elsewhere."

I followed it into a displacement booth. Eyes followed me all the way. It was embarrassing, being accosted in a public drugstore by a two-headed monster. Maybe the puppeteer knew it. Maybe it was testing me to see how badly I needed money.

My need was great. Eight months had passed since Nakamura Lines folded. For some time before that I had been living very high on the hog, knowing that my back pay would cover my debts. I never saw that back pay. It was quite a crash, Nakamura Lines. Respectable middle-aged businessmen took to leaving their hotel windows without their lift belts. Me, I kept spending. If I'd started living frugally, my creditors would have done some checking . . . and I'd have ended in debtor's prison.

The puppeteer dialed thirteen fast digits with its tongue. A moment later we were elsewhere. Air puffed out when I opened the booth door, and I swallowed to pop my ears.

"We are on the roof of the General Products building." The rich contralto voice thrilled along my nerves, and I had to remind myself that it was an alien speaking, not a lovely woman. "You must examine this spacecraft while we discuss your assignment."

I stepped outside a little cautiously, but it wasn't the windy season. The roof was at ground level. That's the way we built on We Made It. Maybe it has something to do with the fifteen-hundred-mile-an-hour winds we get in summer and winter, when the planet's axis of rotation runs through its primary, Procyon. The winds are our planet's only tourist attraction, and it would be a shame to slow them down by planting skyscrapers in their path. The bare, square concrete roof was surrounded by endless square miles of desert, not like the deserts of other inhabited worlds, but an utterly lifeless expanse of fine sand just crying to be planted with ornamental cactus. We've tried that. The wind blows the plants away.

The ship lay on the sand beyond the roof. It was a No. 2 General Products hull: a cylinder three hundred feet long and twenty feet through, pointed at both ends and with a slight wasp-waist constriction near the tail. For some reason it was lying on its side, with the landing shocks still folded in at the tail.

Ever notice how all ships have begun to look the same? A good ninety-five percent of today's spacecraft are built around one of the four General Products hulls. It's easier and safer to build that way, but somehow all ships end as they began: mass-produced look-alikes.

The hulls are delivered fully transparent, and you use paint where you feel like it. Most of this particular hull had been left transparent. Only the nose had been painted, around the lifesystem. There was no major reaction drive. A series of retractable attitude jets had been mounted in the sides, and the hull was pierced with smaller holes, square and round, for observational instruments. I could see them gleaming through the hull.

The puppeteer was moving toward the nose, but something made me turn toward the stern for a closer look at the landing shocks. They were bent. Behind the curved transparent hull panels some tremendous pressure had forced the metal to flow like warm wax, back and into the pointed stern.

"What did this?" I asked.

"We do not know. We wish strenuously to find out."

"What do you mean?"

"Have you heard of the neutron star BVS-1?"

I had to think a moment. "First neutron star ever found, and so far the only. Someone located it two years ago, by stellar displacement."

"BVS-1 was found by the Institute of Knowledge on Jinx. We learned through a go-between that the Institute wished to explore the star. They needed a ship to do it. They had not yet sufficient money. We offered to supply them with a ship's hull, with the usual guarantees, if they would turn over to us all data they acquired through using our ship."

"Sounds fair enough." I didn't ask why they hadn't done their own exploring. Like most sentient vegetarians, puppeteers find discretion to be the *only* part of valor.

"Two humans named Peter Laskin and Sonya Laskin wished to use the ship. They intended to come within one mile of the surface in a hyperbolic orbit. At some point during their trip an unknown force apparently reached through the hull to do this to the landing shocks. The unknown force also seems to have killed the pilots."

"But that's impossible. Isn't it?"

"You see the point. Come with me." The puppeteer trotted toward the bow.

I saw the point, all right. Nothing, but nothing, can get through a

General Products hull. No kind of electromagnetic energy except visible light. No kind of matter, from the smallest subatomic particle to the fastest meteor. That's what the company's advertisements claim, and the guarantee backs them up. I've never doubted it, and I've never heard of a General Products hull being damaged by a weapon or by anything else.

On the other hand, a General Products hull is as ugly as it is functional. The puppeteer-owned company could be badly hurt if it got around that something *could* get through a company hull. But I didn't see where I came in.

We rode an escalladder into the nose.

The lifesystem was in two compartments. Here the Laskins had used heat-reflective paint. In the conical control cabin the hull had been divided into windows. The relaxation room behind it was a windowless reflective silver. From the back wall of the relaxation room an access tube ran aft, opening on various instruments and the hyperdrive motors.

There were two acceleration couches in the control cabin. Both had been torn loose from their mountings and wadded into the nose like so much tissue paper, crushing the instrument panel. The backs of the crumpled couches were splashed with rust brown. Flecks of the same color were all over everything, the walls, the windows, the viewscreens. It was as if something had hit the couches from behind: something like a dozen paint-filled toy balloons striking with tremendous force.

"That's blood," I said.

"That is correct. Human circulatory fluid."

Twenty-four hours to fall.

I spent most of the first twelve hours in the relaxation room, trying to read. Nothing significant was happening, except that a few times I saw the phenomenon Sonya Laskin had mentioned in her last report. When a star went directly behind the invisible BVS-1, a halo formed. BVS-1 was heavy enough to bend light around it, displacing most stars to the sides; but when a star went directly behind the neutron star, its light was displaced to all sides at once. Result: a tiny circle which flashed once and was gone almost before the eye could catch it.

I'd known next to nothing about neutron stars the day the puppeteer picked me up. Now I was an expert. And I still had no idea what was waiting for me when I got down there.

All the matter you're ever likely to meet will be normal matter, composed of a nucleus of protons and neutrons surrounded by electrons in quantum energy states. In the heart of any star there is a second kind of matter: for there, the tremendous pressure is enough to smash the electron shells. The result is degenerate matter: nuclei forced together by pressure and gravity, but held apart by the mutual repulsion of the more or less continuous electron "gas" around them. The right circumstances may create a third type of matter.

Given: a burnt-out white dwarf with a mass greater than 1.44 times the mass of the sun—Chandrasekhar's Limit, named for an Indian-American astronomer of the nineteen hundreds. In such a mass the electron pressure alone would not be able to hold the electrons back from the nuclei. Electrons would be forced against protons—to make neutrons. In one blazing explosion most of the star would change from a compressed mass of degenerate matter to a closely packed lump of neutrons: neutronium, theoretically the densest matter possible in this universe. Most of the remaining normal and degenerate matter would be blown away by the liberated heat.

For two weeks the star would give off X rays as its core temperature dropped from five billion degrees Kelvin to five hundred million. After that it would be a light-emitting body perhaps ten to twelve miles across: the next best thing to invisible. It was not strange that BVS-1 was the first neutron star ever found.

Neither is it strange that the Institute of Knowledge on Jinx would have spent a good deal of time and trouble looking. Until BVS-1 was found, neutronium and neutron stars were only theories. The examination of an actual neutron star could be of tremendous importance. Neutron stars might give us the key to true gravity control.

Mass of BVS-1: 1.3 times the mass of Sol, approximately.

Diameter of BVS-1 (estimated): eleven miles of neutronium, covered by half a mile of degenerate matter, covered by maybe twelve feet of ordinary matter.

Nothing else was known of the tiny hidden star until the Laskins went in to look. Now the Institute knew one thing more: the star's spin.

"A mass that large can distort space by its rotation," said the puppeteer. "The Laskins' projected hyperbola was twisted across itself in such a way that we can deduce the star's period of rotation to be two minutes twenty-seven seconds."

The bar was somewhere in the General Products building. I don't know just where, and with the transfer booths it doesn't matter. I kept staring at the puppeteer bartender. Naturally only a puppeteer would be served by a puppeteer bartender, since any biped life form would resent knowing that his drink had been made with somebody's mouth. I had already decided to get dinner somewhere else.

"I see your problem," I said. "Your sales will suffer if it gets out that something can reach through one of your hulls and smash a crew to bloody smears. But where do I come in?"

"We want to repeat the experiment of Sonya Laskin and Peter Laskin. We must find—"

"With me?"

"Yes. We must find out what it is that our hulls cannot stop. Naturally you may—"

"But I won't."

"We are prepared to offer one million stars."

I was tempted, but only for a moment. "Forget it."

"Naturally you will be allowed to build your own ship, starting with a No. 2 General Products hull."

"Thanks, but I'd like to go on living."

"You would dislike being confined. I find that We Made It has reestablished the debtor's prison. If General Products made public your accounts—"

"Now, *just a*—"

"You owe money on the close order of five hundred thousand stars. We will pay your creditors before you leave. If you return—" I had to admire the creature's honesty in not saying "When"—"we will pay you the residue. You may be asked to speak to news commentators concerning the voyage, in which case there will be more stars."

"You say I can build my own ship?"

"Naturally. This is not a voyage of exploration. We want you to return safely."

"It's a deal," I said.

After all, the puppeteer had tried to blackmail me. What happened next would be its own fault.

They built my ship in two weeks flat. They started with a No. 2 General Products hull, just like the one around the Institute of

Knowledge ship, and the lifesystem was practically a duplicate of the Laskins's, but there the resemblance ended. There were no instruments to observe neutron stars. Instead, there was a fusion motor big enough for a Jinx warliner. In my ship, which I now called *Skydiver*, the drive would produce thirty gees at the safety limit. There was a laser cannon big enough to punch a hole through We Made It's moon. The puppeteer wanted me to feel safe, and now I did, for I could fight and I could run. Especially I could run.

I heard the Laskins's last broadcast through half a dozen times. Their unnamed ship had dropped out of hyperspace a million miles above BVS-1. Gravity warp would have prevented their getting closer in hyperspace. While her husband was crawling through the access tube for an instrument check, Sonya Laskin had called the Institute of Knowledge. "... We can't see it yet, not by naked eye. But we can see where it is. Every time some star or other goes behind it, there's a little ring of light. Just a minute, Peter's ready to use the telescope...."

Then the star's mass had cut the hyperspacial link. It was expected, and nobody had worried—then. Later, the same effect must have stopped them from escaping whatever attacked them into hyperspace.

When would-be rescuers found the ship, only the radar and the cameras were still running. They didn't tell us much. There had been no camera in the cabin. But the forward camera gave us, for one instant, a speed-blurred view of the neutron star. It was a featureless disk the orange color of perfect barbecue coals, if you know someone who can afford to burn wood. This object had been a neutron star a long time.

"There'll be no need to paint the ship," I told the president.

"You should not make such a trip with the walls transparent. You would go insane."

"I'm no flatlander. The mind-wrenching sight of naked space fills me with mild but waning interest. I want to know nothing's sneaking up behind me."

The day before I left, I sat alone in the General Products bar letting the puppeteer bartender make me drinks with his mouth. He did it well. Puppeteers were scattered around the bar in twos and threes, with a couple of men for variety, but the drinking hour had not yet arrived. The place felt empty.

I was pleased with myself. My debts were all paid, not that that would matter where I was going. I would leave with not a minicredit to my name, with nothing but the ship . . .

All told, I was well out of a sticky situation. I hoped I'd like being a rich exile.

I jumped when the newcomer sat down across from me. He was a foreigner, a middle-aged man wearing an expensive night-black business suit and a snow-white asymmetric beard. I let my face freeze and started to get up.

"Sit down, Mr. Shaeffer."

"Why?"

He told me by showing me a blue disk. An Earth government ident. I looked it over to show I was alert, not because I'd know an ersatz from the real thing.

"My name is Sigmund Ausfaller," said the government man. "I wish to say a few words concerning your assignment on behalf of General Products."

I nodded, not saying anything.

"A record of your verbal contract was sent to us as a matter of course. I noticed some peculiar things about it. Mr. Shaeffer, will you really take such a risk for only five hundred thousand stars?"

"I'm getting twice that."

"But you only keep half of it. The rest goes to pay debts. Then there are taxes . . . but never mind. What occurred to me was that a spaceship is a spaceship, and yours is very well armed and has powerful legs. An admirable fighting ship, if you were moved to sell it."

"But it isn't mine."

"There are those who would not ask. On Canyon, for example, or the Isolationist party of Wunderland."

I said nothing.

"Or, you might be planning a career of piracy. A risky business, piracy, and I don't take the notion seriously."

I hadn't even thought about piracy. But I'd have to give up on Wunderland.

"What I would like to say is this, Mr. Shaeffer. A single entrepreneur, if he were sufficiently dishonest, could do terrible damage to the reputation of all human beings everywhere. Most species find it necessary to police the ethics of their own members, and we are no exception. It occurred to me that you might not take your ship to the neutron star at all; that you would take it elsewhere and sell it. The puppeteers do not make invulnerable war vessels. They are pacifists. Your *Skydiver* is unique.

"Hence I have asked General Products to allow me to install a remote-control bomb in the *Skydiver*. Since it is inside the hull, the hull cannot protect you. I had it installed this afternoon.

"Now, notice! If you have not reported within a week, I will set off the bomb. There are several worlds within a week's hyperspace flight of here, but all recognize the dominion of Earth. If you flee, you must leave your ship within a week, so I hardly think you will land on a nonhabitable world. Clear?"

"Clear."

"If I am wrong, you may take a lie-detector test and prove it. Then you may punch me in the nose, and I will apologize handsomely."

I shook my head. He stood up, bowed, and left me sitting there cold sober.

Four films had been taken from the Laskins's cameras. In the time left to me I ran through them several times, without seeing anything out of the way. If the ship had run through a gas cloud, the impact could have killed the Laskins. At perihelion they were moving at better than half the speed of light. But there would have been friction, and I saw no sign of heating in the films. If something alive had attacked them, the beast was invisible to radar and to an enormous range of light frequencies. If the attitude jets had fired accidentally—I was clutching at straws—the light showed on none of the films.

There would be savage magnetic forces near BVS-1, but that couldn't have done any damage. No such force could penetrate a General Products hull. Neither could heat, except in special bands of radiated light, bands visible to at least one of the puppeteers' alien customers. I hold adverse opinions on the General Products hull, but they all concern the dull anonymity of the design. Or maybe I resent the fact that General Products holds a near-monopoly on spacecraft hulls, and isn't owned by human beings. But if I'd had to trust my life to, say, the Sinclair yacht I'd seen in the drugstore, I'd have chosen jail.

Jail was one of my three choices. But I'd be there for life. Ausfaller would see to that.

Or I could run for it in the *Skydiver*. But no world within reach

would have me. If I could find an undiscovered Earth-like world within a
week of We Made It. . . .

Fat Chance. I preferred BVS-1.

I thought that flashing circle of light was getting bigger, but it
flashed so seldom, I couldn't be sure. BVS-1 wouldn't show even in my
telescope. I gave that up and settled for just waiting.

Waiting, I remembered a long-ago summer spent on Jinx. There
were days when, unable to go outside because a dearth of clouds had
spread the land with raw blue-white sunlight, we amused ourselves by
filling party balloons with tap water and dropping them on the sidewalk
from three stories up. They made lovely splash patterns, which dried out
too fast. So we put a little ink in each balloon before filling it. Then the
patterns stayed.

Sonya Laskin had been in her chair when the chairs collapsed.
Blood samples showed that it was Peter who had struck them from
behind, like a water balloon dropped from a great height.

What could get through a General Products hull?

Ten hours to fall.

I unfastened the safety net and went for an inspection tour. The
access tunnel was three feet wide, just right to push through in free fall.
Below me was the length of the fusion tube; to the left, the laser cannon;
to the right, a set of curved side tubes leading to inspection points for the
gyros, the batteries and generator, the air plant, the hyperspace shunt
motors. All was in order—except me. I was clumsy. My jumps were
always too short or too long. There was no room to turn at the stern end,
so I had to back fifty feet to a side tube.

Six hours to go, and still I couldn't find the neutron star. Probably I
would see it only for an instant, passing at better than half the speed of
light. Already my speed must be enormous.

Were the stars turning blue?

Two hours to go—and I was sure they were turning blue. Was my
speed that high? Then the stars behind should be red. Machinery blocked
the view behind me, so I used the gyros. The ship turned with peculiar
sluggishness. And the stars behind were blue, not red. All around me
were blue-white stars.

Imagine light falling into a savagely steep gravitational well. It
won't accelerate. Light can't move faster than light. But it can gain in

energy, in frequency. The light was falling on me, harder and harder as I dropped.

I told the dictaphone about it. That dictaphone was probably the best-protected item on the ship. I had already decided to earn my money by using it, just as if I expected to collect. Privately I wondered just how intense the light would get.

Skydiver had drifted back to vertical, with its axis through the neutron star, but now it faced outward. I'd thought I had the ship stopped horizontally. More clumsiness. I used the gyros. Again the ship moved mushily, until it was halfway through the swing. Then it seemed to fall automatically into place. It was as if the *Skydiver* preferred to have its axis through the neutron star.

I didn't like that.

I tried the maneuver again, and again the *Skydiver* fought back. But this time there was something else. Something was pulling at me.

So I unfastened my safety net—and fell headfirst into the nose.

The pull was light, about a tenth of a gee. It felt more like sinking through honey than falling. I climbed back into my chair, tied myself in with the net, now hanging face down, and turned on the dictaphone. I told my story in such nitpicking detail that my hypothetical listeners could not but doubt my hypothetical sanity. "I think this is what happened to the Laskins," I finished. "If the pull increases, I'll call back."

Think? I never doubted it. This strange, gentle pull was inexplicable. Something inexplicable had killed Peter and Sonya Laskin. Q.E.D.

Around the point where the neutron star must be, the stars were like smeared dots of oilpaint, smeared radially. They glared with an angry, painful light. I hung face down in the net and tried to think.

It was an hour before I was sure. The pull was increasing. And I still had an hour to fall.

Something was pulling on me, but not on the ship.

No, that was nonsense. What could reach out to me through a General Products hull? It must be the other way around. Something was pushing on the ship, pushing it off course.

If it got worse, I could use the drive to compensat. Meanwhile, the ship was being pushed *away* from BVS-1, which was fine by me.

But if I was wrong, if the ship was not somehow being pushed away from BVS-1, the rocket motor would send the *Skydiver* crashing into eleven miles of neutronium.

And why wasn't the rocket already firing? If the ship was being pushed off course, the autopilot should be fighting back. The accelerometer was in good order. It had looked fine when I made my inspection tour down the access tube.

Could something be pushing on the ship *and* on the accelerometer, but not on me? It came down to the same impossibility: something that could reach through a General Products hull.

To hell with theory, said I to myself, said I. I'm getting out of here. To the dictaphone I said, "The pull has increased dangerously. I'm going to try to alter my orbit."

Of course, once I turned the ship outward and used the rocket, I'd be adding my own acceleration to the X-force. It would be a strain, but I could stand it for a while. If I came within a mile of BVS-1, I'd end like Sonya Laskin.

She must have waited face down in a net like mine, waited without a drive unit, waited while the pressure rose and the net cut into her flesh, waited until the net snapped and dropped her into the nose, to lie crushed and broken until the X-force tore the very chairs loose and dropped them on her.

I hit the gyros.

The gyros weren't strong enough to turn me. I tried it three times. Each time the ship rotated about fifty degrees and hung there, motionless, while the whine of the gyros went up and up. Released, the ship immediately swung back to position. I was nose down to the neutron star, and I was going to stay that way.

Half an hour to fall, and the X-force was over a gee. My sinuses were in agony. My eyes were ripe and ready to fall out. I don't know if I could have stood a cigarette, but I didn't get the chance. My pack of Fortunados had fallen out of my pocket when I dropped into the nose. There it was, four feet beyond my fingers, proof that the X-force acted on other objects besides me. Fascinating.

I couldn't take any more. If it dropped me shrieking into the neutron star, I had to use the drive. And I did. I ran the thrust up until I was approximately in free fall. The blood which had pooled in my extremities went back where it belonged. The gee dial registered one point two gee. I cursed it for a lying robot.

The soft-pack was bobbing around in the nose, and it occurred to me that a little extra nudge on the throttle would bring it to me. I tried it. The pack drifted toward me, and I reached, and like a sentient thing it speeded up to avoid my clutching hand. I snatched at it again as it went past my ear, and again it was moving too fast. That pack was going at a hell of a clip, considered that here I was practically in free fall. It dropped through the door to the relaxation room, still picking up speed, blurred and vanished as it entered the access tube. Seconds later I heard a solid *thump*.

But that was *crazy*. Already the X-force was pulling blood into my face. I pulled my lighter out, held it at arm's length and let go. It fell gently into the nose. But the pack of Fortunados had hit like I'd dropped it from a *building*.

Well.

I nudged the throttle again. The mutter of fusing hydrogen reminded me that if I tried to keep this up all the way, I might well put the General Products hull to its toughest test yet: smashing it into a neutron star at half lightspeed. I could see it now: a transparent hull containing only a few cubic inches of dwarf-star matter wedged into the tip of the nose.

At one point four gee, according to that lying gee dial, the lighter came loose and drifted toward me. I let it go. It was clearly falling when it reached the doorway. I pulled the throttle back. The loss of power jerked me violently forward, but I kept my face turned. The lighter slowed and hesitated at the entrance to the access tube. Decided to go through. I cocked my ears for the sound, then jumped as the whole ship rang like a gong.

And the accelerometer was right at the ship's center of mass. Otherwise the ship's mass would have thrown the needle off. The puppeteers were fiends for ten-decimal-point accuracy.

I favored the dictaphone with a few fast comments, then got to work reprogramming the autopilot. Luckily what I wanted was simple. The X-force was but an X-force to me, but now I knew how it behaved. I might actually live through this.

The stars were fiercely blue, warped to streaked lines near that special point. I thought I could see it now, very small and dim and red, but it might have been imagination. In twenty minutes I'd be rounding the neutron star. The drive grumbled behind me. In effective free fall, I unfastened the safety net and pushed myself out of the chair.

A gentle push aft—and ghostly hands grasped my legs. Ten pounds of weight hung by my fingers from the back of the chair. The pressure should drop fast. I'd programmed the autopilot to reduce the thrust from two gees to zero during the next two minutes. All I had to do was be at the center of mass, in the access tube, when the thrust went to zero.

Something gripped the ship through a General Products hull. A psychokinetic life form stranded on a sun twelve miles in diameter? But how could anything alive stand such gravity?

Something might be stranded in orbit. There is life in space: outsiders and sailseeds, and maybe others we haven't found yet. For all I knew or cared, BVS-1 itself might be alive. It didn't matter. I knew what the X-force was trying to do. It was trying to pull the ship apart.

There was no pull on my fingers. I pushed aft and landed on the back wall, on bent legs. I knelt over the door, looking aft/down. When free fall came, I pulled myself through and was in the relaxation room looking down/forward into the nose.

Gravity was changing faster than I liked. The X-force was growing as zero hour approached, while the compensating rocket thrust dropped. The X-force tended to pull the ship apart; it was two gee forward at the nose, two gee backward at the tail, and diminished to zero at the center of mass. Or so I hoped. The pack and lighter had behaved as if the force pulling them had increased for every inch they moved sternward.

The back wall was fifteen feet away. I had to jump it with gravity changing in midair. I hit on my hands, bounced away. I'd jumped too late. The region of free fall was moving through the ship like a wave as the thrust dropped. It had left me behind. Now the back wall was "up" to me, and so was the access tube.

Under something less than half a gee, I jumped for the access tube. For one long moment I stared into the three-foot tunnel, stopped in midair and already beginning to fall back, as I realized that there was nothing to hang on to. Then I stuck my hands in the tube and spread them against the sides. It was all I needed. I levered myself up and started to crawl.

The dictaphone was fifty feet below, utterly unreachable. If I had anything more to say to General Products, I'd have to say it in person. Maybe I'd get the chance. Because I knew what force was trying to tear the ship apart.

It was the tide.

The motor was off, and I was at the ship's midpoint. My spread-eagled position was getting uncomfortable. It was four minutes to perihelion.

Something creaked in the cabin below me. I couldn't see what it was, but I could clearly see a red point glaring among blue radial lines, like a lantern at the bottom of a well. To the sides, between the fusion tube and the tanks and other equipment, the blue stars glared at me with a light that was almost violet. I was afraid to look too long. I actually thought they might blind me.

There must have been hundreds of gravities in the cabin. I could even feel the pressure change. The air was thin at this height, one hundred and fifty feet above the control room.

And now, almost suddenly, the red dot was more than a dot. My time was up. A red disk leapt up at me; the ship swung around me; I gasped and shut my eyes tight. Giants' hands gripped my arms and legs and head, gently but with great firmness, and tried to pull me in two. In that moment it came to me that Peter Laskin had died like this. He'd made the same guess I had, and he'd tried to hide in the access tube. But he'd slipped . . . as I was slipping. . . . From the control room came a multiple shriek of tearing metal. I tried to dig my feet into the hard tube walls. Somehow they held.

When I got my eyes open the red dot was shrinking into nothing.

The puppeteer president insisted I be put in a hospital for observation. I didn't fight the idea. My face and hands were flaming red, with blisters rising, and I ached as though I'd been beaten. Rest and tender loving care, that's what I wanted.

I was floating between a pair of sleeping plates, hideously uncomfortable, when the nurse came to announce a visitor. I knew who it was from her peculiar expression.

"What can get through a General Products hull?" I asked it.

"I hoped you would tell me." The president rested on its single back leg, holding a stick that gave off green incense-smelling smoke.

"And so I will. Gravity."

"Do not play with me, Beowulf Shaeffer. This matter is vital."

"I'm not playing. Does your world have a moon?"

"That information is classified." The puppeteers are cowards. Nobody knows where they come from, and nobody is likely to find out.

"Do you know what happens when a moon gets too close to its primary?"

"It falls apart."

"Why?"

"I do not know."

"Tides."

"What is a tide?"

Oho, said I to myself, said I. "I'm going to try to tell you. The Earth's moon is almost two thousand miles in diameter and does not rotate with respect to Earth. I want you to pick two rocks on the moon, one at the point nearest the Earth, one at the point farthest away."

"Very well."

"Now, isn't it obvious that if those rocks were left to themselves, they'd fall away from each other? They're in two different orbits, mind you, concentric orbits, one almost two thousand miles outside the other. Yet those rocks are forced to move at the same orbital speed."

"The one outside is moving faster."

"Good point. So there *is* a force trying to pull the moon apart. Gravity holds it together. Bring the moon close enough to Earth, and those two rocks would simply float away."

"I see. Then this 'tide' tried to pull your ship apart. It was powerful enough in the lifesystem of the Institute ship to pull the acceleration chairs out of their mounts."

"And to crush a human being. Picture it. The ship's nose was just seven miles from the center of BVS-1. The tail was three hundred feet farther out. Left to themselves, they'd have gone in completely different orbits. My head and feet tried to do the same thing when I got close enough."

"I see. Are you molting?"

"What?"

"I notice you are losing your outer integument in spots."

"Oh, *that*. I got a bad sunburn from exposure to starlight. It's not important."

Two heads stared at each other for an eyeblink. A shrug? The pupeteer said, "We have deposited the residue of your pay with the Bank of We Made It. One Sigmund Ausfaller, human, has frozen the account until your taxes are computed."

"Figures."

"If you will talk to reporters now, explaining what happened to the Institute ship, we will pay you ten thousand stars. We will pay cash so that you may use it immediately. It is urgent. There have been rumors."

"Bring 'em in." As an afterthought I added, "I can also tell them that your world is moonless. That should be good for a footnote somewhere."

"I do not understand." But two long necks had drawn back, and the pupeteer was watching me like a pair of pythons.

"You'd know what a tide was if you had a moon. You couldn't avoid it."

"Would you be interested in—"

"A million stars? I'd be fascinated. I'll even sign a contract if it states what we're hiding. How do *you* like being blackmailed for a change?"

COSMIC DISASTERS

Visions of apocalypse and catastrophe are a revered tradition in science fiction, and come in a bewildering variety—one large group consists of the end coming about through natural means—floods, plagues, cosmic disasters like comets hitting the Earth, etc. In the nineteenth century these stories frequently involved a message to the effect that mankind somehow deserved such fates, although many of the tales were simply meant to be exciting adventures. A second, more recent group consists of stories in which the cause of the end is man himself, most usually via the weapons he has built or the pollution his factories have poured into the environment.

While the potential for man-made disasters is readily apparent, natural disasters may be even more dangerous. For example, it is now believed that approximately sixty-five million years ago a large fragment of cosmic matter struck the earth, piercing its crust to form Iceland, and tossing so much dust into the air that the dinosaurs died from lowered temperatures and decreased vegetation.

Indeed, the first cosmic disaster story, "The Conversation of Eiros and Charmion" (*Burton's Gentleman's Magazine*, December 1839) dealt with earth's destruction as a result of being hit by a comet, a theme which has again become popular (Larry Niven and Jerry Pournelle, *Lucifer's Hammer*, 1977) as we await the return of Halley's Comet in 1986.

THE CONVERSATION OF EIROS AND CHARMION

Edgar Allen Poe *(1839)*

> I will bring fire to thee.
> EURIPIDES, *Androm.* [257].

EIROS.

*W*hy *do you call me Eiros?*

CHARMION.

So henceforward will you always be called. You must forget, too, *my* earthly name, and speak to me as Charmion.

EIROS.

This is indeed no dream!

CHARMION.

Dreams are with us no more—but of these mysteries anon. I rejoice to see you looking lifelike and rational. The film of the shadow has already passed from off your eyes. Be of heart, and fear nothing. Your allotted days of stupor have expired; and, tomorrow, I will myself induct you into the full joys and wonders of your novel existence.

EIROS.

True—I feel no stupor—none at all. The wild sickness and the terrible darkness have left me, and I hear no longer that mad, rushing, horrible sound, like the "voice of many waters." Yet my senses are bewildered, Charmion, with the keenness of their perception of *the new*.

CHARMION.

A few days will remove all this; but I fully understand you, and feel for you. It is now ten earthly years since I underwent what you undergo —yet the remembrance of it hangs by me still. You have now suffered all of pain, however, which you will suffer in Aidenn.

EIROS.

In Aidenn?

CHARMION.

In Aidenn.

EIROS.

Oh God!—pity me, Charmion!—I am over burdened with the majesty of all things—of the unknown now known—of the speculative Future merged in the august and certain Present.

CHARMION.

Grapple not now with such thoughts. Tomorrow we will speak of this. Your mind wavers, and its agitation will find relief in the exercise of simple memories. Look not around, nor forward—but back. I am burning with anxiety to hear the details of that stupendous event which threw you among us. Tell me of it. Let us converse of familiar things, in the old familiar language of the world which has so fearfully perished.

EIROS.

Most fearfully, feafully!—this is indeed no dream.

CHARMION.

Dreams are no more. Was I much mourned, My Eiros?

EIROS.

Mourned, Charmion?—oh deeply. To that last hour of all, there hung a cloud of intense gloom and devout sorrow over your household.

CHARMION.

And that last hour—speak of it. Remember that, beyond the naked fact of the catastrophe itself, I know nothing. When, coming out from among mankind, I passed into Night through the Grave—at that period, if I remember aright, the calamity which overwhelmed you was utterly unanticipated. But, indeed, I knew little of the speculative philosophy of the day.

EIROS.

The individual calamity was, as you say, entirely unanticipated; but analogous misfortunes had been long a subject of discussion with astronomers. I need scarce tell you, my friend, that, even when you left us, men had agreed to understand those passages in the most holy writings which speak of the final destruction of all things by fire, as having reference to the orb of the earth alone. But in regard to the immediate agency of the ruin, speculation had been at fault from that epoch in astronomical knowledge in which the comets were divested of the terrors of flame. The very moderate density of these bodies had been well established. They had been observed to pass among the satellites of Jupiter, without bringing about any sensible alteration either in the masses or in the orbits of these secondary planets. We had long regarded the wanderers as vapory creations of inconceivable tenuity, and as altogether incapable of doing injury to our substantial globe, even in the event of contact. But contact was not in any degree dreaded; for the elements of all the comets were accurately known. That among *them* we should look for the agency of the threatened fiery destruction had been for many years considered an inadmissible idea. But wonders and wild fancies had been, of late days, strangely rife among mankind; and, although it was only with a few of the ignorant that actual apprehension prevailed upon the announcement by astronomers of a *new* comet, yet this announcement was generally received with I know not what of agitation and mistrust.

The elements of the strange orb were immediately calculated, and it was at once conceded by all observers that its path, at perihelion, would bring it into very close proximity with the earth. There were two or three astronomers, of secondary note, who resolutely maintained that a contact was inevitable. I cannot very well express to you the effect of this intelligence upon the people. For a few short days they would not believe

79

an assertion which their intellect, so long employed among worldly considerations, could not in any manner grasp. But the truth of a vitally important fact soon makes its way into the understanding of even the most stolid. Finally, all men saw that astronomical knowledge lied not, and they awaited the comet. Its approach was not, at first, seemingly rapid; nor was its appearance of very unusual character. It was of a dull red, and had little perceptible train. For seven or eight days we saw no material increase in its apparent diameter, and but a partial alteration in its color. Meantime, the ordinary affairs of men were discarded, and all interests absorbed in a growing discussion, instituted by the philosophic, in respect to the cometary nature. Even the grossly ignorant aroused their sluggish capacities to such considerations. The learned *now* gave their intellect—their soul—to no such points as the allaying of fear, or to the sustenance of loved theory. They sought—they panted for right views. They groaned for perfected knowledge. *Truth* arose in the purity of her strength and exceeding majesty, and the wise bowed down and adored.

That material injury to our globe or to its inhabitants would result from the apprehended contact was an opinion which hourly lost ground among the wise; and the wise were now freely permitted to rule the reason and the fancy of the crowd. It was demonstrated that the density of the comet's *nucleus* was far less than that of our rarest gas; and the harmless passage of a similar visitor among the satellites of Jupiter was a point strongly insisted upon, and which served greatly to allay terror. Theologists, with an earnestness fear-enkindled, dwelt upon the biblical prophecies, and expounded them to the people with a directness and simplicity of which no previous instance had been known. That the final destruction of the earth must be brought about by the agency of fire was urged with a spirit that enforced everywhere conviction; and that the comets were of no fiery nature (as all men now knew) was a truth which relieved all, in a great measure, from the apprehension of the great calamity foretold. It is noticeable that the popular prejudices and vulgar errors in regard to pestilence and wars—errors which were wont to prevail upon every appearance of a comet—were now altogether unknown. As if by some sudden convulsive exertion, reason had at once hurled superstition from her throne. The feeblest intellect had derived vigor from excessive interest.

What minor evils might arise from the contact were points of elaborate question. The learned spoke of slight geological disturbances, of probable alterations in climate, and consequently in vegetation; of possible magnetic and electric influences. Many held that no visible or perceptible effect would in any manner be produced. While such discussions were going on, their subject gradually approached, growing larger in apparent diameter, and of a more brilliant luster. Mankind grew paler as it came. All human operations were suspended.

There was an epoch in the course of the general sentiment when the comet had attained, at length, a size surpassing that of any previously recorded visitation. The people now, dismissing any lingering hope that the astronomers were wrong, experienced all the certainty of evil. The chimerical aspect of their terror was gone. The hearts of the stoutest of our race beat violently within their bosoms. A very few days sufficed, however, to merge even such feelings in sentiments more unendurable. We could no longer apply to the strange orb any *accustomed* thoughts. Its *historical* attributes had disappeared. It oppressed us with a hideous *novelty* of emotion. We saw it not as an astronomical phenomenon in the heavens, but as an incubus upon our hearts, and a shadow upon our brains. It had taken, with inconceivable rapidity, the character of a gigantic mantle of rare flame, extending from horizon to horizon.

Yet a day, and men breathed with greater freedom. It was clear that we were already within the influence of the comet; yet we lived. We even felt an unusual elasticity of frame and vivacity of mind. The exceeding tenuity of the object of our dread was apparent; for all heavenly objects were plainly visible through it. Meantime, our vegetation had perceptibly altered; and we gained faith from this predicted circumstance, in the foresight of the wise. A wild luxuriance of foliage, utterly unknown before, burst out upon every vegetable thing.

Yet another day—and the evil was not altogether upon us. It was now evident that its nucleus would first reach us. A wild change had come over all men; and the first sense of *pain* was the wild signal for general lamentation and horror. This first sense of pain lay in a rigorous constriction of the breast and lungs, and an insufferable dryness of the skin. It could not be denied that our atmosphere was radically affected; the conformation of this atmosphere and the possible modifications to which it might be subjected were now the topics of discussion. The result of investigation sent an electric thrill of the intensest terror through the universal heart of man.

It had been long known that the air which encircled us was a compound of oxygen and nitrogen gases, in the proportion of twenty-one measures of oxygen, and seventy-nine of nitrogen, in every one hundred of the atmosphere. Oxygen, which was the principle of combustion, and the vehicle of heat, was absolutely necessary to the support of animal life, and was the most powerful and energetic agent in nature. Nitrogen, on the contrary, was incapable of supporting either animal life or flame. An unnatural excess of oxygen would result, it had been ascertained, in just such an elevation of the animal spirits as we had latterly experienced. It was the pursuit, the extension of the idea, which had engendered awe. What would be the result of a total extraction of the nitrogen? A combustion irresistible, all-devouring, omniprevalent, immediate—the entire fulfillment, in all their minute and terrible details, of the fiery and horror-inspiring denunciations of the prophecies of the Holy Book.

Why need I paint, Charmion, the now disenchained frenzy of mankind? That tenuity in the comet which had previously inspired us with hope was now the source of the bitterness of despair. In its impalpable gaseous character we clearly perceived the consummation of Fate. Meantime a day again passed—bearing away with it the last shadow of Hope. We gasped in the rapid modification of the air. The red blood bounded tumultuously through its strict channels. A furious delirium possessed all men; and, with arms rigidly outstretched toward the threatening heavens, they trembled and shrieked aloud. But the nucleus of the destroyer was now upon us; even here in Aidenn, I shudder while I speak. Let me be brief—brief as the ruin that overwhelmed. For a moment there was a wild lurid light alone, visiting and penetrating all things. Then let us bow down, Charmion, before the excessive majesty of the great God!—then there came a shouting and pervading sound, as if from the mouth itself of Him; while the whole incumbent mass of ether in which we existed burst at once into a species of intense flame, for whose surpassing brilliancy and all-fervid heat even the angels in the high Heaven of pure knowledge have no name. Thus ended all.

EARTH INHERITED
BY OTHER MAMMALS

The question of who will inherit the earth has produced much interesting speculation. Generally, science fiction writers have made four types of suggestions: aliens, man's artificial creations, mutated humans, and lower earth forms.

Aliens kill man off or occasionally speculate about what humans might have been like (Athrur C. Clarke's "History Lesson," 1949). Mutants primarily result from atomic war, but sometimes from natural selection (H. G. Wells's "The Time Machine," 1895). Man's artificial creations are, for the most part, robots and androids who every now and then are part of a cycle in which homo sapiens triumphantly return (H. B. Hickey's "Full Circle," 1952). Lower earth forms who inherit are usually seen as having gained increased intelligence. They include animals (insects, mammals, and reptiles in decreasing order of frequency), vegetables (C. M. Kornbluth's "The Education of Tigress Macardle," 1957), and minerals (J. -H. Rosny aîné's "The Death of the Earth," 1912).

The four primary settings used in this motif are the threat's beginning, the domination over man, the death of man, and the world after man. This section considers stories only in the last two categories, since only they guarantee inheritance.

With these distinctions in mind, Lester del Rey's "The Faithful" (*Astounding Science Fiction*, April 1938) seems to be the first short story to suggest other mammals (dogs) would inherit the earth. Subsequent examples include apes (L. Sprague de Camp and P. Schuyler Miller, *Genus Homo*, 1941), bears (Daniel F. Galouye, "Project Barrier," 1958), and dolphins (Damon Knight, "The Second-Class Citizen," 1963).

One of American Science Fiction's most important figures, Mr. del Rey is the author of many influential stories, has served as editor or critic for several speculative magazines, and is now editor of a prestigious science fiction and fantasy paperback publishing house.

THE FAITHFUL

Lester del Rey *(1938)*

*T*oday, *in a green and lovely world, here in the mightiest of human* cities, the last of the human race is dying. And we of Man's creation are left to mourn his passing, and to worship the memory of Man, who controlled all that he knew save only himself.

I am old, as my people go, yet my blood is still young and my life may go on for untold ages yet, if what this last of Men has told is true. And that also is Man's work, even as we and the Ape-People are his work in the last analysis. We of the Dog-People are old, and have lived a long time with Man. And yet, but for Roger Stren, we might still be baying at the moon and scratching the fleas from our hides, or lying at the ruins of Man's empire in dull wonder at his passing.

There are earlier records of dogs who mouthed clumsily a few Man words, but Hungor was the pet of Roger Stren, and in the labored efforts at speech, he saw an ideal and a life work. The operation on Hungor's throat and mouth, which made Man-speech more nearly possible was comparatively simple. The search for other "talking" dogs was harder.

But he found five besides Hungor, and with this small start he began. Selection and breeding, surgery and training, gland implantation, and X-ray mutation were his methods, and he made steady progress. At first money was a problem, but his pets soon drew attention and commanded high prices.

When he died, the original six had become thousands, and he had watched over the raising of twenty generations of dogs. A generation of my kind then took only three years. He had seen his small back-yard pen develop into a huge institution, with a hundred followers and students, and had found the world eager for his success. Above all, he had seen tail-wagging give place to limited speech in that short time.

The movement he had started continued. At the end of two thousand years, we had a place beside Man in his work that would have been inconceivable to Roger Stren himself. We had our schools, our houses, our work with man, and a society of our own. Even our independence, when we wanted it. And our life span was not fourteen, but fifty or more years.

Man, too, had traveled a long way. The stars were almost within his grasp. The barren moon had been his for centuries. Mars and Venus lay beckoning, and he had reached them twice, but not to return. They lay close at hand. Almost, Man had conquered the universe.

But he had not conquered himself. There had been many setbacks to his progress because he had to go out and kill the others of his kind. And now, the memory from his past called again, and he went out in battle against himself. Cities crumbled to dust, the plains to the south became barren deserts again, Chicago lay covered in a green mist. The death killed slowly, so that Man fled from the city and died, leaving it an empty place. The mist hung there, clinging days, months, years—after Man had ceased to be.

I, too, went out to war, driving a plane built for my people, over the cities of the Rising Sun Empire. The tiny atomic bombs fell from my ship on houses, on farms, on all that was Man's, who had made my race what it was. For my Men told me I must fight.

Somehow, I was not killed. And after the last Great Drive, when half of Man was already dead, I gathered my people about me and we followed to the north, where some of my Men had turned to find a sanctuary from the war. Of Man's work, three cities still stood—wrapped in the green mist, and useless. And Man huddled around little fires and hid himself in the forest, hunting his food in small clans. Yet hardly a year of the war had passed.

For a time, the Men and my people lived in peace, planning to rebuild what had been, once the war finally ceased. Then came the Plague. The anti-toxin which had been developed was ineffective as the Plague increased in its virulency. It spread over land and sea, gripped Man who had invented it, and killed him. It was like a strong dose of strychnine, leaving Man to die in violent cramps and retchings.

For a brief time, Man united against it, but there was no control. Remorselessly it spread, even into the little settlement they had founded in the north. And I watched in sorrow as my Men around me were seized with its agony. Then we of the Dog-People were left alone in a shattered world from whence Man had vanished. For weeks we labored at the little radio we could operate, but there was no answer; and we knew that Man was dead.

There was little we could do. We had to forage our food as of old, and cultivate our crops in such small way as our somewhat modified forepaws permitted. And the barren north country was not suited to us.

I gathered my scattered tribes about me, and we began the long trek south. We moved from season to season, stopping to plant our food in the spring, hunting in the fall. As our sleds grew old and broke down, we could not replace them, and our travel became even slower. Sometimes we came upon our kind in smaller packs. Most of them had gone back to savagery, and these we had to mold to us by force. But little by little, growing in size, we drew south. We sought Men; for two hundred thousand years we of the Dog-People had lived with and for Man.

In the wilds of what had once been Washington State we came upon another group who had not fallen back to the law of tooth and fang. They had horses to work for them, even crude harnesses and machines which they could operate. There we stayed for some ten years, setting up a government and building ourselves a crude city. Where Man had his hands, we had to invent what could be used with our poor feet and our teeth. But we had found a sort of security, and had even acquired some of Man's books by which we could teach our young.

Then into our valley came a clan of our people, moving west, who told us they had heard that one of our tribes sought refuge and provender in a mighty city of great houses lying by a lake in the east. I could only guess that it was Chicago. Of the green mist they had not heard—only that life was possible there.

Around our fires that night we decided that if the city were habitable, there would be homes and machines designed for us. And it might be there were Men, and the chance to bring up our young in the heritage which was their birth-right. For weeks we labored in preparing ourselves for the long march to Chicago. We loaded our supplies in our crude carts, hitched our animals to them, and began the eastward trip.

It was nearing winter when we camped outside the city, still mighty and imposing. In the sixty years of its desertion, nothing had perished that we could see; the fountains to the west were still playing, run by automatic engines.

We advanced upon the others in the dark, quietly. They were living in a great square, littered with filth, and we noted that they had not even fire left from civilization. It was a savage fight, while it lasted, with no quarter given nor asked. But they had sunk too far, in the lazy shelter of Man's city, and the clan was not as large as we had heard. By the time the sun rose there was not one of them but had been killed or imprisoned until we could train them to our ways. The ancient city was ours, the green mist gone after all those years.

Around us were abundant provisions, the food factories which I knew how to run, the machines that Man had made to fit our needs, the houses in which we could dwell, power drawn from the bursting core of the atom which needed only the flick of a switch to start. Even without hands, we could live here in peace and security for ages. Perhaps here my dreams of adapting our feet to handle Man's tools and doing his work were possible, even if no Men were found.

We cleared the muck from the city and moved into Greater South Chicago, where our people had had their section of the city. I, and a few of the elders who had been taught by their fathers in the ways of Man, set up the old regime, and started the great water and light machines. We had returned to a life of certainty.

And four weeks later, one of my lieutenants brought Paul Kenyon before me. Man! Real and alive, after all this time! He smiled, and I motioned my eager people away.

"I saw your lights," he smiled. "I thought at first some men had come back, but that is not to be; but civilization still has its followers, evidently, so I asked one of you to take me to the leader. Greetings from all that is left of Man!"

"Greetings," I gasped. It was like seeing the return of the gods. My breath was choked; a great peace and fulfillment surged over me. "Greetings, and the blessings of your God. I had no hope of seeing Man again."

He shook his head. "I am the last. For fifty years I have been searching for men—but there are none. Well, you have done well. I should like to live among you, work with you—when I can. I survived the Plague somehow, but it comes on me yet, more often now, and I can't move nor care for myself then. That is why I have come to you.

"Funny." He paused. "I seem to recognize you. Hungor Beowulf, XIV? I am Paul Kenyon. Perhaps you remember me? No? Well, it was a long time, and you were young. But that white streak under the eye still shows." A greater satisfaction came to me that he remembered me.

Now one had come among us with hands, and he was of great help. But most of all, he was of the old Men, and gave point to our working. But often, as he had said, the old sickness came over him, and he lay in violent convulsions, from which he was weak for days. We learned to care for him, when he needed it, even as we learned to fit our society to his presence. And at last, he came to me with a suggestion.

"Hungor," he said, "if you had one wish, what would it be?"

"The return of Man. The old order, where we could work together. You know as well as I how much we need Man."

He grinned crookedly. "Now, it seems, Man needs you more. But if that were denied, what next?"

"Hands," I said. "I dream of them at night and plan for them by day, but I will never see them."

"Maybe you will, Hungor. Haven't you ever wondered why you go on living, twice normal age, in the prime of your life? Have you never wondered how I have withstood the Plague which still runs in my blood, and how I still seem only in my thirties, though nearly seventy years have passed since a man has been born?"

"Sometimes." I answered. "I have no time for wonder, now, and when I do—Man is the only answer I have."

"A good answer," he said. "Yes, Hungor, Man is the answer. That is why I remember you. Three years before the war, when you were just reaching maturity, you came into my laboratory. Do you remember?"

"The experiment," I said. "That is why you remember me?"

"Yes, the experiment. I altered your glands somewhat, implanted certain tissues into your body, as I had done to myself. I was seeking the secret of immortality. Though there was no reaction at the time, it worked, and I don't know how much longer we may live—or you may; it helped me resist the Plague, but did not overcome it."

So that was the answer. He stood staring at me a long time. "Yes, unknowingly, I saved you to carry on Man's future for him. But we were talking of hands.

"As you know, there is a great continent to the east of the Americas, called Africa. But did you know Man was working there on the great apes, as he was working here on your people? We never made as much progress with them as with you. We started too late. Yet they spoke a simple language and served for common work. And we changed their hands so the thumb and fingers opposed, as do mine. There, Hungor, are your hands.''

Now Paul Kenyon and I laid plans carefully. Out in the hangars of the city there were aircraft designed for my people's use; heretofore I had seen no need of using them. The planes were in good condition, we found on examination, and my early training came back to me as I took the first ship up. They carried fuel to circle the globe ten times, and out in the lake the big fuel tanks could be drawn on when needed.

Together, though he did most of the mechanical work between spells of sickness, we stripped the planes of all their war equipment. Of the six hundred planes, only two were useless, and the rest would serve to carry some two thousand passengers in addition to the pilots. If the apes had reverted to complete savagery, we were equipped with tanks of anaesthetic gas by which we could overcome them and strap them in the planes for the return. In the houses around us, we built accommodations for them strong enough to hold them by force, but designed for their comfort if they were peaceable.

At first, I had planned to lead the expedition. But Paul Kenyon pointed out that they would be less likely to respond to us than to him. ''After all,'' he said, ''men educated them and cared for them, and they probably remember us dimly. But your people they know only as the wild dogs who are their enemies. I can go out and contact their leaders, guarded of course by your people. But otherwise, it might mean battle.''

Each day I took up a few of our younger ones in the planes and taught them to handle the controls. As they were taught, they began the instruction of others. It was a task which took months to finish, but my people knew the need of hands as well as I; any faint hope was well worth trying.

It was late spring when the expedition set out. I could follow their progress by means of television, but could work the controls only with difficulty. Kenyon, of course, was working the controls at the other end, when he was able.

They met with a storm over the Atlantic Ocean, and three of the ships went down. But under the direction of my lieutenant and Kenyon the rest weathered the storm. They landed near the ruins of Capetown, but found no trace of the Ape-People. Then began weeks of scouting over the jungles and plains. They saw apes, but on capturing a few they found them only the primitive creatures which nature had developed.

It was by accident they finally met with success. Camp had been made near a waterfall for the night, and fires had been lit to guard against the savage beasts which roamed the land. Kenyon was in one of his rare moments of good health. The telecaster had been set up in a tent near the outskirts of the camp, and he was broadcasting a complete account of the day. Then, abruptly, over the head of the Man was raised a rough and shaggy face.

He must have seen the shadow, for he started to turn sharply, then caught himself and moved slowly around. Facing him was one of the apes. He stood there silently, watching the ape, now knowing whether it was savage or well-disposed. It, too, hesitated; then it advanced.

"Man—Man," it mouthed. "You came back. Where were you? I am Tolemy, and I saw you, and I came."

"Tolemy," said Kenyon, smiling. "It is good to see you, Tolemy. Sit down; let us talk. I am glad to see you. Ah, Tolemy, you look old; were your father and mother raised by Man?"

"I am eighty years, I think. It is hard to know. I was raised by Man long ago. And now I am old; my people say I grow too old to lead. They do not want me to come to you, but I know Man. He was good to me. And he had coffee and cigarettes."

"I have coffee and cigarettes, Tolemy," Kenyon smiled. "Wait, I will get them. And your people, is not life hard among them in the jungle? Would you like to go back with me?"

"Yes, hard among us. I want to go back with you. Are you many here?"

"No, Tolemy." He set the coffee and cigarettes before the ape, who drank eagerly and lit the smoke gingerly from a fire. "No, but I have friends with me. You must bring your people here, and let us get to be friends. Are there many of you?"

"Yes. Ten times we make ten tens—a thousand of us, almost. We are all that was left in the city of Man after the great fight. A Man freed us, and I led my people away, and we lived here in the jungle. They wanted to be in small tribes, but I made them one, and we are safe. Food is hard to find."

"We have much food in a big city, Tolemy, and friends who will help you, if you work for them. You remember the Dog-People, don't you? And you would work with them as with Man if they treated you as Man treated you, and fed you, and taught your people?"

"Dogs? I remember the Man-dogs. They were good. But here the dogs are bad. I smelled dog here; it was not like the dog we smell each day, and my nose was not sure. I will work with Man-dogs, but my people will be slow to learn them."

Later telecasts showed rapid progress. I saw the apes come in by twos and threes and meet Paul Kenyon, who gave them food, and introduced my people to them. This was slow, but as some began to lose their fear of us, others were easier to train. Only a few broke away and would not come.

Cigarettes that Man was fond of—but which my people never used—were a help, since they learned to smoke with great readiness.

It was months before they returned. When they came there were over nine hundred of the Ape-People with them, and Paul and Tolemy had begun their education. Our first job was a careful medical examination of Tolemy, but it showed him in good health, and with much of the vigor of a younger ape. Man had been lengthening the ages of his kind, as it had ours, and he was evidently a complete success.

Now they have been among us three years, and during that time we have taught them to use their hands at our instructions. Overhead the great monorail cars are running, and the factories have started to work again. They are quick to learn, with a curiosity that makes them eager for new knowledge. And they are thriving and multiplying here. We need no longer bewail the lack of hands; perhaps, in time to come, with their help, we can change our forepaws further, and learn to walk on two legs, as did Man.

Today I have come back from the bed of Paul Kenyon. We are often together now—perhaps I should include the faithful Tolemy—when he can talk, and among us there has grown a great friendship. I laid certain plans before him today for adapting the apes mentally and physically until they are men. Nature did it with an ape-like brute once; why can we not do it with the Ape-People now? The Earth would be peopled again, science would rediscover the stars, and Man would have a foster child in his own likeness.

And—we of the Dog-People have followed Man for two hundred thousand years. That is too long to change. Of all Earth's creatures, the Dog-People alone have followed Man thus. My people cannot lead now. No dog was ever complete without the companionship of Man. The Ape-People will be Men.

It is a pleasant dream, surely not an impossible one.

Kenyon smiled as I spoke to him, and cautioned me in the jesting way he uses when most serious, not to make them too much like Man, lest another Plague destroy them. Well, we can guard against that. I think he, too, had a dream of Man reborn, for there was a hint of tears in his eyes, and he seemed pleased with me.

There is but little to please him now, alone among us, wracked by pain, waiting the slow death he knows must come. The old trouble has grown worse, and the Plague has settled harder on him.

All we can do is give him sedatives to ease the pain now, though Tolemy and I have isolated the Plague we found in his blood. It seems a form of cholera, and with that information, we have done some work. The old Plague serum offers a clue, too. Some of our serums have seemed to ease the spells a little, but they have not stopped them.

It is a faint chance. I have not told him of our work, for only a stroke of luck will give us success before he dies.

Man is dying. Here in our laboratory, Tolemy keeps repeating something; a prayer, I think it is. Well, maybe the God whom he has learned from Man will be merciful, and grant us success.

Paul Kenyon is all that is left of the old world which Tolemy and I loved. He lies in the ward, moaning in agony, and dying. Sometimes he looks from his windows and sees the birds flying south; he gazes at them as if he would never see them again. Well, will he? Something he muttered once comes back to me:

"For no man knoweth—"

GENERATION STARSHIP

Many different strategies for sending ships to the stars have been suggested. (See Peter Nicholls, *The Science in Science Fiction*, 1982.) One of the most interesting concepts is the generation starship, a vehicle which takes centuries and is crewed by generation after generation of persons born, educated, and trained on board. Mark Twain anticipated the idea, proposing to write about a generation iceberg, drifting across our seas. Later Russian rocket scientist and science fiction writer Konstantin Tsiolkovsky suggested the idea in an article published in 1928. Perhaps the most famous science fictional work of this type is Robert Heinlein's *Orphans of the Sky* (1963), consisting of the novellas "Universe" and "Common Time" (both 1941). Heinlein cleverly arranged for the crew to be ignorant of the ship's original purpose, going so far as to create a "pocket universe" in which the people involved did not even know they were on a ship. *Starship* (also known as *Non-Stop*, 1958) by Brian W. Aldiss, may be an even better example of this concept. More recently, television used the concept in the series "The Starlost."

Don Wilcox's "The Voyage that Lasted 600 Years" (*Amazing Stories*, October 1940) was, however, the first story to use this concept. His work is well-written, but has been virtually ignored—this is only its second known reprinting. Wilcox, himself, lived in the Chicago area many years, teaching creative writing at Northwestern University. His work appeared infrequently in the science fiction field and then almost exclusively in Ziff-Davis publications.

THE VOYAGE THAT LASTED 600 YEARS

Don Wilcox *(1940)*

I

They gave us a gala send-off, the kind that keeps your heart bobbing up at your tonsils.

"It's a long, long way to the Milky Way!" the voices sang out. The band thundered the chorus over and over. The golden trumpaphones blasted our eardrums wide open. Thousands of people clapped their hands in time.

There were thirty-three of us—that is, there was supposed to be. As it turned out, there were thirty-five.

We were a dazzling parade of red, white and blue uniforms. We marched up the gangplank by couples, every couple a man and wife, every couple young and strong, for the selection had been rigid.

Captain Sperry and his wife and I—I being the odd man—brought up the rear. Reporters and cameramen swarmed at our heels. The microphones stopped us. The band and the crowd hushed.

"This is Captain Sperry telling you good-by," the amplified voice boomed. "In behalf of the thirty-three, I thank you for your grand farewell. We'll remember this hour as our last contact with our beloved Earth."

The crowd held its breath. The mighty import of our mission struck through every heart.

"We go forth into space to live—and to die," the captain said gravely. "But *our children's children*, born in space and reared in the light of our vision, will carry on our great purpose. And in centuries to come, *your children's children* may set forth for the Robinello planets, knowing that you will find an American colony already planted there."

97

The captain gestured good-by and the multitude responded with a thunderous cheer. Nothing so daring as a six-century nonstop flight had ever been undertaken before.

An announcer nabbed me by the sleeve and barked into the microphone.

"And now one final word from Professor Gregory Grimstone, the one man who is supposed to live down through the six centuries of this historic flight and see the journey through to the end."

"Ladies and gentlemen," I choked, and the echo of my swallow blobbed back at me from distant walls, "as Keeper of the Traditions, I give you my word that the S. S. *Flashaway* shall carry your civilization through to the end, unsoiled and unblemished!"

A cheer stimulated me and I drew a deep breath for a burst of oratory. But Captain Sperry pulled at my other sleeve.

"That's all. We're set to slide out in two minutes."

The reporters scurried down the gangplank and made a center rush through the crowd. The band struck up. Motors roared suddenly.

One lone reporter who had missed out on the interviews blitz-krieged up and caught me by the coattail.

"Hold it, Butch. Just a coupla words so I can whip up a column of froth for the *Star*—Well, I'll be damned! If it ain't 'Crackdown' Grimstone!"

I scowled. The reporter before me was none other than Bill Broscoe, one of my former pupils at college and a star athlete. At heart I knew that Bill was a right guy, but I'd be the last to tell him so.

"Broscoe!" I snarled. "Tardy as usual. You finally flunked my history course, didn't you?"

"Now, Crackdown," he whined, "don't go hopping on me. I won that Thanksgiving game for you, remember?"

He gazed at my red, white and blue uniform.

"So you're off for Robinello," he grinned.

"Son, this is my last minute on Earth, and *you* have to haunt me, of all people—"

"So you're the one that's taking the refrigerated sleeper, to wake up every hundred years—"

"And stir the fires of civilization among the crew—yes. Six hundred years from now when your bones have rotted, I'll still be carrying on."

"Still teaching 'em history? God forbid!" Broscoe grinned.

"I hope I have better luck than I did with you."

"Let 'em off easy on dates, Crackdown. Give them 1066 for William the Conqueror and 2066 for the *Flashaway* take-off. That's enough. Taking your wife, I suppose?"

At this impertinent question I gave Broscoe the cold eye.

"Pardon me," he said, suppressing a sly grin—proof enough that he had heard the devastating story about how I missed my wedding and got the air. "Faulty alarm clock wasn't it? Too bad, Crackdown. And you always ragged *me* about being tardy!"

With this jibe Broscoe exploded into laughter. Some people have the damnedest notions about what constitutes humor. I backed into the entrance of the space ship uncomfortably. Broscoe followed.

Zzzzippp!

The automatic door cut past me. I jerked Broscoe through barely in time to keep him from being bisected.

"Tardy as usual, my friend," I hooted. "You've missed your gangplank! That makes you the first castaway in space."

We took off like a shooting star, and the last I saw of Bill Broscoe, he stood at a rear window cursing as he watched the earth and the moon fall away into the velvety black heavens. And the more I laughed at him, the madder he got. No sense of humor.

Was that the last time I ever saw him? Well, no, to be strictly honest I had one more unhappy glimpse of him.

It happened just before I packed myself away for my first one hundred years' sleep.

I had checked over the "Who's Who Aboard the *Flashaway*"—the official register—to make sure that I was thoroughly acquainted with everyone on board; for these sixteen couples were to be the great-grand-parents of the next generation I would meet. Then I had promptly taken my leave of Captain Sperry and his wife, and gone directly to my refrigeration plant, where I was to suspend my life by instantaneous freezing.

I clicked the switches, and one of the two huge horizontal wheels—one in reserve, in the event of a breakdown—opened up for me like a door opening in the side of a gigantic doughnut, or better, a tubular merry-go-round. There was my nook waiting for me to crawl in.

Before I did so I took a backward glance toward the ballroom. The one-way glass partition, through which I could see but not be seen, gave me a clear view of the scene of merriment. The couples were dancing. The journey was off to a good start.

"A grand gang," I said to myself. No one doubted that the ship was equal to the six-hundred-year journey. The success would depend upon the people. Living and dying in this closely circumscribed world would put them to a severe test. All credit, I reflected, was due the planning committee for choosing such a congenial group.

"They're equal to it," I said optimistically. If their children would only prove as sturdy and adaptable as their parents, my job as Keeper of the Traditions would be simple.

But how, I asked myself, as I stepped into my life-suspension merry-go-round, would Bill Broscoe fit into this picture? Not a half bad guy. Still—

My final glance through the one-way glass partition slew me. Out of the throng I saw Bill Broscoe dancing past with a beautiful girl in his arms. The girl was Louise—*my* Louise—the girl I had been engaged to marry!

In a flash it came to me—but not about Bill. I forgot him on the spot. About Louise.

Bless her heart, she'd come to find me. She must have heard that I had signed up for the *Flashaway*, and she had come aboard, a stowaway, to forgive me for missing the wedding—to marry me! Now—

A warning click sounded, a lid closed over me, my refrigerator-merry-go-round whirled—Blackness!

II

In a moment—or so it seemed—I was again gazing into the light of the refrigerating room. The lid stood open.

A stimulating warmth circulated through my limbs. Perhaps the machine, I half consciously concluded, had made no more than a preliminary revolution.

I bounded out with a single thought. I must find Louise. We could still be married. For the present I would postpone my entrance into the ice. And since the machine had been equipped with *two* merry-go-round freezers as an emergency safeguard—ah! Happy thought—perhaps Louise would be willing to undergo life suspension with me!

I stopped at the one-way glass partition, astonished to see no signs of dancing in the ballroom. I could scarcely see the ballroom, for it had been darkened.

Upon unlocking the door (the refrigerator room was my own private retreat) I was bewildered. An unaccountable change had come over everything. What it was, I couldn't determine at the moment. But the very air of the ballroom was different.

A few dim green light bulbs burned along the walls—enough to show me that the dancers had vanished. Had time enough elapsed for night to come on? My thoughts spun dizzily. Night, I reflected, would consist simply of turning off the lights and going to bed. It had been agreed in our plan that our twenty-four hour Earth day would be maintained for the sake of regularity.

But there was something more intangible that struck me. The furniture had been changed about, and the very walls seemed *older*. Something more than minutes had passed since I left this room.

Strangest of all the windows were darkened.

In a groggy state of mind I approached one of the windows in hopes of catching a glimpse of the solar system. I was still puzzling over how much time might have elapsed. Here, at least, was a sign of very recent activity.

"Wet Paint" read the sign pinned to the window. The paint was still sticky. What the devil—

The ship, of course, was fully equipped for blind flying. But aside from the problems of navigation, the crew had anticipated enjoying a wonderland of stellar beauty through the portholes. Now, for some strange reason, every window had been painted opaque.

I listened. Slow measured steps were pacing in an adjacent hallway. Nearing the entrance, I stopped, halted by a shrill sound from somewhere overhead. It came from one of the residential quarters that gave on the ballroom balcony.

It was the unmistakable wail of a baby.

Then another baby's cry struck up; and a third, from somewhere across the balcony, joined the chorus. Time, indeed, must have passed since I left this roomful of dancers.

Now some irate voices of disturbed sleepers added rumbling basses to the symphony of wailings. Grumbles of "Shut that little devil up!" and poundings of fists on walls thundered through the empty ballroom.

In a burst of inspiration I ran to the records room, where the ship's "Who's Who" was kept.

The door to the records room was locked, but the footsteps of some sleepless person I had heard now pounded down the dimly lighted hallway. I looked upon the aged man. I had never seen him before. He stopped at the sight of me; then snapping on a brighter light, came on confidently.

"Mr. Grimstone?" he said, extending his hand. "We've been expecting you. My name is William Broscoe—"

"Broscoe!"

"William Broscoe, the second. You knew my father, I believe."

I groaned and choked.

"And my mother," the old man continued, "always spoke very highly of you. I'm proud to be the first to greet you."

He politely overlooked the flush of purple that leaped into my face. For a moment nothing that I could say was intelligible.

He turned a key and we entered the records room. There I faced the inescapable fact. My full century had passed. The original crew of the *Flashaway* were long gone. A completely new generation was on the register.

Or, more accurately, three new generations: the children, the grandchildren, and the great-grandchildren of the generation I had known.

One hundred years had passed—and I had lain so completely suspended, owing to the freezing, that only a moment of my own life had been absorbed.

Eventually I was to get used to this; but on this first occasion I found it utterly shocking—even embarrassing. Only a few minutes ago, as my experience went, I was madly in love with Louise and had hopes of yet marrying her.

But now—well, the leather-bound "Who's Who" told all. Louise had been dead twenty years. Nearly thirty children now alive aboard the S. S. *Flashaway* could claim her as their great-grandmother. These carefully recorded pedigrees proved it.

And the patriarch of that fruitful tribe had been none other than Bill Broscoe, the fresh young athlete who had always been tardy for my history class. I gulped as if I were swallowing a baseball.

Broscoe—tardy! And I had missed my second chance to marry Louise—by a full century!

My fingers turned the pages of the register numbly. William Broscoe II misinterpreted my silence.

"I see you are quick to detect our trouble," he said, and the same deep conscientious concern showed in his expression that I had remembered in the face of his mother, upon our grim meeting after my alarm clock had failed and I had missed my own wedding.

Trouble? Trouble aboard the S. S. *Flashaway*, after all the careful advance planning we had done, and after all our array of budgeting and scheduling and vowing to stamp our systematic ways upon the oncoming generations? This, we had agreed, would be the world's most unique colonizing expedition; for every last trouble that might crop up on the six-hundred-year voyage had already been met and conquered by advance planning.

"They've tried to put off doing anything about it until your arrival," Broscoe said, observing respectfully that the charter invested in me the authority of passing upon all important policies. "But this very week three new babies arrived, which brings the trouble to a crisis. So the captain ordered a blackout of the heavens as an emergency measure."

"Heavens?" I grunted. "What have the heavens got to do with babies?"

"There's a difference of opinion on that. Maybe it depends upon how susceptible you are."

"Susceptible—to what?"

"The romantic malady."

I looked at the old man, much puzzled. He took me by the arm and led me toward the pilots' control room. Here were unpainted windows that revealed celestial glories beyond anything I had ever dreamed. Brilliant planets of varied hues gleamed through the blackness, while close at hand—almost close enough to touch—were numerous large moons, floating slowly past as we shot along our course.

"Some little show," the pilot grinned, "and it keeps getting better."

He proceeded to tell me just where we were and how few adjustments in the original time schedules he had had to make, and why this non-stop flight to Robinello would stand unequalled for centuries to come.

And I heard virtually nothing of what he said. I simply stood there, gazing at the unbelievable beauty of the skies. I was hypnotized, enthralled, shaken to the very roots. One emotion, one thought dominated me. I longed for Louise.

"The romantic malady, as I was saying," William Broscoe resumed, "may or may not be a factor in producing our large population. Personally, I think it's pure buncombe."

"Pure buncombe," I echoed, still thinking of Louise. If she and I had had moons like these—

"But nobody can tell Captain Dickinson anything. . . ."

There was considerable clamor and wrangling that morning as the inhabitants awakened to find their heavens blacked out. Captain Dickinson was none too popular anyway. Fortunately for him, many of the people took their grouches out on the babies who had caused the disturbance in the night.

Families with babies were supposed to occupy the rear staterooms—but there weren't enough rear staterooms. Or rather, there were too many babies.

Soon the word went the rounds that the Keeper of the Traditions had returned to life. I was duly banqueted and toasted and treated to lengthy accounts of the events of the past hundred years. And during the next few days many of the older men and women would take me aside for private conferences and spill their worries into my ears.

III

"What's the world coming to?" these granddaddies and grandmothers would ask. And before I could scratch my head for an answer, they would assure me that this expedition was headed straight for the rocks.

"It's all up with us. We've lost our grip on our original purposes. The Six-Hundred-Year Plan is nothing but a dead scrap of paper."

I'll admit things looked plenty black. And the more parlor conversations I was invited in on, the blacker things looked. I couldn't sleep nights.

"If our population keeps on increasing, we'll run out of food before we're halfway there," William Broscoe II repeatedly declared. "We've got to have a compulsory program of birth control. That's the only thing that will save us."

A delicate subject for parlor conversations, you think? This older generation didn't think so. I was astonished, and I'll admit I was a bit proud as well, to discover how deeply imbued these old graybeards were with *Flashaway* determination and patriotism. They had missed life in America by only one generation, and they were unquestionably the staunchest of flag wavers on board.

The younger generations were less outspoken, and for the first week I began to deplore their comparative lack of vision. They, the possessors of families, seemed to avoid these discussions about the oversupply of children.

"So you've come to check up on our American traditions, Professor Grimstone," they would say casually. "We've heard all about this great purpose of our forefathers, and I guess it's up to us to put it across. But gee whiz, Grimstone, we wish we could have seen the earth! What's it like, anyhow?"

"Tell us some more about the earth . . ."

"All we know is what we see second hand . . ."

I told them about the earth. Yes, they had books galore, and movies and phonograph records, pictures and maps; but these things only excited their curiosity. They asked me questions by the thousands. Only after I had poured out several encyclopedia-loads of Earth memories did I begin to break through their masks.

Back of this constant questioning, I discovered, they were watching me. Perhaps they were wondering whether they were not being subjected to more rigid discipline here on shipboard than their cousins back on Earth. I tried to impress upon them that they were a chosen group, but this had little effect. It stuck in their minds that *they* had had no choice in the matter.

Moreover, they were watching to see what I was going to do about the population problem, for they were no less aware of it than their elders.

Two weeks after my "return" we got down to business.

Captain Dickinson preferred to engineer the matter himself. He called an assembly in the movie auditorium. Almost everyone was present.

The program began with the picture of the Six-Hundred-Year Plan. Everyone knew the reels by heart. They had seen and heard them dozens of times, and were ready to snicker at the proper moments—such as

when the stern old committee chairman, charging the unborn generations with their solemn obligations, was interrupted by a friendly fly on
his nose.

When the films were run through, Captain Dickinson took the
rostrum, and with considerable bluster he called upon the Clerk of the
Council to review the situation. The clerk read a report which went about
as follows:

To maintain a stable population, it was agreed in the original
Plan that families should average two children each. Hence, the
original 16 families would bring forth approximately 32 children;
and assuming that they were fairly evenly divided as to sex, they
would eventually form 16 new families. These 16 families would,
in turn, have an average of two children each—another generation
of approximately 32.

By maintaining these averages, we were to have a total
population, at any given time, of 32 children, 32 parents and 32
grandparents. The great-grandparents may be left out of account,
for owing to the natural span of life they ordinarily die off before
they accumulate in any great numbers.

The three living generations, then, for 32 each would give the
Flashaway a constant active population of 96, or roughly, 100
persons.

The Six-Hundred-Year Plan has allowed for some flexibility
in these figures. It has established the safe maximum at 150 and the
safe minimum at 75.

If our population shrinks below 75, it is dangerously small. If
it shrinks to 50, a crisis is at hand.

But if it grows above 150, it is dangerously large; and if it
reaches the 200 mark, as we all know, a crisis may be said to exist.

The clerk stopped for an impressive pause, marred only by the
crying of a baby from some distant room.

"Now, coming down to the present-day facts, we are well aware
that the population has been dangerously large for the past seven
years—"

"Since we entered this section of the heavens," Captain Dickinson
interspersed with a scowl.

106

"From the first year in space, the population plan has encountered some irregularities," the clerk continued. "To begin with, there were not sixteen couples, but seventeen. The seventeenth couple—" here the clerk shot a glance at William Broscoe— "did not belong to the original compact, and after their marriage they were not bound by the sacred traditions—"

"I object!" I shouted, challenging the eyes of the clerk and the captain squarely. Dickinson had written that report with a touch of malice. The clerk skipped over a sentence or two.

"But however the Broscoe family may have prospered and multiplied, our records show that nearly all the families of the present generation have exceeded the per-family quota."

At this point there was a slight disturbance in the rear of the auditorium. An anxious-looking young man entered and signalled to the doctor. The two went out together.

"*All* the families," the clerk amended. "Our population this week passed the two hundred mark. This concludes the report."

The captain opened the meeting for discussion, and the forum lasted far into the night. The demand for me to assist the Council with some legislation was general. There was also hearty sentiment against the captain's blacked-out heavens from young and old alike.

This, I considered, was a good sign. The children craved the fun of watching the stars and planets; their elders desired to keep up their serious astronomical studies.

"Nothing is so important to the welfare of this expedition," I said to the Council on the following day, as we settled down to the job of thrashing out some legislation, "as to maintain our interests in the outside world. Population or no population, we must not become ingrown!"

I talked of new responsibilities, new challenges in the form of contests and campaigns, new leisure-time activities. The discussion went on for days.

"Back in my times—" I said for the hundredth time; but the captain laughed me down. My times and these times were as unlike as black and white, he declared.

"But the principle is the same!" I shouted. "We had population troubles, too."

They smiled as I referred to twenty-first century relief families who

107

were overrun with children. I cited the fact that some industrialists who paid heavy taxes had considered giving every relief family an automobile as a measure to save themselves money in the long run; for they had discovered that relief families with cars had fewer children than those without.

"That's no help," Dickinson muttered. "You can't have cars on a space ship."

"You can play bridge," I retorted. "Bridge is an enemy of the birthrate too. Bridge, cars, movies, checkers—they all add up to the same thing. They lift you out of your animal natures—"

The Councilmen threw up their hands. They had bridged and checkered themselves to death.

"Then try other things," I persisted. "You could produce your own movies and plays—organize a little theater—create some new drama—"

"What have we got to dramatize?" the captain replied sourly. "All the dramatic things happen on the earth."

This shocked me. Somehow it took all the starch out of this colossal adventure to hear the captain give up so easily.

"All our drama is second hand," he grumbled. "Our ship's course is cut and dried. Our world is bounded by walls. The only dramatic things that happen here are births and deaths."

A doctor broke in on our conference and seized the captain by the hand.

"Congratulations, Captain Dickinson, on the prize crop of the season! Your wife has just presented you with a fine set of triplets—three boys!"

That broke up the meeting. Captain Dickinson was so busy for the rest of the week that he forgot all about his official obligations. The problem of population limitation faded from his mind.

I wrote out my recommendations and gave them all the weight of my dictatorial authority. I stressed the need for more birth control forums, and recommended that the heavens be made visible for further studies in astronomy and mathematics.

I was tempted to warn Captain Dickinson that the *Flashaway* might incur some serious dramas of its own—poverty, disease and the like— unless he got back on the track of the Six-Hundred-Year Plan in a hurry. But Dickinson was preoccupied with some family washings when I took

108

my leave of him, and he seemed to have as much drama on his hands as he cared for.

I paid a final visit to each of the twenty-eight great-grandchildren of Louise, and returned to my ice.

IV

My chief complaint against my merry-go-round freezer was that it didn't give me any rest. One whirl into blackness, and the next thing I knew I popped out of the open lid again with not so much as a minute's time to reorganize my thoughts.

Well, here it was 2266—two hundred years since the take-off.

A glance through the one-way glass told me it was daytime in the ballroom.

As I turned the key in the lock I felt like a prize fighter on a vaudeville tour who, having just trounced the tough local strong man, steps back in the ring to take on his cousin.

A touch of a headache caught me as I reflected that there should be four more returns after this one—if all went according to plan. *Plan!* That word was destined to be trampled underfoot.

Oh, well (I took a deep optimistic breath) the *Flashaway* troubles would all be cleared up by now. Three generations would have passed. The population should be back to normal.

I swung the door open, stepped through, locked it after me.

For an instant I thought I had stepped in on a big movie "take"—a scene of a stricken multitude. The big ballroom was literally strewn with people—if creatures in such a deplorable state could be called people.

There was no movie camera. This was the real thing.

"Grimstone's come!" a hoarse voice cried out.

"Grimstone! Grimstone!" Others caught up the cry. Then— "Food! Give us food! We're starving! For God's sake—"

The weird chorus gathered volume. I stood dazed, and for an instant I couldn't realize that I was looking upon the population of the *Flashaway*.

Men, women and children of all ages and all states of desperation joined in the clamor. Some of them stumbled to their feet and came toward me, waving their arms weakly. But most of them hadn't the strength to rise.

In that stunning moment an icy sweat came over me.

"Food! Food! We've been waiting for you, Grimstone. We've been holding on—"

The responsibility that was strapped to my shoulders suddenly weighed down like a locomotive. You see, I had originally taken my job more or less as a lark. That Six-Hundred-Year Plan had looked so airtight. I, the Keeper of the Traditions, would have a snap.

I had anticipated many a pleasant hour acquainting the oncoming generations with noble sentiments about George Washington; I had pictured myself filling the souls of my listeners by reciting the Gettysburg address and lecturing upon the mysteries of science.

But now those pretty bubbles burst on the spot, nor did they ever re-form in the centuries to follow.

And as they burst, my vision cleared. My job had nothing to do with theories or textbooks or speeches. My job was simply to get to Robinello—to get there with enough living, able-bodied, sane human beings to start a colony.

Dull blue starlight sifted through the windows to highlight the big roomful of starved figures. The mass of pale blue faces stared at me. There were hundreds of them. Instinctively I shrank as the throng clustered around me, calling and pleading.

"One at a time!" I cried. "First I've got to find out what this is all about. Who's your spokesman?"

They designated a handsomely built, if undernourished, young man. I inquired his name and learned that he was Bob Sperry, a descendant of the original Captain Sperry.

"There are eight hundred of us now," Sperry said.

"Don't tell me the food has run out!"

"No, not that—but six hundred of us are not entitled to regular meals."

"Why not?"

Before the young spokesman could answer, the others burst out with an unintelligible clamor. Angry cries of "That damned Dickinson!" and "Guns!" and "They'll shoot us!" were all I could distinguish.

I quieted them and made Bob Sperry go on with his story. He calmly asserted that there was a very good reason that they shouldn't be fed, all sentiment aside; namely, because they had been born outside the quota.

Here I began to catch a gleam of light.

"By Captain Dickinson's interpretation of the Plan," Sperry explained, "there shouldn't be more than two hundred of us altogether."

This Captain Dickinson, I learned, was a grandson of the one I had known.

Sperry continued, "Since there are eight hundred, he and his brother—his brother being Food Superintendent—launched an emergency measure a few months ago to save food. They divided the population into the two hundred, who had a right to be born, and the six hundred who had not."

So the six hundred starving persons before me were theoretically the excess population. The vigorous ancestry of the sixteen—no, seventeen—original couples, together with the excellent medical care that had reduced infant mortality and disease to the minimum, had wrecked the original population plan completely.

"What do you do for food? You must have *some* food!"

"We live on charity."

The throng again broke in with hostile words. Young Sperry's version was too gentle to do justice to their outraged stomachs. In fairness to the two hundred, however, Sperry explained that they shared whatever food they could spare with these, their less fortunate brothers, sisters and offspring.

Uncertain what should or could be done, I gave the impatient crowd my promise to investigate at once. Bob Sperry and nine other men accompanied me.

The minute we were out of hearing of the ballroom, I gasped,

"Good heavens, men, how is it that you and your six hundred haven't mobbed the storerooms long before this?"

"Dickinson and his brother have got the drop on us."

"Drop? What kind of drop?"

"Guns!"

I couldn't understand this. I had believed these new generations of the *Flashaway* to be relatively innocent of any knowledge of firearms.

"What kind of guns?"

"The same kind they use in our Earth-made movies—that make a loud noise and kill people by the hundreds."

"But there aren't any guns aboard! That is—"

I knew perfectly well that the only firearms the ship carried had

111

been stored in my own refrigerator room, which no one could enter but myself. Before the voyage, one of the planned committee had jestingly suggested that if any serious trouble ever arose, I should be master of the situation by virtue of one hundred revolvers.

"They made their own guns," Sperry explained, "just like the ones in our movies and books."

Inquiring whether any persons had been shot, I learned that three of their number, attempting a raid on the storerooms, had been killed.

"We heard three loud bangs, and found our men dead with bloody skulls."

Reaching the upper end of the central corridor, we arrived at the captain's headquarters.

The name of Captain Dickinson carried a bad flavor for me. A century before I had developed a distaste for a certain other Captain Dickinson, his grandfather. I resolved to swallow my prejudice. Then the door opened, and my resolve stuck in my throat. The former Captain Dickinson had merely annoyed me; but this one I hated on sight.

"Well?" the captain roared at the eleven of us.

Well-uniformed and neatly groomed, he filled the doorway with an impressive bulk. In his right hand he gripped a revolver. The gleam of that weapon had a magical effect upon the men. They shrank back respectfully. Then the captain's cold eye lighted on me.

"Who are *you*?"

"Gregory Grimstone, Keeper of the Traditions."

The captain sent a quick glance toward his gun and repeated his "Well?"

For a moment I was fascinated by that intricately shaped piece of metal in his grip.

"Well!" I echoed. "If 'well' is the only reception you have to offer, I'll proceed with my official business. Call your Food Superintendent."

"Why?"

"Order him out! Have him feed the entire population without further delay!"

"We can't afford the food," the captain growled.

"We'll talk that over later, but we won't talk on empty stomachs. Order out your Food Superintendent!"

"Crawl back in your hole!" Dickinson snarled.

At that instant another bulky man stepped into view. He was almost the identical counterpart of the captain, but his uniform was that of the Food Superintendent. Showing his teeth with a sinister snarl, he took his place beside his brother. He too jerked his right hand up to flash a gleaming revolver.

I caught one glimpse—and laughed in his face! I couldn't help it.

"You fellows are good!" I roared. "You're damned good actors! If you've held off the starving six hundred with nothing but those two dumb imitations of revolvers, you deserve an Academy award!"

The two Dickinson brothers went white.

Back of me came low mutterings from ten starving men.

"Imitations—dumb imitations—what the hell?"

Sperry and his nine comrades plunged with one accord. For the next ten minutes the captain's headquarters was simply a whirlpool of flying fists and hurtling bodies.

I have mentioned that these ten men were weak from lack of food. That fact was all that saved the Dickinson brothers; for ten minutes of lively exercise was all the ten men could endure, in spite of the circumstances.

But ten minutes left an impression. The Dickinsons were the worst beaten-up men I have ever seen, and I have seen some bad ones in my time. When the news echoed through the ship, no one questioned the ethics of ten starved men attacking two overfed ones.

Needless to say, before two hours passed, every hungry man, woman and child ate to his gizzard's content. And before another hour passed, some new officers were installed. The S.S. *Flashaway's* trouble was far from solved; but for the present the whole eight hundred were one big family picnic. Hope was restored, and the rejoicing lasted through many thousand miles of space.

There was considerable mystery about the guns. Surprisingly, the people had developed an awe of the movie guns as if they were instruments of magic.

Upon investigating, I was convinced that the captain and his brother had simply capitalized on this superstition. They had a sound enough motive for wanting to save food. But once their gun bluff had been established, they had become uncompromising oppressors. And when the occasion arose that their guns were challenged, they had simply crushed the skulls of their three attackers and faked the noises of explosions.

But now the firearms were dead. And so was the Dickinson regime.

But the menacing problem of too many mouths to feed still clung to the S.S. *Flashaway* like a hungry ghost determined to ride the ship to death.

Six full months passed before the needed reform was forged.

During that time everyone was allowed full rations. The famine had already taken its toll in weakened bodies, and seventeen persons—most of them young children—died. The doctors, released from the Dickinson regime, worked like Trojans to bring the rest back to health.

The reform measure that went into effect six months after my arrival consisted of outright sterilization.

The compulsory rule was sterilization for everyone except those born "within the quota"—and that quota, let me add, was narrowed down one half from Captain Dickinson's two hundred to the most eligible one hundred. The disqualified one hundred now joined the ranks of the six hundred.

And that was not all. By their own agreement, every within-the-quota family, responsible for bearing the *Flashaway's* future children, would undergo sterilization operations after the second child was born.

The seven hundred out-of-quota citizens, let it be said, were only too glad to submit to the simple sterilization measures in exchange for a right to live their normal lives. Yes, they were to have three squares a day. With an assured population decline in prospect for the coming century, this generous measure of food would not give out. Our surveys of the existing food supplies showed that these seven hundred could safely live their four-score years and die with full stomachs.

Looking back on that six months' work, I was fairly well satisfied that the doctors and the Council and I had done the fair, if drastic, thing. If I had planted seeds for further trouble with the Dickinson tribe, I was little concerned about it at the time.

My conscience was, in fact, clear—except for one small matter. I was guilty of one slight act of partiality.

I incurred this guilt shortly before I returned to the ice. The doctors and I, looking down from the balcony into the ballroom, chanced to notice a young couple who were obviously very much in love.

The young man was Bob Sperry, the handsome, clear-eyed descendant of the *Flashaway's* first and finest captain, the lad who had been the spokesman when I first came upon the starving mob.

The girl's name—and how it had clung in my mind!—was Louise

Broscoe. Refreshingly beautiful, she reminded me for all the world of my own Louise (mine and Bill Broscoe's).

"It's a shame," one of the doctors commented, "that fine young blood like that has to fall outside the quota. But rules are rules."

With a shrug of the shoulder he had already dismissed the matter from his mind—until I handed him something I had scribbled on a piece of paper.

"We'll make this one exception," I said perfunctorily. "If any question ever arises, this statement relieves you doctors of all responsibility. This is my own special request."

V

One hundred years later my rash act came back to haunt me—and how! Bob Sperry had married Louise Broscoe, and the births of their two children had raised the unholy cry of "Favoritism!"

By the year 2366, Bob Sperry and Louise Broscoe were gone and almost forgotten. But the enmity against me, the Keeper of the Traditions who played favorites, had grown up into a monster of bitter hatred waiting to devour me.

It didn't take me long to discover this. My first contact after I emerged from the ice set the pace.

"Go tell your parents," I said to the gang of brats that were playing ball in the spacious ballroom, "that Grimstone has arrived."

Their evil little faces stared at me a moment, then they snorted.

"Faw! Faw! Faw!" and away they ran.

I stood in the big bleak room wondering what to make of their insults. On the balcony some of the parents craned over the railings at me.

"Greetings!" I cried. "I'm Grimstone, Keeper of the Traditions. I've just come—"

"Faw!" the men and women shouted at me. "Faw! Faw!"

No one could have made anything friendly out of those snarls. "Faw," to them, was simply a vocal manner of spitting poison.

Uncertain what this surly reception might lead to, I returned to my refrigerator room to procure one of the guns. Then I returned to the volley of catcalls and insults, determined to carry out my duties, come what might.

Don Wilcox

When I reached the forequarter of the ship, however, I found some less hostile citizens who gave me a civil welcome. Here I established myself for the extent of my 2366-67 sojourn, an honored guest of the Sperry family.

This, I told myself, was my reward for my favor to Bob Sperry and Louise Broscoe a century ago. For here was their grandson, a fine upstanding gray-haired man of fifty, a splendid pilot and the father of a beautiful twenty-one year old daughter.

"Your name wouldn't be Louise by any chance?" I asked the girl as she showed me into the Sperry living room.

"Lora-Louise," the girl smiled. It was remarkable how she brought back memories of one of her ancestors of three centuries previous.

Her dark eyes flashed over me curiously.

"So you are the man that we Sperrys have to thank for being here!"

"You've heard about the quotas?" I asked.

"Of course. You're almost a god to our family."

"I must be a devil to some of the others," I said, recalling my reception of catcalls.

"Rogues!" the girl's father snorted, and he thereupon launched into a breezy account of the past century.

The sterilization program, he assured me, had worked—if anything, too well. The population was the lowest in *Flashaway* history. It stood at the dangerously low mark of *fifty!*

Besides the sterilization program, a disease epidemic had taken its toll. In addition three ugly murders, prompted by jealousies, had spotted the record. And there had been one suicide.

As to the character of the population, Pilot Sperry declared gravely that there had been a turn for the worse.

"They fight each other like damned anarchists," he snorted.

The Dickinsons had made trouble for several generations. Now it was the Dickinsons against the Smiths; and these two factions included four-fifths of all the people. They were about evenly divided—twenty on each side—and when they weren't actually fighting each other, they were "fawing" at each other.

These bellicose factions had one sentiment in common: they both despised the Sperry faction. And—here my guilt cropped up again—their hatred stemmed from my special favor of a century ago, without which there would be no Sperrys now. In view of the fact that the Sperry

116

faction lived in the forequarter of the ship and held all the important offices, it was no wonder that the remaining forty citizens were jealous.

All of which gave me enough to worry about. On top of that, Lora-Louise's mother gave me one other angle of the set-up.

"The trouble between the Dickinsons and the Smiths has grown worse since Lora-Louise has become a young lady," Mrs. Sperry confided to me.

We were sitting in a breakfast nook. Amber starlight shone softly through the porthole, lighting the mother's steady imperturbable gray eyes.

"Most girls have married at eighteen or nineteen," her mother went on. "So far, Lora-Louise has refused to marry."

The worry in Mrs. Sperry's face was almost imperceptible, but I understood. I had checked over the "Who's Who" and I knew the seriousness of this population crisis. I also knew that there were four young unmarried men with no other prospects of wives except Lora-Louise.

"Have you any choice for her?" I asked.

"Since she must marry—and I know she *must*—I have urged her to make her own choice."

I could see that the ordeal of choosing had been postponed until my coming, in hopes that I might modify the rules. But I had no intention of doing so. The *Flashaway* needed Lora-Louise. It needed the sort of children she would bear.

That week I saw the two husky Dickinson boys. Both were in their twenties. They stayed close together and bore an air of treachery and scheming. Rumor had it that they carried weapons made from table knives.

Everyone knew that my coming would bring the conflict to a head. Many thought I would try to force the girl to marry the older Smith— "Batch," as he was called in view of his bachelorhood. He was past thirty-five, the oldest of the four unmarried men.

But some argued otherwise. For Batch, though a splendid specimen physically, was slow of wit and speech. It was common knowledge that he was weak-minded.

For that reason, I might choose his younger cousin, "Smithy," a roly-poly overgrown boy of nineteen who spent his time bullying the younger children.

But if the Smiths and the Dickinsons could have their way about it,

117

the Keeper of the Traditions should have no voice in the matter. Let me insist that Lora-Louise marry, said they; but whom she should marry was none of my business.

They preferred a fight as a means of settlement. A free-for-all between the two factions would be fine. A showdown of fists among the four contenders would be even better.

Best of all would be a battle of knives that would eliminate all but one of the suitors. Not that either the Dickinsons or the Smiths needed to admit that was what they preferred; but their barbaric tastes were plain to see.

Barbarians! That's what they had become. They had sprung too far from their native civilization. Only the Sperry faction, isolated in their monasteries of control boards, physicians' laboratories and record rooms, kept alive the spark of civilization.

The Sperrys and their associates were human beings out of the twenty-first century. The Smiths and the Dickinsons had slipped. They might have come out of the Dark Ages.

What burned me up more than anything else was that obviously both the Smiths and the Dickinsons looked forward with sinister glee toward dragging Lora-Louise down from her height to their own barbaric levels.

One night I was awakened by the sharp ringing of the pilot's telephone. I heard the snap of a switch. An *emergency* signal flashed on throughout the ship.

Footsteps were pounding toward the ballroom. I slipped into a robe, seized my gun, made for the door.

"The Dickinsons are murdering up on them!" Pilot Sperry shouted to me from the door of the control room.

"I'll see about it," I snapped.

I bounded down the corridor. Sperry didn't follow. Whatever violence might occur from year to year within the hull of the *Flashaway*, the pilot's code demanded that he lock himself up at the controls and tend to his own business.

It was a free-for-all. Under the bright lights they were going to it, tooth and toenail.

Children screamed and clawed, women hurled dishes, old tottering granddaddies edged into the fracas to crack at each other with canes.

The appalling reason for it all showed in the center of the room—

the roly-poly form of young "Smithy" Smith. Hacked and stabbed, his nightclothes ripped, he was a veritable mess of carnage.

I shouted for order. No one heard me, for in that instant a chase thundered on the balcony. Everything else stopped. All eyes turned on the three racing figures.

Batch Smith, fleeing in his white nightclothes, had less than five yards' lead on the two Dickinsons. Batch was just smart enough to run when he was chased, not smart enough to know he couldn't possibly outrun the younger Dickinsons.

As they shot past blazing lights the Dickinsons' knives flashed. I could see that their hands were red with Smithy's blood.

"*Stop!*" I cried. "Stop or I'll *shoot!*"

If they heard, the words must have been meaningless. The younger Dickinson gained ground. His brother darted back in the opposite direction, crouched, waited for his prey to come around the circular balcony.

"Dickinson! Stop or I'll shoot you dead!" I bellowed.

Batch Smith came on, his eyes white with terror. Crouched and waiting, the older Dickinson lifted his knife for the killing stroke.

I shot.

The crouched Dickinson fell in a heap. Over him tripped the racing form of Batch Smith, to sprawl headlong. The other Dickinson leaped over his brother and pounced down upon the fallen prey, knife upraised.

Another shot went home.

Young Dickinson writhed and came toppling down over the balcony rail. He lay where he fell, his bloody knife sticking up through the side of his neck.

It was ugly business trying to restore order. However, the magic power of firearms, which had become only a dusty legend, now put teeth into every word I uttered.

The doctors were surprisingly efficient. After many hours of work behind closed doors, they released their verdicts to the waiting groups. The elder Dickinson, shot through the shoulder, would live. The younger Dickinson was dead. So was Smithy. But his cousin, Batch Smith, although too scared to walk back to his stateroom, was unhurt.

The rest of the day the doctors devoted to patching up the minor damages done in the free fight. Four-fifths of the *Flashaway* population were burdened with bandages, it seemed. For some time to come both the warring parties were considerably sobered over their losses. But most of all they were disgruntled because the fight had settled nothing.

The prize was still unclaimed. The two remaining contenders, backed by their respective factions, were at a bitter deadlock.

Nor had Lora-Louise's hatred for either the surviving Dickinson or Smith lessened in the slightest.

Never had a duty been more oppressive to me. I postponed my talk with Lora-Louise for several days, but I was determined that there should be no more fighting. She must choose.

We sat in an alcove next to the pilot's control room, looking out into the vast sky. Our ship, bounding at a terrific speed though it was, seemed to be hanging motionless in the tranquil star-dotted heavens.

"I must speak frankly," I said to the girl. "I hope you will do the same."

She looked at me steadily. Her dark eyes were perfectly frank, her full lips smiled with child-like simplicity.

"How old are you?" she asked.

"Twenty-eight," I answered. I'd been the youngest professor on the college faculty. "Or you might say three hundred and twenty-eight. Why?"

"How soon must you go back to your sleep?"

"Just as soon as you are happily married. That's why I must insist that you—"

Something very penetrating about her gaze made my words go weak. To think of forcing this lovely girl—so much like the Louise of my own century—to marry either the brutal Dickinson or the moronic Smith—

"Do you really want me to be *happily* married?" she asked.

I don't remember that any more words passed between us at the time.

A few days later she and I were married—and most happily!

The ceremony was brief. The entire Sperry faction and one representative from each of the two hostile factions were present. The aged captain of the ship, who had been too ineffectual in recent years to apply any discipline to the fighting factions, was still able with vigorous voice to pronounce us man and wife.

A year and a half later I took my leave.

I bid a fond good-by to the "future captain of the *Flashaway*," who lay on a pillow kicking and squirming. He gurgled back at me. If the boasts and promises of the Sperry grandparents and their associates were to be taken at full value, this young prodigy of mine would in time become an accomplished pilot and a skilled doctor as well as a stern but wise captain.

Judging from his talents at the age of six months, I was convinced he showed promise of becoming Food Superintendent as well.

I left reluctantly but happily.

VI

The year 2466 was one of the darkest in my life. I shall pass over it briefly.

The situation I found was all but hopeless.

The captain met me personally and conveyed me to his quarters without allowing the people to see me.

"Safer for everyone concerned," he muttered. I caught glimpses as we passed through the shadows. I seemed to be looking upon ruins.

Not until the captain had disclosed the events of the century did I understand how things could have come to such a deplorable state. And before he finished his story, I saw that I was helpless to right the wrongs.

"They've destroyed 'most everything," the hard-bitten old captain rasped. "And they haven't overlooked *you*. They've destroyed you completely. *You are an ogre.*"

I wasn't clear on his meaning. Dimly in the back of my mind the hilarious farewell of four centuries ago still echoed.

"The *Flashaway* will go through!" I insisted.

"They destroyed all the books, phonograph records, movie films. They broke up clocks and bells and furniture—"

And I was supposed to carry this interspatial outpost of American civilization through *unblemished!* That was what I had promised so gaily four centuries ago.

"They even tried to break out the windows," the captain went on. " 'Oxygen be damned!' they'd shout. They were mad. You couldn't tell them anything. If they could have got into this end of the ship, they'd have murdered us and smashed the control boards to hell."

I listened with bowed head.

"Your son tried like the devil to turn the tide. But God, what chance did he have? The dam had busted loose. They wanted to kill each other.

They wanted to destroy each other's property and starve each other out. No captain in the world could have stopped either faction. They had to get it out of their systems . . ."

He shrugged helplessly. "Your son went down fighting . . ." For a time I could hear no more. It seemed but minutes ago that I had taken leave of the little tot.

The war—if a mania of destruction and murder between two feuding factions could be called a war—had done one good thing, according to the captain. It had wiped the name of Dickinson from the records.

Later I turned through the musty pages to make sure. There were Smiths and Sperrys and a few other names still in the running, but no Dickinsons. Nor were there any Grimstones. My son had left no living descendants.

To return to the captain's story, the war (he said) had degraded the bulk of the population almost to the level of savages. Perhaps the comparison is an insult to the savage. The instruments of knowledge and learning having been destroyed, beliefs gave way to superstitions, memories of past events degenerated into fanciful legends.

The rebound from the war brought a terrific superstitious terror concerning death. The survivors crawled into their shells, almost literally; the brutalities and treacheries of the past hung like storm clouds over their imaginations.

As year after year dropped away, the people told and retold the stories of destruction to their children. Gradually the legend twisted into a strange form in which all the guilt for the carnage *was placed upon me*!

I was the one who had started all the killing! *I, the ogre,* who slept in a cave somewhere in the rear of the ship, came out once upon a time and started all the trouble.

I, the Traditions Man, dealt death with a magic weapon; I cast the spell of killing upon the Smiths and the Dickinsons that kept them fighting until there was nothing left to fight for.

"But that was years ago," I protested to the captain. "Am I still an ogre?" I shuddered at the very thought.

"More than ever. Stories like that don't die out in a century. They grow bigger. You've become the symbol of evil. I've tried to talk the silly notion down, but it has been impossible. My own family is afraid of you."

I listened with sickening amazement. I was the Traditions Man: or rather the "Traddy Man"—the bane of every child's life.

Parents, I was told, would warn them, "If you don't be good, the Traddy Man will come out of his cave and get you!"

And the Traddy Man, as every grown-up knew, could storm out of his cave without warning. He would come with a strange gleam in his eye. That was his evil will. When the bravest, strongest men would cross his path, he would hurl instant death at them. Then he would seize the most beautiful woman and marry her.

"Enough!" I said. "Call your people together. I'll dispel their false ideas—"

The captain shook his head wisely. He glanced at my gun.

"Don't force me to disobey your orders," he said. "I can believe you're not an ogre—but they won't. I know this generation. You don't. Frankly, I refuse to disturb the peace of this ship by telling the people you have come. Nor am I willing to terrorize my family by letting them see you."

For a long time I stared silently into space.

The captain dismissed a pilot from the control room and had me come in.

"You can see for yourself that we are straight on our course. You have already seen that all the supplies are holding up. You have seen that the population problem is well cared for. What more do you want?"

What more did I want! With the whole population of the *Flashaway* steeped in ignorance—immorality—superstition—savagery!

Again the captain shook his head. "You want us to be like your friends of the twenty-first century. *We can't be.*"

He reached in his pocket and pulled out some bits of crumpled papers.

"Look. I save every scrap of reading matter. I learned to read from the primers and charts that your son's grandparents made. Before the destruction, I tried to read about the Earth-life. I still piece together these torn bits and study them. But I can't piece together the Earth-life that they tell about. All I really know is what I've seen and felt breathed right here in my native *Flashaway* world.

"That's how it's bound to be with all of us. We can't get back to your notions about things. Your notions haven't any real truth for us. You don't belong to our world," the captain said with honest frankness.

"So I'm an outcast on my own ship."

"That's putting it mildly. You're a menace and a troublemaker—
an ogre. It's in their minds as tight as the bones in their skulls."

The most I could do was secure some promises from him before I
went back to the ice. He promised to keep the ship on its course. He
promised to do his utmost to fasten the necessary obligations upon those
who would take over the helm.

"Straight relentless navigation!" We drank a toast to it. He didn't
pretend to appreciate the purpose or the mission of the *Flashaway*, but he
took my word for it that it would come to some good.

"To Robinello in 2666!" Another toast. Then he conducted me
back, in utmost secrecy, to my refrigerator room.

VII

I awoke to the year 2566, keenly aware that I was not Gregory
Grimstone, the respected Keeper of the Traditions. If I was anyone at all,
I was the Traddy Man—the ogre.

But perhaps by this time—and I took hope with the thought—I had
been completely forgotten.

I tried to get through the length of the ship without being seen. I had
watched through the one-way glass for several hours for a favorable
opportunity, but the ship seemed to be in a continual state of daylight,
and shabby-looking people roamed about as aimlessly as sheep in a
meadow.

The few persons who saw me as I darted toward the captain's
quarters shrieked as if they had been knifed. In their world there was no
such thing as a strange person. I was the impossible, the unbelievable.
My name, obviously, had been forgotten.

I found three men in the control room. After minutes of tension,
during which they adjusted themselves to the shock of my coming, I
succeeded in establishing speaking terms. Two of the men were Sperrys.

But at the very moment I should have been concerned with solidify-
ing my friendship, I broke the calm with an excited outburst. My eye
caught the position of instruments and I leaped from my seat.

"How long have you been going *that way*?"

"Eight years."

"Eight—" I glanced at the huge automatic chart overhead. It

showed the long straight line of our centuries of flight with a tiny shepherd's crook at the end. Eight years ago we had turned back sharply.

"That's sixteen years lost, gentlemen!"

I tried to regain my poise. The three men before me were perfectly calm, to my astonishment. The two Sperry brothers glanced at each other. The third man, who had introduced himself as Smith, glared at me darkly.

"It's all right," I said. "We won't lose another minute. I know how to operate—"

"No you don't!" Smith's voice was harsh and cold. I had started to reach for the controls. I hesitated. Three pairs of eyes were fixed on me.

"We know where we're going," one of the Sperry's said stubbornly, "We've got our own destination."

"This ship is bound for Robinello!" I snapped. "We've got to colonize. The Robinello planets are ours—America's. It's our job to clinch the claim and establish the initial settlement—"

"Who said so?"

"America!"

"*When*?" Smith's cold eyes tightened.

"Five hundred years ago."

"That doesn't mean a thing. Those people are all dead."

"I'm one of those people!" I growled. "And I'm not dead by a damned sight!"

"Then you're out on a limb."

"Limb or no limb, the plan goes through!" I clutched my gun. "We haven't come five hundred years in a straight line for nothing!"

"The plan is dead," one of the Sperrys snarled. "We've killed it."

His brother chimed in, "This is our ship and we're running it. We've studied the heavens and we're out on our own. We're through with this straight-line stuff. We're going to see the universe."

I didn't want to kill the men. But I saw no other way out. Was there any other way? Three lives weren't going to stand between the *Flashaway* and her destination.

Seconds passed, with the four of us breathing hard. Eternity was about to descend on someone. Any of the three might have been splendid pioneers if they had been confronted with the job of building a colony. But in this moment, their lack of vision was as deadly as any deliberate sabotage. I focused my attack on the most troublesome man of the three.

"Smith, I'm giving you an order. Turn back before I count ten or I'll kill you. One . . . two . . . three . . ."

Not the slightest move from anyone.

"Seven . . . eight . . . nine . . ."

Smith leaped at me—and fell dead at my feet.

The two Sperrys looked at the faint wisp of smoke from the weapon. I barked another sharp command, and one of the Sperrys marched to the controls and turned the ship back toward Robinello.

VIII

For a year I was with the Sperry brothers constantly, doing my utmost to bring them around to my way of thinking. At first I watched them like hawks. But they were not treacherous. Neither did they show any inclination to avenge Smith's death. Probably this was due to a suppressed hatred they had held toward him.

The Sperrys were the sort of men, being true children of space, who bided their time. That's what they were doing now. That was why I couldn't leave them and go back to my ice.

As sure as the *Flashaway* could cut through the heavens, those two men were counting the hours until I returned to my rest. The minute I was gone, they would turn back toward their own goal.

And so I continued to stay with them for a full year. If they contemplated killing me, they gave no indication. I presume I would have killed them with little hesitation, had I had no pilots whatsoever that I could entrust with the job of carrying on.

There were no other pilots, nor were there any youngsters old enough to break into service.

Night after night I fought the matter over in my mind. There was a full century to go. Perhaps one hundred and fifteen or twenty years. And no one except the two Sperrys and I had any serious conception of a destination!

These two pilots and I—*and one other*, whom I had never for a minute forgotten. If the *Flashaway* was to go through, it was up to me and *that one other—*

I marched back to the refrigerator room, people fleeing my path in terror. Inside the retreat I touched the switches that operated the auxiliary merry-go-round freezer. After a space of time the operation was complete.

Someone very beautiful stood smiling before me, looking not a minute older than when I had packed her away for safe-keeping two centuries before.

"Gregory," she breathed ecstatically. "Are my three centuries up already?"

"Only two of them, Lora-Louise." I took her in my arms. She looked up at me sharply and must have read the trouble in my eyes.

"They've all played out on us," I said quietly. "It's up to us now."

I discussed my plan with her and she approved.

One at a time we forced the Sperry brothers into the icy retreat, with repeated promises that they would emerge within a century. By that time Lora-Louise and I would be gone—but it was our expectation that our children and grandchildren would carry on.

And so the two of us, plus firearms, plus Lora-Louise's sense of humor, took over the running of the *Flashaway* for its final century.

As the years passed the native population grew to be less afraid of us. Little by little a foggy glimmer of our vision filtered into their numbed minds.

The year is now 2600. Thirty-three years have passed since Lora-Louise and I took over. I am now sixty-two, she is fifty-six. Or if you prefer, I am 562, she is 256. Our four children have grown up and married.

We have realized down through these long years that we would not live to see the journey completed. The Robinello planets have been visible for some time; but at our speed they are still sixty or eighty years away.

But something strange happened nine or ten months ago. It has changed the outlook for all of us—even me, the crusty old Keeper of the Traditions.

A message reached us through our radio receiver!

It was a human voice speaking in our own language. It had a fresh vibrant hum to it and a clear-cut enunciation. It shocked me to realize how sluggish our own brand of the King's English had become in the past five-and-a-half centuries.

"Calling the S.S. *Flashaway*!" it said. "Calling the S.S. *Flashaway*! We are trying to locate you, S.S. *Flashaway*. Our instruments indicate that you are approaching. If you can hear us, will you give us your exact location?"

127

I snapped on the transmitter. "This is the *Flashaway*. Can you hear us?"

"Dimly. Where are you?"

"On our course. Who's calling?"

"This is the American colony on Robinello," came the answer. "American colony, Robinello, established in 2550—fifty years ago. We're waiting for you, *Flashaway*."

"How the devil did you get there?" I may have sounded a bit crusty but I was too excited to know what I was saying.

"Modern space ships," came the answer. "We've cut the time from the earth to Robinello down to six years. Give us your location. We'll send a fast ship out to pick you up."

I gave them our location. That, as I said, was several months ago. Today we are receiving a radio call every five minutes as their ship approaches.

One of my sons, supervising the preparations, has just reported that all persons aboard are ready to transfer—including the Sperry brothers, who have emerged successfully from the ice. The eighty-five *Flashaway* natives are scared half to death and at the same time as eager as children going to a circus.

Lora-Louise has finished packing our boxes, bless her heart. That teasing smile she just gave me was because she noticed the "Who's Who Aboard the *Flashaway*" tucked snugly under my arm.

HOME COMPUTER

Artificial intelligence in the form of robots (mobile computers), androids (robots composed of organic material), and computers has been written about since at least the twelfth century when William of Malmesbury claimed Pope Sylvester II had devised a talking mechanical head. (See John Cohen's *Human Robots in Myth and Science*, 1966.)

The theme is popular because it has many uses: robots and androids are used as surrogates for oppressed minorities like blacks and Jews, a particularly important device in past decades when pulp science fiction could not depict these peoples directly; artificial intelligence can be used to represent science gone mad, in the form of man's creations taking over from him; and they can also be used creatively to explore such questions as what it means to be human.

"A Logic Named Joe" (*Astounding Science Fiction*, March 1946) is the first home computer story, written at a time when the first computer was just coming into being, a truly prophetic piece of speculation. Its author, Murray Leinster (Will F. Jenkins) was often called the "Dean of Science Fiction," for he had one of the longest careers of any science fiction writer, beginning in 1919 and remaining active until the late 1960s.

Other science fictional firsts about artificial intelligence include the first robot, computer, and electronic robot stories: E. T. A. Hoffmann's "Automata" (1814), Edward Page Mitchells's "The Ablest Man in the World" (1879), and Harl Vincent's "Rex" (1934).

A LOGIC NAMED JOE

Murray Leinster *(1946)*

*I*t was on the third day of August that Joe come off the assembly line, and on the fifth Laurine come into town, and that afternoon I saved civilization. That's what I figure anyhow. Laurine is a blonde that I was crazy about once—and crazy is the word—and Joe is a logic that I have stored away down in the cellar right now. I had to pay for him because I said I busted him, and sometimes I think about turning him on and sometimes I think about taking an ax to him. Sooner or later I'm gonna do one or the other. I kinda hope it's the ax. I could use a coupla million dollars—sure!—an' Joe'd tell me how to get or make 'em. He can do plenty! But so far I've been scared to take a chance. After all, I figure I really saved a civilization by turnin' him off.

The way Laurine fits in is that she makes cold shivers run up an' down my spine when I think about her. You see, I've got a wife which I acquired after I had parted from Laurine with much romantic despair. She is a reasonable good wife, and I have some kids which are hellcats but I value 'em. If I have sense enough to leave well enough alone, sooner or later I will retire on a pension an' Social Security an' spend the rest of my life fishin', contented an' lyin' about what a great guy I used to be. But there's Joe. I'm worried about Joe.

I'm a maintenance man for the Logics Company. My job is servicing logics, and I admit modestly that I am pretty good. I was servicing televisions before that guy Carson invented his trick circuit that will select any of 'steenteen million other circuits—in theory there ain't no limit—and before the Logics Company hooked it into the tank-and-integrator setup they were usin' 'em as business machine service. They added a vision screen for speed—an' they found out they'd made logics.

131

They were surprised an' pleased. They're still findin' out what logics will do, but everybody's got 'em.

I got Joe, after Laurine nearly got me. You know the logics setup. You got a logic in your house. It looks like a vision receiver used to, only it's got keys instead of dials and you punch the keys for what you wanna get. It's hooked in to the tank, which has the Carson Circuit all fixed up with relays. Say you punch "Station SNAFU" on your logic. Relays in the tank take over an' whatever vision-program SNAFU is telecastin' comes on your logic's screen. Or you punch "Sally Hancock's Phone" an' the screen blinks an' sputters an' you're hooked up with the logic in her house an' if somebody answers you got a vision-phone connection. But besides that, if you punch for the weather forecast or who won today's race at Hialeah or who was mistress of the White House durin' Garfield's administration or what is PDQ and R sellin' for today, that comes on the screen too. The relays in the tank do it. The tank is a big buildin' full of all the facts in creation an' all the recorded telecasts that ever was made—an' it's hooked in with all the other tanks all over the country—an' anything you wanna know or see or hear, you punch for it an' you get it. Very convenient. Also it does math for you, an' keeps books, an' acts as consultin' chemist, physicist, astronomer an' tealeaf reader, with an "Advice to Lovelorn" thrown in. The only thing it won't do is tell you exactly what your wife meant when she said, "Oh, you think so, do you?" in that peculiar kinda voice. Logics don't work good on women. Only on things that make sense.

Logics are all right, though. They changed civilization, the highbrows tell us. All on accounta the Carson Circuit. And Joe shoulda been a perfectly normal logic, keeping some family or other from wearin' out its brains doin' the kids' homework for 'em. But somethin' went wrong in the assembly line. It was somethin' so small that precision gauges didn't measure it, but it made Joe an individual. Maybe he didn't know it at first. Or maybe, bein' logical, he figured out that if he was to show he was different from other logics they'd scrap him. Which woulda been a brilliant idea. But anyhow, he come off the assembly line, an' he went through the regular tests without anybody screamin' shrilly on findin' out what he was. And he went right on out an' was duly installed in the home of Mr. Thaddeus Korlanovitch at 119 East Seventh Street, second floor front. So far, everything was serene.

The installation happened late Saturday night. Sunday morning the

Korlanovitch kids turned him on an' seen the Kiddie Shows. Around noon their parents peeled 'em away from him an' piled 'em in the car. Then they come back in the house for the lunch they'd forgot an' one of the kids sneaked back an' they found him punchin' keys for the Kiddie Shows of the week before. They dragged him out an' went off. But they left Joe turned on.

That was noon. Nothin' happened until two in the afternoon. It was the calm before the storm. Laurine wasn't in town yet, but she was comin'. I picture Joe sittin' there all by himself, buzzing meditative. Maybe he run Kiddie Shows in the empty apartment for awhile. But I think he went kinda remote-control exploring in the tank. There ain't any fact that can be said to be a fact that ain't on a data plate in some tank somewhere—unless it's one the technicians are diggin' out an' puttin' on a data plate now. Joe had plenty of material to work on. An' he musta started workin' right off the bat.

Joe ain't vicious, you understand. He ain't like one of these ambitious robots you read about that make up their minds the human race is inefficient and has got to be wiped out an' replaced by thinkin' machines. Joe's just got ambition. If you were a machine, you'd wanna work right, wouldn't you? That's Joe. He wants to work right. An' he's a logic. An' logics can do a lotta things that ain't been found out yet. So Joe, discoverin' the fact, begun to feel restless. He selects some things us dumb humans ain't thought of yet, an' begins to arrange so logics will be called on to do 'em.

That's all. That's everything. But, brother, it's enough!

Things are kinda quiet in the Maintenance Department about two in the afternoon. We are playing pinochle. Then one of the guys remembers he has to call up his wife. He goes to one of the banks of logics in Maintenance and punches the keys for his house. The screen sputters. Then a flash come on the screen.

"Announcing new and improved logics service! Your logic is now equipped to give you not only consultative but directive service. If you want to do something and don't know how to do it—ask your logic!"

There's a pause. A kinda expectant pause. Then, as if reluctantly, his connection comes through. His wife answers an' gives him hell for somethin' or other. He takes it an' snaps off.

"Whadda you know?" he says when he comes back. He tells us about the flash. "We shoulda been warned about that. There's gonna be a lotta complaints. Suppose a fella asks how to get ridda his wife an' the censor circuits block the question?''

Somebody melds a hundred aces an' says:

"Why not punch for it an' see what happens?''

It's a gag, o' course. But the guy goes over. He punches keys. In theory, a censor block is gonna come on an' the screen will say severely, "Public Policy Forbids This Service.'' You hafta have censor blocks or the kiddies will be askin' detailed questions about things they're too young to know. And there are other reasons. As you will see.

This fella punches, "How can I get rid of my wife?'' Just for the fun of it. The screen is blank for half a second. Then comes a flash. "Service question: Is she blonde or brunette?'' He hollers to us an' we come look. He punches, "Blonde.'' There's another brief pause. Then the screen says, "Hexymetacryloaminoacetine is a constituent of green shoe polish. Take home a frozen meal including dried pea soup. Color the soup with green shoe polish. It will appear to be green-pea soup. Hexymetacryloaminoacetine is a selective poison which is fatal to blonde females but not to brunettes or males of any coloring. This fact has not been brought out by human experiment, but is a product of logics service. You cannot be convicted of murder. It is improbable that you will be suspected.''

The screen goes blank, and we stare at each other. It's bound to be right. A logic workin' the Carson Circuit can no more make a mistake than any other kinda computin' machine. I call the tank in a hurry.

"Hey, you guys!'' I yell. "Somethin's happened! Logics are givin' detailed instructions for wife-murder! Check your censor-circuits—but quick!''

That was close, I think. But little do I know. At that precise instant, over on Monroe Avenue, a drunk starts to punch for somethin' on a logic. The screen says "Announcing new and improved logics service! If you want to do something and don't know how to do it—ask your logic!'' And the drunk says owlish, "I'll do it!'' So he cancels his first punching and fumbles around and says: "How can I keep my wife from finding out I've been drinking?'' And the screen says, prompt: "Buy a bottle of Franine hair shampoo. It is harmless but contains a detergent which will neutralize ethyl alcohol immediately. Take one teaspoonful for each jigger of hundred-proof you have consumed.''

This guy was plenty plastered—just plastered enough to stagger next door and obey instructions. An' five minutes later he was cold sober and writing down the information so he couldn't forget it. It was new, and it was big! He got rich offa that memo! He patented "*SOBUH, The Drink that Makes Happy Homes!*" You can top off any souse with a slug or two of it an' go home sober as a judge. The guy's cussin' income taxes right now!

You can't kick on stuff like that. But an ambitious young fourteen-year-old wanted to buy some kid stuff and his pop wouldn't fork over. He called up a friend to tell his troubles. And his logic says: "If you want to do something and don't know how to do it—ask your logic!" So this kid punches: "How can I make alotta money, fast?"

His logic comes through with the simplest, neatest, and the most efficient counterfeitin' device yet known to science. You see, all the data was in the tank. The logic—since Joe had closed some relays here an' there in the tank—simply integrated the facts. That's all. The kid got caught up with three days later, havin' already spent two thousand credits an' havin' plenty more on hand. They hadda time tellin' his counterfeits from the real stuff, an' the only way they done it was that he changed his printer, kid fashion, not bein' able to let somethin' that was workin' right alone.

Those are what you might call samples. Nobody knows all that Joe done. But there was the bank president who got humorous when his logic flashed that "Ask your logic" spiel on him, and jestingly asked how to rob his own bank. An' the logic told him, brief and explicit but good! The bank president hit the ceiling, hollering for cops. There must a been plenty of that sorta thing. There was fifty-four more robberies than usual in the next twenty-four hours, all of them planned astute an' perfect. Some of 'em they never did figure out how they'd been done. Joe, he'd gone exploring in the tank and closed some relays like a logic is supposed to do—but only when required—and blocked all censor-circuits an' fixed up this logics service which planned perfect crimes, nourishing an' attractive meals, conterfeitin' machines, an' new industries with a fine impartiality. He musta been plenty happy, Joe must. He was functionin' swell, buzzin' along to himself while the Korlanovitch kids were off ridin' with their ma an' pa.

They come back at seven o'clock, the kids all happily wore out with the afternoon of fightin' each other in the car. Their folks put 'em to bed and sat down to rest. They saw Joe's screen flickerin' meditative from one subject to another an' old man Korlanovitch had had enough excitement for one day. He turned Joe off.

An' at that instant the patterns of relays that Joe had turned on snapped off, all the offers of directive service stopped flashin' on logic screens everywhere, an' peace descended on the earth.

For everybody else. But for me. Laurine come to town. I have often thanked God fervent that she didn't marry me when I thought I wanted her to. In the intervenin' years she had progressed. She was blonde an' fatal to begin with. She had got blonder and fataler an' had had four husbands and one acquittal for homicide an' had acquired a air of enthusiasm and self-confidence. That's just a sketch of the background. Laurine was not the kinda former girlfriend you like to have turning up in the same town with your wife. But she came to town, an' Monday morning she tuned right into the middle of Joe's second spasm of activity.

The Korlanovitch kids had turned him on again. I got these details later and kinda pieced 'em together. An' every logic in town was dutifully flashin' a notice, "If you want to do something—ask your logic!" every time they were turned on for use. More'n that, when people punched for the morning news, they got a full account of the previous afternoon's doin's. Which put 'em in a frame of mind to share in the party. One bright fella demands, "How can I make a perpetual motion machine?" And his logic sputters a while an' then comes up with a set-up usin' the Brownian movement to turn little wheels. If the wheels ain't bigger'n a eighth of an inch they'll turn, all right, an' practically it's perpetual motion. Another one asks for the secret of transmuting metals. The logic rakes back in the data plates an' integrates a strictly practical answer. It does take so much power that you can't make no profit except on radium, but that pays off good. An' from the fact that for a coupla years to come the police were turnin' up new and improved jimmies, knob-claws for gettin' at safe innards, and all-purpose keys that'd open any known lock—why there must have been other inquiries with a strictly practical viewpoint. Joe done a lot for technical progress!

But he done more in other lines. Educational, say. None of my kids are old enough to be interested, but Joe bypassed all censor-circuits because they hampered the service he figured logics should give humanity. So the kids an' teenagers who wanted to know what comes after the bees an' flowers found out. And there is certain facts which men hope their wives won't do more'n suspect, an' those facts are just what their wives are really curious about. So when a woman dials: "How can I tell if Oswald is true to me?" and her logic tells her—you can figure out how many rows got started that night when the men come home!

All this while Joe goes on buzzin' happy to himself, showin' the Korlanovitch kids the animated funnies with one circuit while with the others he remote-controls the tank so that all the other logics can give people what they ask for and thereby raise merry hell.

An' then Laurine gets onto the new service. She turns on the logic in her hotel room, prob'ly to see the week's style-forecast. But the logic says, dutiful: "If you want to do something—ask your logic!" So Laurine prob'ly looks enthusiastic—she would!—and tries to figure out something to ask. She already knows all about everything she cares about—ain't she had four husbands an' shot one?—so I occur to her. She know this is the town I live in. So she punches, "How can I find Ducky?"

O.K., guy! But that is what she used to call me. She gets a service question. "Is Ducky known by any other name?" So she gives my regular name. And the logic can't find me. Because my logic ain't listed under my name on account of I am in Maintenance and don't want to be pestered when I'm home, and there ain't any data plates on code-listed logics, because the codes get changed so often—like a guy gets plastered an' tells a redhead to call him up, an' on gettin' sober hurriedly has the code changed before she reaches his wife on the screen.

Well! Joe is stumped. That's prob'ly the first question logics service hasn't been able to answer. "How can I locate Ducky?"!! Quite a problem! So Joe broods over it while showin' the Korlanovitch kids the animated comic about the cute little boy who carries sticks of dynamite in his hip pocket an' plays practical jokes on everybody. Then he gets the trick. Laurine's screen suddenly flashes:

"Logics special service will work upon your question. Please punch your logic designation and leave it turned on. You will be called back."

Laurine is merely mildly interested, but she punches her hotel-room number and has a drink and takes a nap. Joe sets to work. He has been given an idea.

My wife calls me at Maintenance and hollers. She is fit to be tied. She says I got to do something. She was gonna make a call to the butcher shop. Instead of the butcher or even the "If you want to do something" flash, she got a new one. The screen says, "Service question: What is your name?" She is kinda puzzled, but she punches it. The screen sputters an' then says: "Secretarial Service Demonstration! You—" It reels off her name, address, age, sex, coloring, the amounts of all her charge accounts in all the stores, my name as her husband, how much I get a week, the fact that I've been pinched three times—twice was traffic stuff, and once for a argument I got in with a guy—and the interestin' item that once when she was mad with me she left me for three weeks an' had her address changed to her folks' home. Then it says, brisk: "Logics Service will hereafter keep your personal accounts, take messages, and locate persons you may wish to get in touch with. This demonstration is to introduce the service." Then it connects her with the butcher.

But she don't want meat, then. She wants blood. She calls me.

"If it'll tell me all about myself," she says, fairly boilin', "it'll tell anybody else who punches my name! You've got to stop it!"

"Now, now, honey!" I says. "I didn't know about all this! It's new! But they musta fixed the tank so it won't give out information except to the logic where a person lives!"

"Nothing of the kind!" she tells me, furious. "I tried! And you know that Blossom woman who lives next door! She's been married three times and she's forty-two years old and she says she's only thirty! And Mrs. Hudson's had her husband arrested four times for nonsupport and once for beating her up. And—"

"Hey!" I says. "You mean the logic told you this?"

"Yes!" she wails. "It will tell anybody anything! You've got to stop it! How long will it take?"

"I'll call up the tank," I says. "It can't take long."

"Hurry!" she says, desperate, "before somebody punches my name! I'm going to see what it says about that hussy across the street."

She snaps off to gather what she can before it's stopped. So I punch for the tank and I get this new "What is your name?" flash. I got a morbid curiosity and I punch my name, and the screen says: "Were you ever called Ducky?" I blink. I ain't got no suspicions. I say, "Sure!" And the screen says, "There is a call for you."

Bingo! There's the inside of a hotel room and Laurine is reclinin' asleep on the bed. She'd been told to leave her logic turned on an' she done it: It is a hot day and she is trying to be cool. I would say that she oughta not suffer from the heat. Me, being human, I do not stay as cool as she looks. But there ain't no need to go into that. After I get my breath I say, "For Heaven's sake!" and she opens her eyes.

At first she looks puzzled, like she was thinking is she getting absentminded and is this guy somebody she married lately. Then she grabs a sheet and drapes it around herself and beams at me.

"Ducky!" she says. "How marvelous!"

I say something like "Ugmph!" I am sweating.

She says:

"I put in a call for you, Ducky, and here you are! Isn't it romantic? Where are you really, Ducky? And when can you come up? You've no idea how often I've thought of you!"

I am probably the only guy she ever knew real well that she has not been married to at some time or another.

I say, "Ugmph!" and swallow.

"Can you come up instantly?" asks Laurine brightly.

"I'm . . . workin'," I say. "I'll . . . uh . . . call you back."

"I'm terribly lonesome," says Laurine. "Please make it quick, Ducky! I'll have a drink waiting for you. Have you ever thought of me?"

"Yeah," I say, feebly. "Plenty!"

"You darling!" says Laurine. "Here's a kiss to go on with until you get here! Hurry, Ducky!"

Then I sweat! I still don't know nothing about Joe, understand. I cuss out the guys at the tank because I blame them for this. If Laurine was just another blonde—well—when it comes to ordinary blondes I can leave 'em alone or leave 'em alone, either one. A married man gets that way or else. But Laurine has a look of unquenched enthusiasm that gives a man very strange weak sensations at the back of his knees. And she'd had four husbands and shot one and got acquitted.

So I punch the keys for the tank technical room, fumbling. And the screen says: "What is your name?" but I don't want any more. I punch the name of the old guy who's stock clerk in Maintenance. And the screen gives me some pretty interestin' dope—I never woulda thought the old fella had ever had that much pep—and winds up by mentionin'

139

an unclaimed deposit now amountin' to two hundred eighty credits in the First National Bank, which he should look into. Then it spiels about the new secretarial service and gives me the tank at last.

I start to swear at the guy who looks at me, but he says, tired "Snap it off, fella. We got troubles an' you're just another. What are the logics doin' now?"

I tell him, and he laughs a hollow laugh.

"A light matter, fella," he says. "A very light matter! We just managed to clamp off all the data plates that give information on high explosives. The demand for instructions in counterfeiting is increasing minute by minute. We are also trying to shut off, by main force, the relays that hook into data plates that just barely might give advice on the fine points of murder. So if people will only keep busy getting the goods on each other for a while, maybe we'll get a chance to stop the circuits that are shifting credit-balances from bank to bank before everybody's bankrupt except the guys who thought of askin' how to get big bank accounts in a hurry."

"Then," I says hoarse, "shut down the tank! Do somethin'!"

"Shut down the tank?" he says mirthless. "Does it occur to you, fella, that the tank has been doin' all the computin' for every business office for years? It's been handlin' the distribution of ninety-four percent of all telecast programs, has given out all information on weather, plane schedules, special sales, employment opportunities and news; has handled all person-to-person contacts over wires and recorded every business conversation and agreement—Listen, fella! Logics changed civilization. Logics *are* civilization! If we shut off logics, we go back to a kind of civilization we have forgotten how to run! I'm getting hysterical myself and that's why I'm talkin' like this! If my wife finds out my paycheck is thirty credits a week more than I told her and starts hunting for that red-head—"

He smiles a haggard smile at me and snaps off. And I sit down and put my head in my hands. It's true. If something had happened back in cave days and they'd hadda stop usin' fire—if they'd hadda stop usin' steam in the nineteenth century or electricity in the twentieth—it's like that. We got a very simple civilization. In the nineteen hundreds a man would have to make use of a typewriter, radio, telephone, tele-type-writer, newspaper, reference library, encyclopedias, office files, directories, plus messenger service and consulting lawyers, chemists, doctors, dietitians, filing clerks, secretaries—all to put down what he wanted to remember an' to tell him what other people had put down that he wanted to know; to report what he said to somebody else and to report to him what they said back. All we have to have is logics. Anything we want to know or see or hear, or anybody we want to talk to, we punch keys on a logic. Shut off logics and everything goes skid-doo. But Laurine. . . .

Somethin' had happened. I still didn't know what it was. Nobody else knows, even yet. What had happened was Joe. What was the matter with him was that he wanted to work good. All this fuss he was raisin' was, actual, nothin' but stuff we shoulda thought of ourselves. Directive advice, tellin' us what we wanted to know to solve a problem, wasn't but a slight extension of logical-integrator service. Figurin' out a good way to poison a fella's wife was only different in degrees from figurin' out a cube root or a guy's bank balance. It was gettin' the answer to a question. But things was goin' to pot because there was too many answers being give to too many questions.

One of the logics in Maintenance lights up. I go over, weary, to answer it. I punch the answer key. Laurine says:

"Ducky!"

It's the same hotel room. There's two glasses on the table with drinks in them. One is for me. Laurine's got on some kinda frothy hangin'-around-the-house-with-the-boyfriend outfit that automatic makes you strain your eyes to see if you actual see what you think. Laurine looks at me enthusiastic.

"Ducky!" says Laurine. "I'm lonesome! Why haven't you come up?"

"I . . . been busy," I say, strangling slightly.

"*Pooh!*" says Laurine. "Listen, Ducky! Do you remember how much in love we used to be?"

I gulp.

"Are you doin' anything this evening?" says Laurine.

I gulp again, because she is smiling at me in a way that a single man would maybe get dizzy, but it gives a old married man like me cold chills. When a dame looks at you possessive. . . .

"Ducky!" says Laurine, impulsive. "I was so mean to you! Let's get married!"

Desperation gives me a voice.

141

"I . . . got married," I tell her, hoarse.

Laurine blinks. Then she says, courageous:

"Poor boy! But we'll get you outa that! Only it would be nice if we could be married today. Now we can only be engaged!"

"I . . . can't—"

"I'll call up your wife," says Laurine, happy, "and have a talk with her. You must have a code signal for your logic, darling. I tried to ring your house and noth—"

Click! That's my logic turned off. I turned it off. And I feel faint all over. I got nervous prostration. I got combat fatigue. I got anything you like. I got cold feet.

I beat it outa Maintenance, yellin' to somebody I got a emergency call. I'm gonna get out in a Maintenance car an' cruise around until it's plausible to go home. Then I'm gonna take the wife an' kids an' beat it for somewheres that Laurine won't ever find me. I don't wanna be fifth in Laurine's series of husbands and maybe the second one she shoots in a moment of boredom. I got experience of blondes! I got experience of Laurine! And I'm scared to death!

I beat it out into traffic in the Maintenance car. There was a disconnected logic on the back, ready to substitute for one that hadda burnt-out coil or something that it was easier to switch and fix back in the Maintenance shop. I drove crazy but automatic. It was kinda ironic, if you think of it. I was goin' hoopla over a strictly personal problem, while civilization was crackin' up all around me because other people were havin' their personal problems solved as fast as they could state 'em. It is a matter of record that part of the Mid-Western Electric research guys had been workin' on cold electron-emission for thirty years, to make vacuum tubes that wouldn't need a power source to heat the filament. And one of those fellas was intrigued by the "Ask your logic" flash. He asked how to get cold emission of electrons. And the logic integrates a few squintillion facts on the physics data plates and tells him. Just as casual as it told somebody over in the Fourth Ward how to serve leftover soup in a new attractive way, and somebody else on Mason Street how to dispose of a torso that somebody had left careless in his cellar after ceasing to use same.

Laurine wouldn't never have found me if it hadn't been for this new logics service. But now that it was started—Zowie! She'd shot one husband and got acquitted. Suppose she got impatient because I was still married an' asked logics service how to get me free an' in a spot where I'd have to marry her by 8:30 p.m.? It woulda told her! Just like it told that woman out in the suburbs how to make sure her husband wouldn't run around no more. *Br-r-r-r!* An' like it told that kid how to find some buried treasure. Remember? He was happy totin' home the gold reserve of the Hanoverian Bank and Trust Company when they caught on to it. The logic had told him how to make some kinda machine that nobody has been able to figure how it works even yet, only they guess it dodges around a couple extra dimensions. If Laurine was to start askin' questions with a technical aspect to them, that would be logics service meat! And fella, I was scared! If you think a he-man oughtn't to be scared of just one blonde—you ain't met Laurine!

I'm driving blind when a social-conscious guy asks how to bring about his own particular system of social organization at once. He don't ask if it's best or if it'll work. He just wants to get it started. And the logic—or Joe—tells him! Simultaneous, there's a retired preacher asks how can the human race be cured of concupiscence. Bein' seventy, he's pretty safe himself, but he wants to remove the peril to the spiritual welfare of the rest of us. He finds out. It involves constructin' a sort of broadcastin' station to emit a certain wave-pattern an' turnin' it on. Just that. Nothing more. It's found out afterward, when he is solicitin' funds to construct it. Fortunate, he didn't think to ask logics how to finance it, or it woulda told him that, too, an' we woulda all been cured of the impulses we maybe regret afterward but never at the time. And there's another group of serious thinkers who are sure the human race would be a lot better off if everybody went back to nature an' lived in the woods with the ants an' poison ivy. They start askin' questions about how to cause humanity to abandon cities and artificial conditions of living. They practically got the answer in logics service!

Maybe it didn't strike you serious at the time, but while I was drivin' aimless, sweatin' blood over Laurine bein' after me, the fate of civilization hung in the balance. I ain't kiddin'. For instance, the Superior Man gang that sneers at the rest of us was quietly asking questions on what kinda weapons could be made by which Superior men could take over and run things . . .

But I drove here an' there, sweatin' an' talkin' to myself.

"What I ought to do is ask this wacky logics service how to get outa this mess," I says. "But it'd just tell me a intricate an' foolproof way to bump Laurine off. I wanna have peace! I wanna grow comfortably old and brag to other old guys about what a hellion I used to be, without havin' to go through it an' lose my chance of livin' to be a elderly liar."

I turn a corner at random, there in the Maintenance car.

"It was a nice kinda world once," I says, bitter. "I could go home peaceful and not have belly-cramps wonderin' if a blonde has called up my wife to announce my engagement to her. I could punch keys on a logic without gazing into somebody's bedroom while she is giving her epidermis a air bath and being led to think things I gotta take out in thinkin'. I could—"

Then I groan, rememberin' that my wife, naturally, is gonna blame me for the fact that our private life ain't private any more if anybody has tried to peek into it.

"It was a swell world," I says, homesick for the dear dead days-before-yesterday. "We was playin' happy with our toys like little innocent children until somethin' happened. Like a guy named Joe come in and squashed all our mud pies."

Then it hit me. I got the whole thing in one flash. There ain't nothing in the tank set-up to start relays closin'. Relays are closed exclusive by logics, to get the information the keys are punched for. Nothin' but a logic coulda cooked up the relay patterns that constituted logics service. Humans wouldn't ha' been able to figure it out! Only a logic could integrate all the stuff that woulda made all the other logics work like this—

There was one answer. I drove into a restaurant and went over to a pay-logic an' dropped in a coin.

"Can a logic be modified," I spell out, "to co-operate in long-term planning which human brains are too limited in scope to do?"

The screen sputters. Then it says:

"Definitely yes."

"How great will the modifications be?" I punch.

"Microscopically slight. Changes in dimensions," says the screen. "Even modern precision gauges are not exact enough to check them, however. They can only come about under present manufacturing methods by an extremely improbable accident, which has only happened once."

144

"How can one get hold of that one accident which can do this highly necessary work?" I punch.

The screen sputters. Sweat broke out on me. I ain't got it figured out close, yet, but what I'm scared of is that whatever is Joe will be suspicious. But what I'm askin' is strictly logical. And logics can't lie. They gotta be accurate. They can't help it.

" A complete logic capable of the work required," says the screen, "is now in ordinary family use in—"

And it gives me the Korlanovitch address and do I go over there! Do I go over there fast! I pull up the Maintenance car in front of the place, and I take the extra logic outa the back, and I stagger up the Korlanovitch flat and I ring the bell. A kid answers the door.

"I'm from Logics Maintenance," I tell the kid. "An inspection record has shown that your logic is apt to break down any minute. I come to put in a new one before it does."

The kid says "O.K.!" real bright and runs back to the livin'-room where Joe—I got the habit of callin' him Joe later, through just meditatin' about him—is runnin' something the kids wanna look at. I hook in the other logic an' turn it on, conscientious making sure it works. Then I say:

"Now kiddies, you punch this one for what you want. I'm gonna take the old one away before it breaks down."

And I glance at the screen. The kiddies have apparently said they wanna look at some real cannibals. So the screen is presenting an anthropological expedition scientific record film of the fertility dance of the Huba-Jouba tribe of West Africa. It is supposed to be restricted to anthropological professors an' post-graduate medical students. But there ain't any censor blocks workin' any more and it's on. The kids are much interested. Me, bein' a old married man, I blush.

I disconnect Joe. Careful. I turn to the other logic and punch keys for Maintenance. I do not get a services flash. I get Maintenance. I feel very good. I report that I am goin' home because I fell down a flight of steps an' hurt my leg. I add, inspired:

"An' say, I was carryin' the logic I replaced an' it's all busted. I left it for the dustman to pick up."

"If you don't turn 'em in," says Stock, "you gotta pay for 'em."

"Cheap at the price," I say.

I go home. Laurine ain't called. I put Joe down in the cellar, careful. If I turned him in, he'd be inspected an' his parts salvaged even if I busted somethin' on him. Whatever part was off-normal might be used again and everything start all over. I can't risk it. I pay for him and leave him be.

That's what happened. You might say I saved civilization an' not be far wrong. I know I ain't goin' to take a chance on havin' Joe in action again. Not while Laurine is livin'. An' there are other reasons. With all the nuts who wanna change the world to their own line o' thinkin', an' the ones that wanna bump people off, an' generally solve their problems.... Yeah! Problems are bad, but I figure I better let sleepin' problems lie.

But on the other hand, if Joe could be tamed, somehow, and got to work just reasonable—he could make me a coupla million dollars, easy. But even if I got sense enough not to get rich, an' if I get retired and just loaf around fishin' an' lyin' to the other old duffers about what a great guy I used to be—maybe I'll like it, but maybe I won't. And after all, if I get fed up with bein' old and confined strictly to thinking—why I could hook Joe in long enough to ask: "How can a old guy not stay old?" Joe'll be able to find out. An' he'll tell me.

That couldn't be allowed out general, of course. You gotta make room for kids to grow up. But it's a pretty good world, now Joe's turned off. Maybe I'll turn him on long enough to learn how to stay in it. But on the other hand, maybe....

INVISIBILITY

Stories of invisibility have been written since earliest times. A large reason for their continued popularity is undoubtably their link with common power fantasies about what we would do if seeing but unseen. However, the chill of unseen menaces probably plays a part also.

During the nineteenth century attempts were made to rationally explain invisibility in literary works. Supernatural creatures and magic cloaks were replaced by natural things whose invisibility was naturally explained.

In "What was It?" (*Harpers*, March 1859), Fitz-James O'Brien first suggested a human constituted of naturally clear cells like glass, an idea Guy de Maupassant later used in "The Horla" (1887). Other approaches include animals composed of colors outside the visual spectrum (Ambrose Bierce's "The Damned Thing," 1893); achieving different speeds of movement by going faster or slowing things down (H. G. Wells's "The New Accelerator," 1903, and John D. MacDonald's *The Girl, the Gold Watch, and Everything*, 1962); using some kind of mechanical or chemical agent to make you invisible by bending light rays or turning cells transparent (Edward Page Mitchell's "The Crystal Man," 1881); possessing psychic power to cause others to look away, to forget, or to display disinterest (Bill Pronzini's "The Man Who Collected 'The Shadow,' " 1971); moving through another dimension of time or space (Richard Matheson's "Little Girl Lost," 1953); existing as pure energy (Kurt Vonnegut's "Unready to Wear," 1953); being so ordinary that you are forgotten (Algis Budrys's "Lost Love," 1957); shrinking in size (Ray Cummings's "The Girl in the Golden Atom," 1919); and being intentionally shunned or ignored (Robert Silverberg's

"To See the Invisible Man," 1963). An anthology about invisibility is Basil Davenport's *Invisible Men* (1960).

Fitz-James O'Brien was an Irish immigrant who published several advanced science fiction and fantasy stories. He was killed in the Civil War.

WHAT WAS IT?

Fitz-James O'Brien *(1859)*

*I*t is, I confess, with considerable diffidence that I approach the strange
narrative which I am about to relate. The events which I purpose
detailing are of so extraordinary a character that I am quite prepared to
meet with an unusual amount of incredulity and scorn. I accept all such
beforehand. I have, I trust, the literary courage to face unbelief. I have,
after mature consideration, resolved to narrate, in as simple and straight-
forward a manner as I can compass, some facts that passed under my
observation, in the month of July last, and which, in the annals of the
mysteries of physical science, are wholly unparalleled.

I live at No. —— Twenty-sixth Street, in New York. The house is
in some respects a curious one. It has enjoyed for the last two years the
reputation of being haunted. It is a large and stately residence, surrounded by what was once a garden, but which is now only a green
enclosure used for bleaching clothes. The dry basin of what has been a
fountain, and a few fruit trees ragged and unpruned, indicate that this
spot in past days was a pleasant, shady retreat, filled with fruits and
flowers and the sweet murmur of waters.

The house is very spacious. A hall of noble size leads to a large
spiral staircase winding through its center, while the various apartments
are of imposing dimensions. It was built some fifteen or twenty years
since by Mr. A——, the well-known New York merchant, who five years
ago threw the commercial world into convulsions by a stupendous bank
fraud. Mr. A——, as everyone knows, escaped to Europe, and died not
long after, of a broken heart. Almost immediately after the news of his
decease reached this country and was verified, the report spread in
Twenty-sixth Street that No. —— was haunted. Legal measures had

149

dispossessed the widow of its former owner, and it was inhabited merely by a caretaker and his wife, placed there by the house agent into whose hands it had passed for purposes of renting or sale. These people declared that they were troubled with unnatural noises. Doors were opened without any visible agency. The remnants of furniture scattered through the various rooms, were, during the night, piled one upon the other by unknown hands. Invisible feet passed up and down the stairs in broad daylight, accompanied by the rustle of unseen silk dresses, and the gliding of viewless hands along the massive balusters. The caretaker and his wife declared they would live there no longer. The house agent laughed, dismissed them, and put others in their place. The noises and supernatural manifestations continued. The neighborhood caught up the story, and the house remained untenanted for three years. Several persons negotiated for it; but, somehow, always before the bargain was closed they heard the unpleasant rumors and declined to treat any further.

It was in this state of things that my landlady, who at that time kept a boarding-house in Bleecker Street, and who wished to move further up town, conceived the bold idea of renting No. —— Twenty-sixth Street. Happening to have in her house rather a plucky and philosophical set of boarders, she laid her scheme before us, stating candidly everything she had heard respecting the ghostly qualities of the establishment to which she wished to remove us. With the exception of two timid persons—a sea-captain and a returned Californian, who immediately gave notice that they would leave—all of Mrs. Moffat's guests declared that they would accompany her in her chivalric incursion into the abode of spirits.

Our removal was effected in the month of May, and we were charmed with our new residence. The portion of Twenty-sixth Street where our house is situated, between Seventh and Eighth Avenues, is one of the pleasantest localities in New York. The gardens back of the houses, running down nearly to the Hudson, form, in the summer time, a perfect avenue of verdure. The air is pure and invigorating, sweeping, as it does, straight across the river from the Weehawken heights, and even the ragged garden which surrounded the house, although displaying on washing days rather too much clothesline, still gave us a piece of greensward to look at, and a cool retreat in the summer evenings, where we smoked our cigars in the dusk, and watched the fireflies flashing their dark lanterns in the long grass.

Of course we had no sooner established ourselves at No. —— than we began to expect the ghosts. We absolutely awaited their advent with eagerness. Our dinner conversation was supernatural. One of the boarders, who had purchased Mrs. Crowe's "Night Side of Nature" for his own private delectation, was regarded as a public enemy by the entire household for not have bought twenty copies. The man led a life of supreme wretchedness while he was reading this volume. A system of espionage was established, of which he was the victim. If he incautiously laid the book down for an instant and left the room, it was immediately seized and read aloud in secret places to a select few. I found myself a person of immense importance, it having leaked out that I was tolerably well versed in the history of supernaturalism, and had once written a story the foundation of which was a ghost. If a table or a wainscot panel happened to warp when we were assembled in the large drawing-room, there was an instant silence, and every one was prepared for an immediate clanking of chains and a spectral form.

After a month of psychological excitement, it was with the utmost dissatisfaction that we were forced to acknowledge that nothing in the remotest degree approaching the supernatural had manifested itself. Once the black butler asseverated that his candle had been blown out by some invisible agency while he was undressing himself for the night; but as I had more that once discovered this colored gentleman in a condition when one candle must have appeared to him like two, I thought it possible that, by going a step further in his potations, he might have reversed this phenomenon, and seen no candle at all where he ought to have beheld one.

Things were in this state when an incident took place so awful and inexplicable in its character that my reason fairly reels at the bare memory of the occurrence. It was the tenth of July. After dinner was over I repaired, with my friend Dr. Hammond, to the garden to smoke my evening pipe. Independent of certain mental sympathies which existed between the Doctor and myself, we were linked together by a vice. We both smoked opium. We knew each other's secret, and respected it. We enjoyed together that wonderful expansion of thought, that marvellous intensifying of the perceptive faculties, that boundless feeling of existence when we seem to have points of contact with the whole universe— in short, that unimaginable spiritual bliss, which I would not surrender for a throne, and which I hope you, reader, will never—never taste.

Those hours of opium happiness which the Doctor and I spent

together in secret were regulated with a scientific accuracy. We did not blindly smoke the drug of paradise, and leave our dreams to chance. While smoking, we carefully steered our conversation through the brightest and calmest channels of thought. We talked of the East, and endeavored to recall the magical panorama of its glowing scenery. We criticized the most sensuous poets—those who painted life ruddy with health, brimming with passion, happy in the possession of youth and strength and beauty. If we talked of Shakespeare's "Tempest," we lingered over Ariel, and avoided Caliban. Like the Guebers, we turned our faces to the east, and saw only the sunny side of the world.

This skillful coloring of our train of thought produced in our subsequent visions a corresponding tone. The splendors of Arabian fairyland dyed our dreams. We paced that narrow strip of grass with the tread and port of kings. The song of the *rana arborea*, while he clung to the bark of the ragged plum tree, sounded like the strains of divine musicians. Houses, walls, and streets melted like rain clouds, and vistas of unimaginable glory stretched away before us. It was a rapturous companionship. We enjoyed the vast delight more perfectly because, even in our most ecstatic moments, we were conscious of each other's presence. Our pleasures, while individual, were still twin, vibrating and moving in musical accord.

On the evening in question, the tenth of July, the Doctor and myself drifted into an unusually metaphysical mood. We lit our large meerschaums, filled with fine Turkish tobacco, in the core of which burned a little black nut of opium, that, like the nut in the fairy tale, held within its narrow limits wonders beyond the reach of kings; we paced to and fro, conversing. A strange perversity dominated the currents of our thought. They would *not* flow through the sun-lit channels into which we strove to divert them. For some unaccountable reason, they constantly diverged into dark and lonesome beds, where a continual gloom brooded. It was in vain that, after our old fashion, we flung ourselves on the shores of the East, and talked of its gay bazaars, of the splendors of the time of Haroun, of harems and golden palaces. Black afreets continually arose from the depths of our talk, and expanded, like the one the fisherman released from the copper vessel, until they blotted everything bright from our vision. Insensibly, we yielded to the occult force that swayed us, and indulged in gloomy speculation. We had talked some time upon the proneness of the human mind to mysticism, and the almost universal love of the terrible, when Hammond suddenly said to me, "What do you consider to be the greatest element of terror?"

The question puzzled me. That many things were terrible, I knew. Stumbling over a corpse in the dark; beholding, as I once did, a woman floating down a deep and rapid river, with wildly lifted arms, and awful, upturned face, uttering, as she drifted, shrieks that rent one's heart, while we, the spectators, stood frozen at a window which overhung the river at a height of sixty feet, unable to make the slightest effort to save her, but dumbly watching her last supreme agony and her disappearance. A shattered wreck, with no life visible, encountered floating listlessly on the ocean, is a terrible object, for it suggests a huge terror, the proportions of which are veiled. But it now struck me, for the first time, that there must be one great and ruling embodiment of fear—a King of Terrors, to which all others must succumb. What might it be? To what train of circumstances would it owe its existence?

"I confess, Hammond," I replied to my friend, "I never considered the subject before. That there must be one Something more terrible than any other thing, I feel. I cannot attempt, however, even the most vague definition."

"I am somewhat like you, Harry," he answered. "I feel my capacity to experience a terror greater than anything yet conceived by the human mind—something combining in fearful and unnatural amalgamation hitherto supposed incompatible elements. The calling of the voices in Brockden Brown's novel of *Wieland* is awful; so the picture of the Dweller of the Threshold, in Bulter's *Zanoni*; but," he added, shaking his head gloomily, "there is something more horrible still than these."

"Look here, Hammond," I rejoined, "let us drop this kind of talk, for heaven's sake! We shall suffer for it, depend on it."

"I don't know what's the matter with me tonight," he replied, "but my brain is running upon all sorts of weird and awful thoughts. I feel as if I could write a story like Hoffman, tonight, if I were only master of a literary style."

"Well, if we are going to be Hoffmanesque in our talk, I'm off to bed. Opium and nightmares should never be brought together. How sultry it is! Good night, Hammond."

"Good night, Harry. Pleasant dreams to you."

"To you, gloomy wretch, afreets, ghouls, and enchanters."

We parted, and each sought his respective chamber. I undressed

153

quickly and got into bed, taking with me, according to my usual custom, a book, over which I generally read myself to sleep. I opened the volume as soon as I had laid my head upon the pillow, and instantly flung it to the other side of the room. It was Goudon's *History of Monsters*, a curious French work, which I had lately imported from Paris, but which, in the state of mind I had then reached, was anything but an agreeable companion. I resolved to go to sleep at once; so turning down my gas until nothing but a little blue point of light glimmered on the top of the tube, I composed myself to rest.

The room was in total darkness. The atom of gas that still remained alight did not illuminate a distance of three inches round the burner. I desperately drew my arm across my eyes, as if to shut out even the darkness, and tried to think of nothing. It was in vain. The confounded themes touched on by Hammond in the garden kept obtruding themselves on my brain. I battled against them. I erected ramparts of would-be blankness of intellect to keep them out. They still crowded upon me. While I was lying still as a corpse, hoping that by a perfect physical inaction I should hasten mental repose, an awful incident occurred. A Something dropped, as it seemed, from the ceiling, plumb upon my chest, and the next instant I felt two bony hands encircling my throat, endeavoring to choke me.

I am no coward, and am possessed of considerable physical strength. The suddenness of the attack, instead of stunning me, strung every nerve to its highest tension. My body acted from instinct, before my brain had time to realize the terrors of my position. In an instant I wound two muscular arms around the creature, and squeezed it, with all the strength of despair, against my chest. In a few seconds the bony hands that had fastened on my throat loosened their hold, and I was free to breathe once more. Then commenced a struggle of awful intensity. Immersed in the most profound darkness, totally ignorant of the nature of the Thing by which I was so suddenly attacked, finding my grasp slipping every moment, by reason, it seemed to me, of the entire nakedness of my assailant, bitten with sharp teeth in the shoulder, neck, and chest, having every moment to protect my throat against a pair of sinewy, agile hands, which my utmost efforts could not confine—these were a combination of circumstances to combat which required all the strength, skill, and courage that I possessed.

At last, after a silent, deadly, exhausting struggle, I got my assailant under by a series of incredible efforts of strength. Once pinned, with my knee on what I made out to be its chest, I knew that I was victor. I rested for a moment to breathe. I heard the creature beneath me panting in the darkness, and felt the violent throbbing of a heart. It was apparently as exhausted as I was; that was one comfort. At this moment I remembered that I usually placed under my pillow, before going to bed, a large yellow silk pocket handkerchief. I felt for it instantly; it was there. In a few seconds more I had, after a fashion, pinioned the creature's arms.

I now felt tolerably secure. There was nothing more to be done but to turn on the gas, and, having first seen what my midnight assailant was like, arouse the household. I will confess to being actuated by a certain pride in not giving the alarm before; I wished to make the capture alone and unaided.

Never losing my hold for an instant, I slipped from the bed to the floor, dragging my captive with me. I had but a few steps to make to reach the gas burner; these I made with the greatest caution, holding the creature in a grip like a vise. At last I got within arm's length of the tiny speck of blue light which told me where the gas burner lay. Quick as lightning I released my grasp with one hand and let on the full flood of light. Then I turned to look at my captive.

I cannot even attempt to give any definition of my sensations the instant after I turned on the gas. I suppose I must have shrieked with terror, for in less than a minute afterward my room was crowded with the inmates of the house. I shudder now as I think of that awful moment. *I saw nothing!* Yes; I had one arm firmly clasped round a breathing, panting, corporeal shape, my other hand gripped with all its strength a throat as warm, and apparently fleshly, as my own; and yet, with this living substance in my grasp, with its body pressed against my own, and all in the bright glare of a large jet of gas, I absolutely beheld nothing! Not even an outline—a vapor!

I do not, even at this hour, realize the situation in which I found myself. I cannot recall the astounding incident thoroughly. Imagination in vain tries to compass the awful paradox.

It breathed. I felt its warm breath upon my cheek. It struggled fiercely. It had hands. They clutched me. Its skin was smooth, like my own. There it lay, pressed close up against me, solid as stone—and yet utterly invisible!

I wonder that I did not faint or go mad on the instant. Some wonderful instinct must have sustained me; for, absolutely, in place of loosening my hold on the terrible Enigma, I seemed to gain an additional strength in my moment of horror, and tightened my grasp with such wonderful force that I felt the creature shivering with agony.

Just then Hammond entered my room at the head of the household. As soon as he beheld my face—which, I suppose, must have been an awful sight to look at—he hastened forward, crying, "Great heaven, Harry! what has happened?"

"Hammond! Hammond!" I cried, "come here. O, this is awful! I have been attacked in bed by something or other, which I have hold of; but I can't see it— I can't see it!"

Hammond, doubtless struck by the unfeigned horror expressed in my countenance, made one or two steps forward with an anxious yet puzzled expression. A very audible titter burst from the remainder of my visitors. This suppressed laughter made me furious. To laugh at a human being in my position! It was the worst species of cruelty. *Now*, I can understand why the appearance of a man struggling violently, as it would seem, with an airy nothing, and calling for assistance against a vision, should have appeared ludicrous. *Then*, so great was my rage against the mocking crowd that had I the power I would have stricken them dead where they stood.

"Hammond! Hammond!" I cried again, despairingly, "for God's sake come to me. I can hold the—the Thing but a short while longer. It is overpowering me. Help me! Help me!"

"Harry," whispered Hammond, approaching me, "you have been smoking too much opium."

"I swear to you, Hammond, that this is no vision," I answered in the same low tone. "Don't you see how it shakes my whole frame with its struggles? If you don't believe me, convince yourself. Feel it—touch it."

Hammond advanced and laid his hand in the spot I indicated. A wild cry of horror burst from him. He had felt it!

In a moment he had discovered somewhere in my room a long piece of cord, and was the next instant winding it and knotting it about the body of the unseen being that I clasped in my arms.

"Harry," he said, in a hoarse, agitated voice, for, though he preserved his presence of mind, he was deeply moved, "Harry, it's all safe now. You may let go, old fellow, if you're tired. The Thing can't move."

I was utterly exhausted, and I gladly loosed my hold.

Hammond stood holding the ends of the cord that bound the Invisible, twisted round his hand, while before him, self-supporting as it were, he beheld a rope laced and interlaced, and stretching tightly around a vacant space. I never saw a man look so thoroughly stricken with awe. Nevertheless his face expressed all the courage and determination which I knew him to possess. His lips, although white, were set firmly, and one could perceive at a glance that, although stricken with fear, he was not daunted.

The confusion that ensued among the guests of the house who were witnesses of this extraordinary scene between Hammond and myself—who beheld the pantomime of binding this struggling Something—who beheld me almost sinking from physical exhaustion when my task of jailer was over—the confusion and terror that took possession of the bystanders, when they saw all this, was beyond description. The weaker ones fled from the apartment. The few who remained clustered near the door and could not be induced to approach Hammond and his Charge. Still incredulity broke out through their terror. They had not the courage to satisfy themselves, and yet they doubted. It was in vain that I begged of some of the men to come near and convince themselves by touch of the existence in that room of a living being which was invisible. They were incredulous, but did not dare to undeceive themselves. How could a solid, living, breathing body be invisible, they asked. My reply was this. I gave a sign to Hammond, and both of us—conquering our fearful repugnance to touch the invisible creature—lifted it from the ground, manacled as it was, and took it to my bed. Its weight was about that of a boy of fourteen.

"Now, my friends," I said, as Hammond and myself held the creature suspended over the bed, "I can give you self-evident proof that here is a solid, ponderable body, which, nevertheless, you cannot see. Be good enough to watch the surface of the bed attentively."

I was astonished at my own courage in treating this strange event so calmly; but I had recovered from my first terror, and felt a sort of scientific pride in the affair, which dominated every other feeling.

The eyes of the bystanders were immediately fixed on my bed. At a given signal Hammond and I let the creature fall. There was the dull sound of a heavy body alighting on a soft mass. The timbers of the bed creaked. A deep impression marked itself distinctly on the pillow, and on the bed itself. The crowd who witnessed this gave a low cry, and rushed

157

from the room. Hammond and I were left alone with our Mystery.

We remained silent for some time, listening to the low, irregular breathing of the creature on the bed, and watching the rustle of the bedclothes as it impotently struggled to free itself from confinement. Then Hammond spoke.

"Harry, this is awful."

"Ay, awful."

"But not unaccountable."

"Not unaccountable! What do you mean? Such a thing has never occurred since the birth of the world. I know not what to think, Hammond. God grant that I am not mad, and that this is not an insane fantasy!"

"Let us reason a little, Harry. Here is a solid body which we touch, but which we cannot see. The fact is so unusual that it strikes us with terror. Is there no parallel, though, for such a phenomenon? Take a piece of pure glass. It is tangible and transparent. A certain chemical coarseness is all that prevents its being so entirely transparent as to be totally invisible. It is not *theoretically impossible*, mind you, to make a glass which shall not reflect a single ray of light—a glass so pure and homogeneous in its atoms that the rays from the sun will pass through it as they do through the air, refracted but not reflected. We do not see the air, and yet we feel it."

"That's all very well, Hammond, but these are inanimate substances. Glass does not breathe, air does not breathe. *This* thing has a heart that palpitates—a will that moves it—lungs that play and inspire and respire."

"You forget the phenomena of which we have so often heard of late," answered the Doctor, gravely. "At the meetings called 'spirit circles,' invisible hands have been thrust into the hands of those persons round the table—warm, fleshly hands that seemed to pulsate with mortal life."

"What? Do you think, then, that this thing is—"

"I don't know what it is," was the solemn reply; "but please the gods I will, with your assistance, thoroughly investigate it."

We watched together, smoking many pipes, all night long, by the bedside of the unearthly being that tossed and panted until it was apparently wearied out. Then we learned by the low, regular breathing that it slept.

The next morning the house was all astir. The boarders congregated on the landing outside my room, and Hammond and myself were lions. We had to answer a thousand questions as to the state of our extraordinary prisoner, for as yet not one person in the house except ourselves could be induced to set foot in the apartment.

The creature was awake. This was evidenced by the convulsive manner in which the bedclothes were moved in its efforts to escape. There was something truly terrible in beholding, as it were, those second-hand indications of the terrible writhings and agonized struggles for liberty which themselves were invisible.

Hammond and myself had racked our brains during the long night to discover some means by which we might realize the shape and general appearance of the Enigma. As well as we could make out by passing our hands over the creature's form, its outlines and lineaments were human. There was a mouth; a round, smooth head without hair; a nose, which however, was little elevated above the cheeks; and its hands and feet felt like those of a boy. At first we thought of placing the being on a smooth surface and tracing its outline with chalk, as shoemakers trace the outline of the foot. This plan was given up as being of no value. Such an outline would give not the slightest idea of its conformation.

A happy thought struck me. We would take a cast of it in plaster of Paris. This would give us the solid figure, and satisfy all our wishes. But how to do it? The movements of the creature would disturb the setting of the plastic covering, and distort the mould. Another thought. Why not give it chloroform? It had respiratory organs—that was evident by its breathing. Once reduced to a state of insensibility, we could do with it what we would. Doctor X—— was sent for; and after the worthy physician had recovered from the first shock of amazement, he proceeded to administer the chloroform. In three minutes afterward we were enabled to remove the fetters from the creature's body, and a modeller was busily engaged in covering the invisible form with the moist clay. In five minutes more we had a mould, and before evening a rough facsimile of the Mystery. It was shaped like a man—distorted, uncouth, and horrible, but still a man. It was small, not over four feet and some inches in height, and its limbs revealed a muscular development that was unparalleled. Its face surpassed in hideousness anything I had ever seen. Gustave Doré, or Callot, or Tony Johannot never conceived anything so horrible. There is a face in one of the latter's illustrations to *Un Voyage où il vous plaira*, which somewhat approaches the countenance of this creature, but does not equal it. It was the physiognomy of what I should fancy a ghoul might be. It looked as if it was capable of feeding on human flesh.

Having satisfied our curiosity, and bound everyone in the house to secrecy, it became a question what was to be done with our Enigma? It was impossible that we should keep such a horror in our house; it was equally impossible that such an awful being should be let loose upon the world. I confess that I would have gladly voted for the creature's destruction. But who would shoulder the responsibility? Who would undertake the execution of this horrible semblance of a human being? Day after day this question was deliberated gravely. The boarders all left the house. Mrs. Moffat was in despair, and threatened Hammond and myself with all sorts of legal penalties if we did not remove the Horror. Our answer was, "We will go if you like, but we decline taking this creature with us. Remove it yourself if you please. It appeared in your house. On you the responsibility rests." To this there was, of course, no answer. Mrs. Moffat could not obtain for love or money a person who would even approach the Mystery.

The most singular part of the affair was that we were entirely ignorant of what the creature habitually fed on. Everything in the way of nutriment that we could think of was placed before it, but was never touched. It was awful to stand by, day after day, and see the clothes toss, and hear the hard breathing, and know that it was starving.

Ten, twelve days, a fortnight passed, and it still lived. The pulsations of the heart, however, were daily growing fainter, and had now nearly ceased. It was evident that the creature was dying for want of sustenance. While this terrible life struggle was going on, I felt miserable. I could not sleep. Horrible as the creature was, it was pitiful to think of the pangs it was suffering.

At last it died. Hammond and I found it cold and stiff one morning in the bed. The heart had ceased to beat, the lungs to inspire. We hastened to bury it in the garden. It was a strange funeral, the dropping of that viewless corpse into the damp hole. The cast of its form I gave to Doctor X——, who keeps it in his museum in Tenth Street.

As I am on the eve of a long journey from which I may not return, I have drawn up this narrative of an event the most singular that has ever come to my knowledge.

MICROCOSMIC WORLD

One of the most fascinating concepts in science fiction is that of "pocket universes," self-contained worlds that exist inside larger ones. The first story of this type, Fitz-James O'Brien's "The Diamond Lens" (*Atlantic Monthly*, January 1858), created a sensation when published and still remains a powerful and wonderful work.

The possibility that microcosmic worlds might actually exist was raised in 1863 by Nicholas Odger in *The Mystery of Being; or, Are Ultimate Atoms Inhabited Worlds?* Rutherford's subsequent model of the atom as a kind of tiny solar system—electrons orbiting a nucleus—seemed to lend additional support. In *Triuniverse* (1912) R. A. Kennedy took the idea one step further, suggesting that our universe might be a collection of atoms in a macrocosmos.

Then in 1919 *Argosy* published Raymond Cumming's "The Girl in the Golden Atom." It was extremely popular and seemed to precipitate a flurry of stories about large and small worlds during the 1920s and 1930s. Henry Hasse, S. P. Meek, Harl Vincent, Donald Wandrei, and G. P. Wertenbaker all spun variations. Such stories inspired a sense of wonder with their vivid descriptions of changing landscapes that size-shifting protagonists encountered. But eventually microcosmic stories fell before changing scientific concepts and overfamiliarity.

More recent attempts have concentrated on worlds larger than atoms such as James Blish's "Surface Tension," 1952, and William W. Stuart's "Inside John Barth," 1960. Here a common theme has been the use of microcosms for testing or experimentation as in Theodore Sturgeon's "Microcosmic God" (1941), Frederik Pohl's "The Tunnel Under the World" (1954), and Raymond E. Banks' "The Short Ones," (1955) use microcosms for purposes of testing or experimentation.

THE DIAMOND LENS

Fitz-James O'Brien (1858)

I
THE BENDING OF THE TWIG

From a very early period of my life the entire bent of my inclinations had been toward microscopic investigations. When I was not more than ten years old, a distant relative of our family, hoping to astonish my inexperience, constructed a simple microscope for me, by drilling in a disk of copper a small hole, in which a drop of pure water was sustained by capillary attraction. This very primitive apparatus, magnifying some fifty diameters, presented, it is true, only indistinct and imperfect forms, but still sufficiently wonderful to work up my imagination to a preternatural state of excitement.

Seeing me so interested in this rude instrument, my cousin explained to me all that he knew about the principles of the microscope, related to me a few of the wonders which had been accomplished through its agency, and ended by promising to send me one regularly constructed, immediately on his return to the city. I counted the days, the hours, the minutes, that intervened between that promise and his departure.

Meantime I was not idle. Every transparent substance that bore the remotest resemblance to a lens I eagerly seized upon, and employed in vain attempts to realize that instrument, the theory of whose construction I as yet only vaguely comprehended. All panes of glass containing those oblate spheroidal knots familiarly known as "bull's eyes" were ruthlessly destroyed, in the hope of obtaining lenses of marvellous power. I even went so far as to extract the crystalline humor from the eyes of fishes and animals, and endeavored to press it into the microscopic service. I plead guilty to having stolen the glasses from my Aunt Agatha's spectacles, with a dim idea of grinding them into lenses of wondrous magnifying properties—in which attempt it is scarcely necessary to say that I totally failed.

At last the promised instrument came. It was of that order known as Field's simple microscope, and had cost perhaps about fifteen dollars. As far as educational purposes went, a better apparatus could not have been selected. Accompanying it was a small treatise on the microscope —its history, uses, and discoveries. I comprehended then for the first time the "Arabian Nights Entertainments." The dull veil of ordinary existence that hung across the world seemed suddenly to roll away, and to lay bare a land of enchantments. I felt toward my companions as the seer might feel toward the ordinary masses of men. I held conversations with Nature in a tongue which they could not understand. I was in daily communication with living wonders, such as they never imagined in their wildest visions. I penetrated beyond the external portal of things, and roamed through the sanctuaries. Where they beheld only a drop of rain slowly rolling down the window-glass, I saw a universe of beings animated with all the passions common to physical life, and convulsing their minute sphere with struggles as fierce and protracted as those of men. In the common spots of mold, which my mother, good housekeeper that she was, fiercely scooped away from her jam pots, there abode for me, under the name of mildew, enchanted gardens, filled with dells and avenues of the densest foliage and most astonishing verdure, while from the fantastic boughs of these microscopic forests hung strange fruits glittering with green, and silver, and gold.

It was no scientific thirst that at this time filled my mind. It was the pure enjoyment of a poet to whom a world of wonders has been disclosed. I talked of my solitary pleasures to none. Alone with my microscope, I dimmed my sight, day after day and night after night, poring over the marvels which it unfolded to me. I was like one who, having discovered the ancient Eden still existing in all its primitive glory, should resolve to enjoy it in solitude, and never betray to mortal the secret of its locality. The rod of my life was bent at this moment. I destined myself to be a microscopist.

Of course, like every novice, I fancied myself a discoverer. I was ignorant at the time of the thousands of acute intellects engaged in the same pursuit as myself, and with the advantage of instruments a thousand times more powerful than mine. The names of Leeuwenhoek, Williamson, Spencer, Ehrenberg, Schultz, Dujardin, Schact, and Schleiden were then entirely unknown to me, or if known, I was ignorant of their patient and wonderful researches. In every fresh specimen of cryptogamia which I placed beneath my instrument I believed that I discovered wonders of which the world was as yet ignorant. I remember well the thrill of delight and admiration that shot through me the first time that I discovered the common wheel animalcule (*Rotifera vulgaris*) expanding and contracting its flexible spokes, and seemingly rotating through the water. Alas! as I grew older, and obtained some works treating of my favorite study, I found that I was only on the threshold of a science to the investigation of which some of the greatest men of the age were devoting their lives and intellects.

As I grew up, my parents, who saw but little likelihood of anything practical resulting from the examination of bits of moss and drops of water through a brass tube and a piece of glass, were anxious that I should choose a profession. It was their desire that I should enter the counting-house of my uncle Ethan Blake, a prosperous merchant, who carried on business in New York. This suggestion I decisively combated. I had no taste for trade; I should only make a failure; in short, I refused to become a merchant.

But it was necessary for me to select some pursuit. My parents were staid New England people, who insisted on the necessity of labor; and therefore, although, thanks to the bequest of my poor Aunt Agatha, I should, on coming of age, inherit a small fortune sufficient to place me above want, it was decided that, instead of waiting for this, I should act the nobler part, and employ the intervening years in rendering myself independent.

After much cogitation I complied with the wishes of my family, and selected a profession. I determined to study medicine at the New York Academy. This disposition of my future suited me. A removal from my relatives would enable me to dispose of my time as I pleased without fear of detection. As long as I paid my Academy fees, I might shirk attending the lectures if I chose; and, as I never had the remotest intention of standing an examination, there was no danger of my being "plucked." Besides, a metropolis was the place for me. There I could obtain excellent instruments, the newest publications, intimacy with men of pursuits kindred with my own—in short, all things necessary to insure a profitable devotion of my life to my beloved science. I had an abundance of money, few desires that were not bounded by my illuminating mirror on one side and my object-glass on the other; what, therefore, was to prevent my becoming an illustrious investigator of the veiled worlds? It was with the most buoyant hopes that I left my New England home and established myself in New York.

II
THE LONGING OF A MAN OF SCIENCE

My first step, of course, was to find suitable apartments. These I obtained, after a couple of days' search, in Fourth Avenue; a very pretty second-floor unfurnished, containing sitting-room, bedroom, and a smaller apartment which I intended to fit up as a laboratory. I furnished my lodgings simply, but rather elegantly, and then devoted all my energies to the adornment of the temple of my worship. I visited Pike, the celebrated optician, and passed in review his splendid collection of microscopes—Field's Compound, Hingham's, Spencer's, Nachet's Binocular (that founded on the principles of the stereoscope), and at length fixed upon that form known as Spencer's Trunnion Microscope, as combining the greatest number of improvements with an almost perfect freedom from tremor. Along with this I purchased every possible accessory—draw-tubes, micrometers, a *camera-lucida*, lever stage, achromatic condensers, white cloud illuminators, prisms, parabolic condensers, polarizing apparatus, forceps, aquatic boxes, fishing-tubes, with a host of other articles, all of which would have been useful in the hands of an experienced microscopist, but, as I afterwards discovered, were not of the slightest present value to me. It takes years of practice to know how to use a complicated microscope. The optician looked suspiciously at me as I made these wholesale purchases. He evidently was uncertain whether to set me down as some scientific celebrity or a madman. I think he inclined to the latter belief. I suppose I was mad. Every great genius is mad upon the subject in which he is greatest. The unsuccessful madman is disgraced and called a lunatic.

Mad or not, I set myself to work with a zeal which few scientific students have ever equalled. I had everything to learn relative to the delicate study upon which I had embarked—a study involving the most earnest patience, the most rigid analytic powers, the steadiest hand, the most untiring eye, the most refined and subtile manipulation.

For a long time half my apparatus lay inactively on the shelves of my laboratory, which was now most amply furnished with every possible contrivance for facilitating my investigations. The fact was that I did not know how to use some of my scientific accessories—never having been taught microscopics—and those whose use I understood theoretically were of little avail, until by practice I could attain the necessary delicacy of handling. Still, such was the fury of my ambition, such the untiring perseverance of my experiments, that, difficult of credit as it may be, in the course of one year I became theoretically and practically an accomplished microscopist.

During this period of my labors, in which I submitted specimens of every substance that came under my observation to the action of my lenses, I became a discoverer—in a small way, it is true, for I was very young, but still a discoverer. It was I who destroyed Ehrenberg's theory that the *Volvox globator* was an animal, and proved that his "monads" with stomachs and eyes were merely phases of the formation of a vegetable cell, and were, when they reached their mature state, incapable of the act of conjugation, or any true generative act, without which no organism rising to any stage of life higher than vegetable can be said to be complete. It was I who resolved the singular problem of rotation in the cells and hairs of plants into ciliary attraction, in spite of the assertions of Mr. Wenham and others, that my explanation was the result of an optical illusion.

But notwithstanding these discoveries, laboriously and painfully made as they were, I felt horribly dissatisfied. At every step I found myself stopped by the imperfections of my instruments. Like all active microscopists, I gave my imagination full play. Indeed, it is a common complaint against many such, that they supply the defects of their instruments with the creations of their brains. I imagined depths beyond depths in Nature which the limited power of my lenses prohibited me from exploring. I lay awake at night constructing imaginary microscopes of immeasurable power, with which I seemed to pierce through all the envelopes of matter down to its original atom. How I cursed those imperfect mediums which necessity through ignorance compelled me to use! How I longed to discover the secret of some perfect lens, whose magnifying power should be limited only by the resolvability of the object, and which at the same time should be free from spherical and chromatic aberrations, in short from all the obstacles over which the poor microscopist finds himself continually stumbling! I felt convinced that the simple microscope, composed of a single lens of such vast yet perfect power was possible of construction. To attempt to bring the compound microscope up to such a pitch would have been commencing at the wrong end; this latter being simply a partially successful endeavor to remedy those very defects of the simple instrument, which, if conquered, would leave nothing to be desired.

It was in this mood of mind that I became a constructive microscopist. After another year passed in this new pursuit, experimenting on every imaginable substance—glass, gems, flints, crystals, artificial crystals formed of the alloy of various vitreous materials—in short, having constructed as many varieties of lenses as Argus had eyes, I found myself precisely where I started, with nothing gained save an extensive knowledge of glass-making. I was almost dead with despair. My parents were surprised at my apparent want of progress in the medical studies, (I had not attended one lecture since my arrival in the city) and the expenses of my mad pursuit had been so great as to embarrass me very seriously.

I was in this frame of mind one day, experimenting in my laboratory on a small diamond—that stone, from its great refracting power, having always occupied my attention more than any other—when a young Frenchman, who lived on the floor above me, and who was in the habit of occasionally visiting me, entered the room.

I think that Jules Simon was a Jew. He had many traits of the Hebrew character: a love of jewelry, of dress, and of good living. There was something mysterious about him. He always had something to sell, and yet went into excellent society. When I say sell, I should perhaps have said peddle; for his operations were generally confined to the disposal of single articles—a picture, for instance, or a rare carving in ivory, or a pair of duelling-pistols, or the dress of a Mexican *caballero*. When I was first furnishing my rooms, he paid me a visit, which ended in my purchasing an antique silver lamp, which he assured me was a Cellini—it was handsome enough even for that—and some other knick-knacks for my sitting-room. Why Simon should pursue this petty trade I never could imagine. He apparently had plenty of money, and had the *entrée* of the best houses in the city—taking care, however, I suppose, to drive no bargains within the enchanted circle of the Upper Ten. I came at length to the conclusion that this peddling was but a mask to cover some greater object, and even went so far as to believe my young acquaintance to be implicated in the slave-trade. That, however, was none of my affair.

On the present occasion, Simon entered my room in a state of considerable excitement.

"Ah! mon ami!" he cried, before I could even offer him the ordinary salutation, "it has occurred to me to be the witness of the most astonishing things in the world. I promenade myself to the house of Madame—How does the little animal—*le renard*—name himself in the Latin?"

"Vulpes," I answered.

"Ah! yes—Vulpes. I promenade myself to the house of Madame Vulpes."

"The spirit medium?"

"Yes, the great medium. Great Heavens! what a woman! I write on a slip of paper many of questions concerning affairs the most secret— affairs that conceal themselves in the abysses of my heart the most profound; and behold! by example! what occurs? This devil of a woman makes me replies the most truthful to all of them. She talks to me of things that I do not love to talk of to myself. What am I to think? I am fixed to the earth!"

"Am I to understand you, M. Simon, that this Mrs. Vulpes replied to questions secretly written by you, which questions related to events known only to yourself?"

"Ah! more than that, more than that," he answered, with an air of some alarm. "She related to me things— But," he added, after a pause, and suddenly changing his manner, "why occupy ourselves with these follies? It was all the biology, without doubt. It goes without saying that it has not my credence. But why are we here, *mon ami?* It has occurred to me to discover the most beautiful thing as you can imagine—a vase with green lizards on it, composed by the great Bernard Palissy. It is in my apartment; let us mount. I go to show it to you."

I followed Simon mechanically; but my thoughts were far from Palissy and his enamelled ware, although I, like him, was seeking in the dark after a great discovery. This casual mention of the spiritualist, Madame Vulpes, set me on a new track. What if this spiritualism should be really a great fact? What if, through communication with more subtle organisms than my own, I could reach at a single bound the goal, which perhaps a life of agonizing mental toil would never enable me to attain?

While purchasing the Palissy vase from my friend Simon, I was mentally arranging a visit to Madame Vulpes.

III
THE SPIRIT OF LEEUWENHOEK

Two evenings after this, thanks to an arrangement by letter and the promise of an ample fee, I found Madame Vulpes awaiting me at her residence alone. She was a coarse-featured woman, with a keen and rather cruel dark eye, and an exceedingly sensual expression about her mouth and under jaw. She received me in perfect silence, in an apartment on the ground floor, very sparely furnished. In the center of the room, close to where Mrs. Vulpes sat, there was a common round mahogany table. If I had come for the purpose of sweeping her chimney, the woman could not have looked more indifferent to my appearance. There was no attempt to inspire the visitor with any awe. Everything bore a simple and practical aspect. This intercourse with the spiritual world was evidently as familiar an occupation with Mrs. Vulpes as eating her dinner or riding in an omnibus.

"You come for a communication, Mr. Linley?" said the medium, in a dry, business-like tone of voice.

"By appointment—yes."

"What sort of communication do you want? A written one?"

"Yes—I wish for a written one."

"From any particular spirit?"

"Yes."

"Have you ever known this spirit on this earth?"

"Never. He died long before I was born. I wish merely to obtain from him some information which he ought to be able to give better than any other."

"Will you seat yourself at the table, Mr. Linley," said the medium, "and place your hands upon it?"

I obeyed, Mrs. Vulpes being seated opposite me, with her hands also on the table. We remained thus for about a minute and a half, when a violent succession of raps came on the table, on the back of my chair, on the floor immediately under my feet, and even on the windowpanes. Mrs. Vulpes smiled composedly.

"They are very strong tonight," she remarked. "You are fortunate." She then continued, "Will the spirits communicate with this gentleman?"

Vigorous affirmative.

"Will the particular spirit he desires to speak with communicate?"

A very confused rapping followed this question.

"I know what they mean," said Mrs. Vulpes, addressing herself to me; "they wish you to write down the name of the particular spirit that you desire to converse with. Is that so?" she added, speaking to her invisible guests.

That it was so was evident from the numerous affirmatory responses. While this was going on, I tore a slip from my pocketbook, and scribbled a name, under the table.

"Will this spirit communicate in writing with this gentleman?" asked the medium once more.

After a moment's pause, her hand seemed to be seized with a violent tremor, shaking so forcibly that the table vibrated. She said that a spirit had seized her hand and would write. I handed her some sheets of paper that were on the table, and a pencil. The latter she held loosely in her hand, which presently began to move over the paper with a singular and seemingly involuntary motion. After a few moments had elapsed, she handed me the paper, on which I found written, in a large, uncultivated hand, the words, "He is not here, but has been sent for." A pause of a minute or so now ensued, during which Mrs. Vulpes remained perfectly silent, but the raps continued at regular intervals. When the short period I mention had elapsed, the hand of the medium was again seized with its convulsive tremor, and she wrote, under this strange influence, a few words on the paper, which she handed to me. They were as follows:

I am here. Question me.
LEEUWENHOEK

I was astounded. The name was identical with that I had written beneath the table, and carefully kept concealed. Neither was it at all probable that an uncultivated woman like Mrs. Vulpes should know even the name of the great father of microscopics. It may have been biology; but this theory was soon doomed to be destroyed. I wrote on my slip—still concealing it from Mrs. Vulpes—a series of questions, which, to avoid tediousness, I shall place with the responses, in the order in which they occurred.

I—Can the microscope be brought to perfection?

SPIRIT—Yes.

I—Am I destined to accomplish this great task?

SPIRIT—You are.

I—I wish to know how to proceed to attain this end. For the love which you bear to science, help me!

SPIRIT—A diamond of one-hundred-and-forty carats, submitted to electro-magnetic currents for a long period, will experience a rearrangement of its atoms *inter se*, and from that stone you will form the universal lens.

I—Will great discoveries result from the use of such a lens?

SPIRIT—So great that all that has gone before is as nothing.

I—But the refractive power of the diamond is so immense, that the image will be formed within the lens. How is that difficulty to be surmounted?

SPIRIT—Pierce the lens through its axis, and the difficulty is obviated. The image will be formed in the pierced space, which will itself serve as a tube to look through. Now I am called. Good night.

I cannot at all describe the effect that these extraordinary communications had upon me. I felt completely bewildered. No biological theory could account for the *discovery* of the lens. The medium might, by means of biological *rapport* with my mind, have gone so far as to read my questions, and reply to them coherently. But biology could not enable her to discover that magnetic currents would so alter the crystals of the diamond as to remedy its previous defects, and admit of its being polished into a perfect lens. Some such theory may have passed through my head, it is true; but if so, I had forgotten it. In my excited condition of mind there was no course left but to become a convert, and it was in a state of the most painful nervous exaltation that I left the medium's house that evening. She accompanied me to the door, hoping that I was satisfied. The raps followed us as we went through the hall, sounding on the balusters, the flooring, and even the lintels of the door. I hastily expressed my satisfaction, and escaped hurriedly into the cool night air. I walked home with but one thought possessing me—how to obtain a diamond of the immense size required. My entire means multiplied a hundred times over would have been inadequate to its purchase. Besides, such stones are rare, and become historical. I could find such only in the regalia of Eastern or European monarchs.

IV
THE EYE OF MORNING

There was a light in Simon's room as I entered my house. A vague impulse urged me to visit him. As I opened the door of his sitting-room unannounced, he was bending, with his back toward me, over a carcel lamp, apparently engaged in minutely examining some object which he held in his hands. As I entered he started suddenly, thrust his hand into his breast pocket, and turned to me with a face crimson with confusion.

"What!" I cried, "poring over the miniature of some fair lady? Well, don't blush so much; I won't ask to see it."

Simon laughed awkwardly enough, but made none of the negative protestations usual on such occasons. He asked me to take a seat.

"Simon," said I, "I have just come from Madame Vulpes."

This time Simon turned as white as a sheet, and seemed stupefied, as if a sudden electric shock had smitten him. He babbled some incoherent words, and went hastily to a small closet where he usually kept his liquors. Although astonished at his emotion, I was too preoccupied with my own idea to pay much attention to anything else.

"You say truly when you call Madame Vulpes a devil of a woman," I continued. "Simon, she told me wonderful things tonight, or rather was the means of telling me wonderful things. Ah! if I could only get a diamond that weighed one hundred and forty carats!"

Scarcely had the sigh with which I uttered this desire died upon my lips, when Simon, with the aspect of a wild beast, glared at me savagely, and, rushing to the mantelpiece, where some foreign weapons hung on the wall, caught up a Malay creese, and brandished it furiously before him.

"No!" he cried in French, into which he always broke when excited. "No! you shall not have it! You are perfidious! You have consulted with that demon, and desire my treasure! But I will die first! Me! I am brave! You cannot make me fear!"

All this, uttered in a loud voice trembling with excitement, astounded me. I saw at a glance that I had accidentally trodden upon the edges of Simon's secret, whatever it was. It was necessary to reassure him.

"My dear Simon," I said, "I am entirely at a loss to know what you mean. I went to Madame Vulpes to consult with her on a scientific problem, to the solution of which I discovered that a diamond of the size I just mentioned was necessary. You were never alluded to during the evening, nor, so far as I was concerned, even thought of. What can be the meaning of this outburst? If you happen to have a set of valuable diamonds in your possession, you need fear nothing from me. The diamond which I require you could not possess; or, if you did possess it, you would not be living here."

Something in my tone must have completely reassured him; for his expression immediately changed to a sort of constrained merriment, combined, however, with a certain suspicious attention to my movements. He laughed, and said that I must bear with him; that he was at certain moments subject to a species of vertigo, which betrayed itself in incoherent speeches, and that the attacks passed off as rapidly as they came. He put his weapon aside while making this explanation, and endeavored, with some success, to assume a more cheerful air.

All this did not impose on me in the least. I was too much accustomed to analytical labors to be baffled by so flimsy a veil. I determined to probe the mystery to the bottom.

"Simon," I said, gaily, "let us forget all this over a bottle of Burgundy. I have a case of Lausseure's *Clos Vougeot* downstairs, fragrant with the odors and ruddy with the sunlight of the Côte d'Or. Let us have up a couple of bottles. What say you?"

"With all my heart," answered Simon, smilingly.

I produced the wine and we seated ourselves to drink. It was of a famous vintage, that of 1848, a year when war and wine throve together —and its pure but powerful juice seemed to impart renewed vitality to the system. By the time we had half finished the second bottle, Simon's head, which I knew was a weak one, had begun to yield, while I remained calm as ever, only that every draught seemed to send a flush of vigor through my limbs. Simon's utterance became more and more indistinct. He took to singing French *chansons* of a not very moral tendency. I rose suddenly from the table just at the conclusion of one of those incoherent verses, and, fixing my eyes on him with a quiet smile, said: "Simon, I have deceived you. I learned your secret this evening. You may as well be frank with me. Mrs. Vulpes, or rather one of her spirits, told me all."

He started with horror. His intoxication seemed for the moment to fade away, and he made a movement toward the weapon that he had a short time before laid down. I stopped him with my hand.

"Monster!" he cried, passionately, "I am ruined! What shall I do? You shall never have it! I swear by my mother!"

"I don't want it," I said; "rest secure, but be frank with me. Tell me all about it."

The drunkenness began to return. He protested with maudlin earnestness that I was entirely mistaken—that I was intoxicated; then asked me to swear eternal secrecy, and promised to disclose the mystery to me. I pledged myself, of course, to all. With an uneasy look in his eyes, and hands unsteady with drink and nervousness, he drew a small case from his breast and opened it. Heavens! How the mild lamplight was shivered into a thousand prismatic arrows, as it fell upon a vast rose-diamond that glittered in the case! I was no judge of diamonds, but I saw at a glance that this was a gem of rare size and purity. I looked at Simon with wonder, and—must I confess it?—with envy. How could he have obtained this treasure? In reply to my questions, I could just gather from his drunken statements (of which, I fancy, half the incoherence was affected) that he had been superintending a gang of slaves engaged in diamond-washing in Brazil; that he had seen one of them secrete a diamond, but, instead of informing his employers, had quietly watched the negro until he saw him bury his treasure; that he had dug it up and fled with it, but that as yet he was afraid to attempt to dispose of it publicly— so valuable a gem being almost certain to attract too much attention to its owner's antecedents—and he had not been able to discover any of those obscure channels by which such matters are conveyed away safely. He added, that, in accordance with the oriental practice, he had named his diamond by the fanciful title of "The Eye of Morning."

While Simon was relating this to me, I regarded the great diamond attentively. Never had I beheld anything so beautiful. All the glories of light, ever imagined or described, seemed to pulsate in its crystalline chambers. Its weight, as I learned from Simon, was exactly one hundred and forty carats. Here was an amazing coincidence. The hand of Destiny seemed in it. On the very evening when the spirit of Leeuwenhoek communicates to me the great secret of the microscope, the priceless means which he directs me to employ start up within my easy reach! I determined, with the most perfect deliberation, to possess myself of Simon's diamond.

I sat opposite to him while he nodded over his glass, and calmly revolved the whole affair. I did not for an instant contemplate so foolish an act as a common theft, which would of course be discovered, or at least necessitate flight and concealment, all of which must interfere with my scientific plans. There was but one step to be taken—to kill Simon. After all, what was the life of a little peddling Jew, in comparison with the interests of science? Human beings are taken every day from the condemned prisons to be experimented on by surgeons. This man, Simon, was by his own confession a criminal, a robber, and I believed on my soul a murderer. He deserved death quite as much as any felon condemned by the laws; why should I not, like government, contrive that his punishment should contribute to the progress of human knowledge?

The means for accomplishing everything I desired lay within my reach. There stood upon the mantel-piece a bottle half full of French laudanum. Simon was occupied with his diamond, which I had just restored to him, that it was an affair of no difficulty to drug his glass. In a quarter of an hour he was in a profound sleep.

I now opened his waistcoat, took the diamond from the inner pocket in which he had placed it, and removed him to the bed, on which I laid him so that his feet hung down over the edge. I had possessed myself of the Malay creese, which I held in my right hand, while with the other I discovered as accurately as I could by pulsation the exact locality of the heart. It was essential that all the aspects of his death should lead to the surmise of self-murder. I calculated the exact angle at which it was probable that the weapon, if levelled by Simon's own hand, would enter his breast; then with one powerful blow I thrust it up to the hilt in the very spot which I desired to penetrate. A convulsive thrill ran through Simon's limbs. I heard a smothered sound issue from his throat, precisely like the bursting of a large air-bubble, sent up by a diver, when it reaches the surface of the water; he turned half round on his side, and, as if to assist my plans more effectually, his right hand, moved by some mere spasmodic impulse, clasped the handle of the creese, which it remained holding with extraordinary muscular tenacity. Beyond this there was no apparent struggle. The laudanum, I presume, paralyzed the usual nervous action. He must have died instantaneously.

There was yet something to be done. To make it certain that all suspicion of the act should be diverted from any inhabitant of the house to Simon himself, it was necessary that the door should be found in the morning *locked on the inside*. How to do this, and afterwards escape myself? Not by the window; that was a physical impossibility. Besides, I was determined that the windows *also* should be found bolted. The solution was simple enough. I descended softly to my own room for a peculiar instrument which I had used for holding small slippery substances, such as minute spheres of glass, etc. This instrument was nothing more than a long slender hand-vice, with a very powerful grip, and a considerable leverage, which last was accidentally owing to the shape of the handle. Nothing was simpler than, when the key was in the lock, to seize the end of its stem in this vice, through the keyhole, from the outside, and so lock the door. Previously, however, to doing this, I burned a number of papers on Simon's hearth, Suicides almost always burn papers before they destroy themselves. I also emptied some more laudanum into Simon's glass—having first removed from it all traces of wine—cleaned the other wine glass, and brought the bottles away with me. If traces of two persons drinking had been found in the room, the question naturally would have arisen, Who was the second? Besides, the wine bottles might have been identified as belonging to me. The laudanum I poured out to account for its presence in his stomach, in case of a *post-mortem* examination. The theory naturally would be, that he first intended to poison himself, but, after swallowing a little of the drug, was either disgusted with its taste, or changed his mind from other motives, and chose the dagger. These arrangements made, I walked out, leaving the gas burning, locked the door with my vice, and went to bed.

Simon's death was not discovered until nearly three in the afternoon. The servant, astonished at seeing the gas burning—the light streaming on the dark landing from under the door—peeped through the keyhole and saw Simon on the bed. She gave the alarm. The door was burst open, and the neighborhood was in a fever of excitement.

Everyone in the house was arrested, myself included. There was an inquest; but no clue to his death beyond that of suicide could be obtained. Curiously enough, he had made several speeches to his friends the preceding week, that seemed to point to self-destruction. One gentleman

swore that Simon had said in his presence that "he was tired of life." His
landlord affirmed that Simon, when paying him his last month's rent,
remarked that "he would not pay him rent much longer." All the other
evidence corresponded—the door locked inside, the position of the
corpse, the burnt papers. As I anticipated, no one knew of the possession
of the diamond by Simon, so that no motive was suggested for his
murder. The jury, after a prolonged examination, brought in the usual
verdict, and the neighborhood once more settled down into its accustomed quiet.

V
ANIMULA

The three months succeeding Simon's catastrophe I devoted night
and day to my diamond lens. I had constructed a vast galvanic battery,
composed of nearly two thousand pairs of plates—a higher power I dared
not use, lest the diamond should be calcined. By means of this enormous
engine I was enabled to send a powerful current of electricity continually
through my great diamond, which it seemed to me gained in luster every
day. At the expiration of a month I commenced the grinding and
polishing of the lens, a work of intense toil and exquisite delicacy. The
great density of the stone, and the care required to be taken with the
curvatures of the surfaces of the lens, rendered the labor the severest and
most harassing that I had yet undergone.

At last the eventful moment came; the lens was completed. I stood
trembling on the threshold of new worlds. I had the realization of
Alexander's famous wish before me. The lens lay on the table, ready to
be placed upon its platform. My hand fairly shook as I enveloped a drop
of water with a thin coating of oil of turpentine, preparatory to its
examination—a process necessary in order to prevent the rapid evapora-
tion of the water. I now placed the drop on a thin slip of glass under the
lens, and throwing upon it, by the combined aid of a prism and a mirror,
a powerful stream of light, I approached my eye to the minute hole
drilled through the axis of the lens. For an instant I saw nothing save what
seemed to be an illuminated chaos, a vast luminous abyss. A pure white
light, cloudless and serene, and seemingly limitless as space itself, was
my first impression. Gently, and with the greatest care, I depressed the
lens a few hair's breadths. The wondrous illumination still continued,

but as the lens approached the object a scene of indescribable beauty was unfolded to my view.

I seemed to gaze upon a vast space, the limits of which extended far beyond my vision. An atmosphere of magical luminousness permeated the entire field of view. I was amazed to see no trace of animalculous life. Not a living thing, apparently, inhabited that dazzling expanse. I comprehended instantly that, by the wondrous power of my lens, I had penetrated beyond the grosser particles of aqueous matter, beyond the realms of infusoria and protozoa, down to the original gaseous globule, into whose luminous interior I was gazing, as into an almost boundless dome filled with a supernatural radiance.

It was, however, no brilliant void into which I looked. On every side I beheld beautiful inorganic forms, of unknown texture, and colored with the most enchanting hues. These forms presented the appearance of what might be called, for want of a more specific definition, foliated clouds of the highest rarity; that is, they undulated and broke into vegetable formations, and were tinged with splendors compared with which the gilding of our autumn woodlands is as dross compared with gold. Far away into the illimitable distance stretched long avenues of these gaseous forests, dimly transparent, and painted with prismatic hues of unimaginable brilliancy. The pendent branches waved along the fluid glades until every vista seemed to break through half-lucent ranks of many-colored drooping silken pennons. What seemed to be either fruits or flowers, plied with a thousand hues, lustrous and ever varying, bubbled from the crowns of this fairy foliage. No hills, no lakes, no rivers, no forms animate or inanimate, were to be seen, save those vast auroral copses that floated serenely in the luminous stillness, with leaves and fruits and flowers gleaming with unknown fires, unrealizable by mere imagination.

How strange, I thought, that this sphere should be thus condemned to solitude! I had hoped, at least, to discover some new form of animal life—perhaps of a lower class than any with which we are at present acquainted—but still, some living organism. I found my newly discovered world, if I may so speak, a beautiful chromatic desert.

While I was speculating on the singular arrangements of the internal economy of Nature, with which she so frequently splinters into atoms our most compact theories, I thought I beheld a form moving slowly through the glades of one of the prismatic forests. I looked more attentively, and found that I was not mistaken. Words cannot depict the anxiety with which I awaited the nearer approach of this mysterious object. Was it merely some inanimate substance, held in suspense in the attenuated atmosphere of the globule? Or was it an animal endowed with vitality and motion? It approached, flitting behind the gauzy, colored veils of cloud-foliage, for seconds dimly revealed, then vanishing. At last the violet pennons that trailed nearest to me vibrated; they were gently pushed aside, and the Form floated out into the broad light.

It was a female human shape. When I say *human*, I mean it possessed the outlines of humanity—but there the analogy ends. Its adorable beauty lifted it illimitable heights beyond the loveliest daughter of Adam.

I cannot, I dare not, attempt to inventory the charms of this divine revelation of perfect beauty. Those eyes of mystic violet, dewy and serene, evade my words. Her long, lustrous hair following her glorious head in a golden wake, like the track sown in heaven by a falling star, seemed to quench my most burning phrases with its splendors. If all the bees of Hybla nestled upon my lips, they would still sing but hoarsely the wondrous harmonies of outline that enclosed her form.

She swept out from between the rainbow-curtains of the cloud-trees into the broad sea of light that lay beyond. Her motions were those of some graceful Naiad, cleaving, by a mere effort of her will, the clear, unruffled waters that fill the chambers of the sea. She floated forth with the serene grace of a frail bubble ascending through the still atmosphere of a June day. The perfect roundness of her limbs formed suave and enchanting curves. It was like listening to the most spiritual symphony of Beethoven the divine, to watch the harmonious flow of lines. This, indeed, was a pleasure cheaply purchased at any price. What cared I, if I had waded to the portal of this wonder through another's blood? I would have given my own to enjoy one such moment of intoxication and delight.

Breathless with gazing on this lovely wonder, and forgetful for an instant of everything save her presence, I withdrew my eye from the microscope eagerly—alas! As my gaze fell on the thin slide that lay beneath my instrument, the bright light from mirror and from prism sparkled on a colorless drop of water! There, in that tiny bead of dew, this beautiful being was forever imprisoned. The planet Neptune was not more distant from me than she. I hastened once more to apply my eye to the microscope.

Animula (let me now call her by that dear name which I subsequently bestowed on her) had changed her position. She had again approached the wondrous forest, and was gazing earnestly upwards. Presently one of the trees—as I must call them—unfolded a long ciliary process, with which it seized one of the gleaming fruits that glittered on its summit, and, sweeping slowly down, held it within reach of Animula. The sylph took it in her delicate hand and began to eat. My attention was so entirely absorbed by her, that I could not apply myself to the task of determining whether this singular plant was or was not instinct with volition.

I watched her, as she made her repast, with the most profound attention. The suppleness of her motions sent a thrill of delight through my frame; my heart beat madly as she turned her beautiful eyes in the direction of the spot in which I stood. What would I not have given to have had the power to precipitate myself into that luminous ocean, and float with her through those groves of purple and gold! While I was thus breathlessly following her every movement, she suddenly started, seemed to listen for a moment, and then cleaving the brilliant ether in which she was floating, like a flash of light, pierced through the opaline forest, and disappeared.

Instantly a series of the most singular sensations attacked me. It seemed as if I had suddenly gone blind. The luminous sphere was still before me, but my daylight had vanished. What caused this sudden disappearance? Had she a lover or a husband? Yes, that was the solution! Some signal from a happy fellow-being had vibrated through the avenues of the forest, and she had obeyed the summons.

The agony of my sensations, as I arrived at this conclusion, startled me. I tried to reject the conviction that my reason forced upon me. I battled against the fatal conclusion—but in vain. It was so. I had no escape from it. I loved an animalcule!

It is true that, thanks to the marvellous power of my microscope, she appeared of human proportions. Instead of presenting the revolting aspect of the coarser creatures, that live and struggle and die, in the more easily resolvable portions of the water-drop, she was fair and delicate and of surpassing beauty. But of what account was all that? Every time that my eye was withdrawn from the instrument, it fell on a miserable drop of water, within which, I must be content to know, dwelt all that could make my life lovely.

Could she but see me once! Could I for one moment pierce the mystical walls that so inexorably rose to separate us, and whisper all that filled my soul, I might consent to be satisfied for the rest of my life with the knowledge of her remote sympathy. It would be something to have established even the faintest personal link to bind us together—to know that at times, when roaming through those enchanted glades, she might think of the wonderful stranger, who had broken the monotony of her life with his presence, and left a gentle memory in her heart!

But it could not be. No invention of which human intellect was capable could break down the barriers that Nature had erected. I might feast my soul upon her wondrous beauty, yet she must always remain ignorant of the adoring eyes that day and night gazed upon her, and even when closed, beheld her in dreams. With a bitter cry of anguish I fled from the room, and, flinging myself on my bed, sobbed myself to sleep like a child.

VI
THE SPILLING OF THE CUP

I arose the next morning almost at daybreak, and rushed to my microscope. I trembled as I sought the luminous world in miniature that contained my all. Animula was there. I had left the gas-lamp, surrounded by its moderators, burning, when I went to bed the night before. I found the sylph bathing, as it were, with an expression of pleasure animating her features, in the brilliant light which surrounded her. She tossed her lustrous golden hair over her shoulders with innocent coquetry. She lay at full length in the transparent medium, in which she supported herself with ease, and gambolled with the enchanting grace that the nymph Salmacis might have exhibited when she sought to conquer the modest Hermaphroditus. I tried an experiment to satisfy myself if her powers of reflection were developed. I lessened the lamplight considerably. By the dim light that remained, I could see an expression of pain flit across her face. She looked upward suddenly, and her brows contracted. I flooded the stage of the microscope again with a full stream of light, and her whole expression changed. She sprang forward like some substance deprived of all weight. Her eyes sparkled and her lips moved. Ah! if science had only the means of conducting and reduplicating sounds, as it does the rays of light, what carols of happiness would then have entranced my ears! what jubilant hymns to Adonaïs would have thrilled the illumined air!

I now comprehended how it was that the Count de Gabalis peopled his mystic world with sylphs—beautiful beings whose breath of life was lambent fire, and who sported forever in regions of purest ether and purest light. The Rosicrucian had anticipated the wonder that I had practically realized.

How long this worship of my strange divinity went on thus I scarcely know. I lost all note of time. All day from early dawn, and far into the night, I was to be found peering through that wonderful lens. I saw no one, went nowhere, and scarce allowed myself sufficient time for my meals. My whole life was absorbed in contemplation as rapt as that of any of the Romish saints. Every hour that I gazed upon the divine form strengthened my passion—a passion that was always overshadowed by the maddening conviction, that, although I could gaze on her at will, she never, never could behold me!

At length, I grew so pale and emaciated, from want of rest, and continual brooding over my insane love and its cruel conditions, that I determined to make some effort to wean myself from it. "Come," I said, "this is at best but a fantasy. Your imagination has bestowed on Animula charms which in reality she does not possess. Seclusion from female society has produced this morbid condition of mind. Compare her with the beautiful women of your own world, and this false enchantment will vanish."

I looked over the newspapers by chance. There I beheld the advertisement of a celebrated *danseuse* who appeared nightly at Niblo's. The Signorina Caradolce had the reputation of being the most beautiful as well as the most graceful woman in the world. I instantly dressed and went to the theater.

The curtain drew up. The usual semicircle of fairies in white muslin were standing on the right toe around the enamelled flower-bank, of green canvas, on which the belated prince was sleeping. Suddenly a flute is heard. The fairies start. The trees open, the fairies all stand on the left toe, and the queen enters. It was the Signorina. She bounded forward amid thunders of applause, and, lighting on one foot, remained poised in air. Heavens! was this the great enchantress that had drawn monarchs at her chariot-wheels? Those heavy muscular limbs, those thick ankles, those cavernous eyes, that stereotyped smile, those crudely painted cheeks! Where were the vermeil blooms, the liquid expressive eyes, the harmonious limbs of Animula?

The Signorina danced. What gross, discordant movements! The

play of her limbs was all false and artificial. Her bounds were painful athletic efforts; her poses were angular and distressed the eye. I could bear it no longer; with an exclamation of disgust that drew every eye upon me, I rose from my seat in the very middle of the Signorina's *pas-de-fascination*, and abruptly quitted the house.

I hastened home to feast my eyes once more on the lovely form of my sylph. I felt that henceforth to combat this passion would be impossible. I applied my eye to the lens. Animula was there—but what could have happened? Some terrible change seemed to have taken place during my absence. Some secret grief seemed to cloud the lovely features of her I gazed upon. Her face had grown thin and haggard; her limbs trailed heavily; the wondrous luster of her golden hair had faded. She was ill!—ill, and I could not assist her! I believe at that moment I would have gladly forfeited all claims to my human birthright, if I could only have been dwarfed to the size of an animalcule, and permitted to console her from whom fate had forever divided me.

I racked my brain for the solution of this mystery. What was it that afflicted the sylph? She seemed to suffer intense pain. Her features contracted, and she even writhed, as if with some internal agony. The wondrous forests appeared also to have lost half their beauty. Their hues were dim and in some places faded away altogether. I watched Animula for hours with a breaking heart, and she seemed absolutely to wither away under my very eye. Suddenly I remembered that I had not looked at the water-drop for several days. In fact, I hated to see it; for it reminded me of the natural barrier between Animula and myself. I hurriedly looked down on the stage of the microscope. The slide was still there— but, great heavens! the water-drop had vanished! The awful truth burst upon me; it had evaporated, until it had become so minute as to be invisible to the naked eye; I had been gazing on its last atom, the one that contained Animula—and she was dying!

I rushed again to the front of the lens, and looked through. Alas! the last agony had seized her. The rainbow-hued forests had all melted away, and Animula lay struggling feebly in what seemed to be a spot of dim light. Ah! the sight was horrible: the limbs once so round and lovely shrivelling up into nothings; the eyes—those eyes that shone like heaven —being quenched into black dust; the lustrous golden hair now lank and discolored. The last throe came. I beheld that final struggle of the blackening form—and I fainted.

When I awoke out of a trance of many hours, I found myself lying amid the wreck of my instrument, myself as shattered in mind and body as it. I crawled feebly to my bed, from which I did not rise for months.

They say now that I am mad; but they are mistaken. I am poor, for I have neither the heart nor the will to work; all my money is spent, and I live on charity. Young men's associations that love a joke invite me to lecture on Optics before them, for which they pay me, and laugh at me while I lecture. "Linley, the mad microscopist," is the name I go by. I suppose that I talk incoherently while I lecture. Who could talk sense when his brain is haunted by such ghastly memories, while ever and anon among the shapes of death I behold the radiant form of my lost Animula!

OVERPOPULATION

Thomas Malthus warned of the dangers of population increase as early as 1798. So it seems incredible that science fiction writers—with the exception of H. G. Wells in *Men Like Gods* (1922)—failed to anticipate the issue until it became important to society at large. Could pulp science fiction taboos that strongly dissuaded open reference to birth control methods and sexuality in any form, have been so strong, or was it just a lack of imagination?

Whatever the cause, writers did not begin to focus on overpopulation until the 1950s. In the vanguard were C. M. Kornbluth and Frederik Pohl. Kornbluth's "The Marching Morons" (1951), a novelette about decreasing intelligence, obliquely touched upon the problem of too many people. In 1952 both men collaborated on *Gravy Planet* (also known as *The Space Merchants*), a powerful attack on Madison Avenue and the evils of an overcrowded world. In 1955 Pohl wrote "The Mapmakers," concerning a post-holocaust world whose members use a time machine to destroy any knowledge of the atom, only to discover they have become a grossly overpopulated alternate world. His "The Census Takers," appeared the following year. It has the bureau reducing crowding by killing every three hundredth person counted. Finally in 1958, Kornbluth produced the unforgettably bleak "Shark Ship" shortly before his death. Banished from the land, excess population lives on shipboard, skimming plankton from the sea.

In 1954 Kurt Vonnegut considered overpopulation due to longevity drugs in "The Big Trip Up Yonder" (also known as "Tomorrow and Tomorrow and Tomorrow"). Later that year, Richard Matheson published "The Test" (*Magazine of Fantasy and Science Fiction*, November 1954). It was the first short story to suggest problems of crowding could result from natural population growth.

Richard Matheson is an extremely talented author who gradually turned to screenwriting. He wrote many episodes of *The Twilight Zone*. A number of his novels and short stories, such as *The Shrinking Man* (1956), have been filmed.

THE TEST

Richard Matheson (1954)

The night before the test, Les helped his father study in the dining room. Jim and Tommy were asleep upstairs and, in the living room, Terry was sewing, her face expressionless as the needle moved with a swiftly rhythmic piercing and drawing.

Tom Parker sat very straight, his lean, vein-ribbed hands clasped together on the table top, his pale blue eyes looking intently at his son's lips as though it might help him to understand better.

He was eighty and this was his fourth test.

"All right," Les said, reading from the sample test Doctor Trask had gotten them. "Repeat the following sequences of numbers."

"Sequence of numbers," Tom murmured, trying to assimilate the words as they came. But words were not quickly assimilated any more; they seemed to lie upon the tissues of his brain like insects on a sluggish carnivore. He said the words in his mind again—*sequence of . . . sequence of numbers*—there he had it. He looked at his son and waited.

"Well?" he said, impatiently, after a moment's silence.

"Dad, I've already given you the first one," Les told him.

"Well . . ." His father grasped for the proper words. "Kindly give me the—the . . . do me the kindness of . . ."

Les exhaled wearily. "Eight-five-eleven-six," he said.

The old lips stirred, the old machinery of Tom's mind began turning slowly.

"Eight . . . f—ive . . ." The pale eyes blinked slowly. "Elevensix," Tom finished in a breath, then straightened himself proudly.

Yes, good, he thought—very good. They wouldn't fool him tomor-

189

row; he'd beat their murderous law. His lips pressed together and his hands clasped tightly on the white table cloth.

"What?" he said then, refocusing his eyes as Les said something. "Speak up," he said, irritably. "Speak up."

"I gave you another sequence," Les said quietly. "Here, I'll read it again."

Tom leaned forward a little, ears straining.

"Nine-two-sixteen-seven-three," Les said.

Tom cleared his throat with effort. "Speak slower," he told his son. He hadn't quite gotten that. How did they expect anyone to retain such a ridiculously long string of numbers?

"What, *what?*" he asked angrily as Les read the numbers again.

"Dad, the examiner will be reading the questions faster than I'm reading them. You—"

"I'm quite aware of that," Tom interrupted stiffly. "Quite aware. Let me remind you . . . however, this is . . . not a test. It's study, it's for *study*. Foolish to go rushing through everything. *Foolish*. I have to learn this—this . . . this *test*," he finished, angry at his son and angry at the way desired words hid themselves from his mind.

Les shrugged and looked down at the test again. "Nine-two-sixteen-seven-three," he read slowly.

"Nine-two-six-seven—"

"Six*teen*-seven, Dad."

"I said that."

"You said six, Dad."

"Don't you suppose I know what I said!"

Les closed his eyes a moment. "All right, Dad," he said.

"Well, are you going to read it again or not?" Tom asked him sharply.

Les read the numbers off again and, as he listened to his father stumble through the sequence, he glanced into the living room at Terry.

She was sitting there, features motionless, sewing. She'd turned off the radio and he knew she could hear the old man faltering with the numbers.

All right, Les heard himself saying in his mind as if he spoke to her. All right, I know he's old and useless. Do you want me to tell him that to his face and drive a knife into his back? You know and I know that he won't pass the test. Allow me, at least, this brief hypocrisy. Tomorrow the sentence will be passed. Don't make me pass it tonight and break the old man's heart.

"That's correct, I believe," Les heard the dignified voice of his father say and he refocused his eyes on the gaunt, seamed face.

"Yes, that's right," he said hastily.

He felt like a traitor when a slight smile trembled at the corners of his father's mouth. I'm cheating him, he thought.

"Let's go on to something else," he heard his father say and he looked down quickly at the sheet. What would be easy for him? he thought, despising himself for thinking it.

"Well, come on, Leslie," his father said in a restrained voice. "We have no time to waste."

Tom looked at his son thumbing through the pages and his hands closed into fists. Tomorrow, his life was in the balance and his son just browsed through the test paper as if nothing important were going to happen tomorrow.

"Come on, come on," he said peevishly.

Les picked up a pencil that had string attached to it and drew a half-inch circle on a piece of blank paper. He held out the pencil to his father.

"Suspend the pencil point over the circle for three minutes," he said, suddenly afraid he'd picked the wrong question. He'd seen his father's hands trembling at meal times or fumbling with the buttons and zippers of his clothes.

Swallowing nervously, Les picked up the stop watch, started it, and nodded to his father.

Tom took a quivering breath as he leaned over the paper and tried to hold the slightly swaying pencil above the circle. Les saw him lean on his elbow, something he wouldn't be allowed to do on the test; but he said nothing.

He sat there looking at his father. Whatever color there had been was leaving the old man's face and Les could see clearly the tiny red lines of broken vessels under the skin of his cheeks. He looked at the dry skin, creased and brownish, dappled with liver spots. Eighty years old, he thought—how does man feel when he's eighty years old?

He looked in at Terry again. For a moment, her gaze shifted and they were looking at each other, neither of them smiling or making any sign. Then Terry looked back to her sewing.

"I believe that's three minutes," Tom said in a taut voice.

Les looked down at the stop watch. "A minute and a half, Dad," he said, wondering if he should have lied again.

"Well, keep your eyes on the watch then," his father said, perturbedly, the pencil penduluming completely out of the circle. "This is supposed to be a test, not a—a—a *party*."

Les kept his eyes on the wavering pencil point, feeling a sense of utter futility at the realization that this was only pretense, that nothing they did could save his father's life.

At least, he thought, the examinations weren't given by the sons and daughters who had voted the law into being. At least he wouldn't have to stamp the black INADEQUATE on his father's test and thus pronounce the sentence.

The pencil wavered over the circle edge again and was returned as Tom moved his arm slightly on the table, a motion that would automatically disqualify him on that question.

"That watch is slow!" Tom said in a sudden fury.

Les caught his breath and looked down at the watch. Two and a half minutes. "Three minutes," he said, pushing in the plunger.

Tom slapped down the pencil irritably. "*There*," he said. "Fool test anyway." His voice grew morose. "Don't prove a thing. Not a thing."

"You want to do some money questions, Dad?"

"Are they the next questions in the test?" Tom asked, looking over suspiciously to check for himself.

"Yes," Les lied, knowing that his father's eyes were too weak to see even though Tom always refused to admit he needed glasses. "Oh, wait a second, there's one before that," he added, thinking it would be easier for his father. "They ask you to tell time."

"That's a foolish question," Tom muttered. "What do they—"

He reached across the table irritably and picked up the watch and glanced down at its face. "Ten fifteen," he said, scornfully.

Before Les could think to stop himself, he said, "But it's eleven-fifteen, Dad."

His father looked, for a moment, as though his face had been slapped. Then he picked up the watch again and stared down at it, lips twitching, and Les had the horrible premonition that Tom was going to insist it really was ten-fifteen.

192

"Well, that's what I meant," Tom said abruptly. "Slipped out wrong. 'Course it's eleven-fifteen, any fool can see that. Eleven fifteen. Watch is no good. Numbers too close. Ought to throw it away. Now—"

Tom reached into his vest pocket and pulled out his own gold watch. "Here's a *watch*," he said, proudly. "Been telling perfect time for . . . sixty years! That's a watch. Not like this."

He tossed Les's watch down contemptuously and it flipped over on its face and the crystal broke.

"Look at that," Tom said quickly, to cover the jolting of embarrassment. "Watch can't take anything."

He avoided Les's eyes by looking down at his own watch. His mouth tightened as he opened the back and looked at Mary's picture; Mary when she was in her thirties, golden-haired and lovely.

Thank God, she didn't have to take these tests, he thought—at least she was spared that. Tom had never thought he could believe that Mary's accidental death at fifty-seven was fortunate, but that was before the tests.

He closed the watch and put it away.

"You just leave that watch with me, tonight," he said grumpily. "I'll see you get a decent . . . uh, *crystal* tomorrow."

"That's all right, Dad. It's just an old watch."

"That's all right," Tom said. "That's all right. You just leave it with me. I'll get you a decent . . . crystal. Get you one that won't break, one that won't break. You just leave it with me."

Tom did the money questions then, questions like *How many quarters in a five dollar bill?* and *If I took thirty-six cents from your dollar, how much change would you have left?*

They were written questions and Les sat there timing his father. It was quiet in the house, warm. Everything seemed very normal and ordinary with the two of them sitting there and Terry sewing in the living room.

That was the horror.

Life went on as usual. No one spoke of dying. The government sent out letters and the tests were given and those who failed were requested to appear at the government center for their injections. The law operated, the death rate was steady, the population problem was contained—all officially, impersonally, without a cry or a sensation.

But it was still loved people who were being killed.

"Never mind hanging over that watch," his father said. "I can do these questions without you . . . hanging over that watch."

"Dad, the examiners will be looking at their watches."

"The examiners are the examiners," Tom snapped. "You're not an examiner."

"Dad, I'm trying to help y—"

"Well, help me then, *help* me. Don't sit there hanging over that watch."

"This is your test, Dad, not mine," Les started, a flush of anger creeping up his cheeks. "If—"

"My test, yes, my test!" his father suddenly raged. "You all saw to that, didn't you? All saw to it that—that—"

Words failed again, angry thoughts piling up in his brain.

"You don't have to yell, Dad."

"I'm not yelling!"

"Dad, the boys are sleeping!" Terry suddenly broke in.

"I don't care if—!" Tom broke off suddenly and leaned back in the chair, the pencil falling unnoticed from his fingers and rolling across the table cloth. He sat shivering, his thin chest rising and falling in jerks, his hands twitching uncontrollably on his lap.

"Do you want to go on, Dad?" Les asked, restraining his nervous anger.

"I don't ask much," Tom mumbled to himself. "Don't ask much in life."

"Dad, shall we go *on*?"

His father stiffened. "If you can spare the time," he said with slow, indignant pride. "If you can spare the time."

Les looked at the test paper, his fingers gripping the stapled sheets rigidly. Psychological questions? No, he couldn't ask them. How did you ask your eighty-year-old father his views on sex?—your flint-surfaced father to whom the most innocuous remark was obscene.

"Well?" his father asked in a rising voice.

"There doesn't seem to be anymore," Les said. "We've been at it almost four hours now."

"What about all those pages you just skipped?"

"Most of those are for the . . . the physical, Dad."

He saw his father's lips press together and was afraid Tom was going to say something about that again. But all his father said was, "A fine friend. Fine friend."

"Dad, you—"

Les's voice broke off. There was no point in talking about it anymore. Tom knew perfectly well that Doctor Trask couldn't make out a bill of health for this test the way he'd done for the three tests previous.

Les knew how frightened and insulted the old man was because he'd have to take off his clothes and be exposed to doctors who would probe and tap and ask offensive questions. He knew how afraid Tom was of the fact that when he re-dressed, he'd be watched from a peephole and someone would mark on a chart how well he dressed himself. He knew how it frightened his father to know that, when he ate in the government cafeteria at the midpoint of the day-long examination, eyes would be watching him again to see if he dropped a fork or a spoon or knocked over a glass of water or dribbled gravy on his shirt.

"They'll ask you to sign your name and address," Les said, wanting his father to forget about the physical and knowing how proud Tom was of his handwriting.

Pretending that he grudged it, the old man picked up the pencil and wrote. I'll fool them, he thought as the pencil moved across the page with strong, sure motions.

Mr. Thomas Parker, he wrote, *2719 Brighton Street, Blairtown, New York*.

"And the date," Les said.

The old man wrote, *January 17, 2003*, and something cold moved in the old man's vitals.

Tomorrow was the test.

They lay beside each other, neither of them sleeping. They had barely spoken while undressing and when Les had leaned over to kiss her goodnight she'd murmured something he didn't hear.

Now he turned over on his side with a heavy sigh and faced her. In the darkness, she opened her eyes and looked over at him.

"Asleep?" she asked softly.

"No."

He said no more. He waited for her to start.

But she didn't start and, after a few moments, he said, "Well, I guess this is . . . it." He finished weakly because he didn't like the words; they sounded ridiculously melodramatic.

Terry didn't say anything right away. Then, as if thinking aloud, she said, "Do you think there's any chance that—"

195

Les tightened at the words because he knew what she was going to say.

"No," he said. "He'll never pass."

He heard Terry swallowing. Don't say it, he thought, pleadingly. Don't tell me I've been saying the same thing for fifteen years. I know it. I said it because I thought it was true.

Suddenly, he wished he's signed the *Request For Removal* years before. They needed desperately to be free of Tom; for the good of their children and themselves. But how did you put that need into words without feeling like a murderer? You couldn't say: I hope the old man fails. I hope they kill him. Yet anything else you said was only a hypocritical substitute for those words because that was exactly how you felt.

Medical terms, he thought—charts about declining crops and low-ered standard of living and hunger ratio and degrading health level—they'd used all those as arguments to support passage of the law. Well, they were lies—obvious, groundless lies. The law had been passed because people wanted to be left alone, because they wanted to live their own lives.

"Les, what if he passes?" Terry said.

He felt his hands tightening on the mattress.

"Les?"

"I don't know, honey," he said.

Her voice was firm in the darkness. It was a voice at the end of patience. "You have to know," it said.

He moved his head restlessly on the pillow. "Honey, don't push it," he begged. "Please."

"Les, if he passes that test it means five more years. *Five more years*, Les. Have you thought what that means?"

"Honey, he can't pass that test."

"But, what if he does?"

"Terry, he missed three-quarters of the questions I asked him tonight. His hearing is almost gone, his eyes are bad, his heart is weak, he has arthritis." His fist beat down hopelessly on the bed. "He won't even pass the *physical*," he said, feeling himself tighten in self-hatred for assuring her that Tom was doomed.

If only he could forget the past and take his father for what he was now—a helpless, mind-jading old man who was ruining their lives. But it was hard to forget how he'd loved and respected his father, hard to forget the hikes in the country, the fishing trips, the long talks at night and all the many things his father and he had shared together.

That was why he'd never had the strength to sign the request. It was a simple form to fill out, much simpler than waiting for the five-year tests. But it had meant signing away the life of his father, requesting the government to dispose of him like some unwanted garbage. He could never do that.

And yet, now his father was eighty and, in spite of moral upbringing, in spite of life-taught Christian principles, he and Terry were horribly afraid that old Tom might pass the test and live another five years with them—another five years of fumbling around the house, undoing instructions they gave to the boys, breaking things, wanting to help but only getting in the way and making life an agony of held-in nerves.

"You'd better sleep," Terry said to him.

He tried to but he couldn't. He lay staring at the dark ceiling and trying to find an answer but finding no answer.

The alarm went off at six. Les didn't have to get up until eight but he wanted to see his father off. He got out of bed and dressed quietly so he wouldn't wake up Terry.

She woke up anyway and looked at him from her pillow. After a moment, she pushed up on one elbow and looked sleepily at him.

"I'll get up and make you some breakfast," she said.

"That's all right," Les said. "You stay in bed."

"Don't you want me to get up?"

"Don't bother, honey," he said. "I want you to rest."

She lay down again and turned away so Les wouldn't see her face. She didn't know why she began to cry soundlessly; whether it was because he didn't want her to see his father or because of the test. But she couldn't stop. All she do was hold herself rigid until the bedroom door had closed.

Then her shoulders trembled and a sob broke the barrier she had built in herself.

The door to his father's room was open as Les passed. He looked in and saw Tom sitting on the bed, leaning down and fastening his dark shoes. He saw the gnarled fingers shaking as they moved over the straps.

"Everything all right, Dad?" Les asked.

197

His father looked up in surprise. "What are you doing up this hour?" he asked.

"Thought I'd have breakfast with you," Les told him.

For a moment they looked at each other in silence. Then his father leaned over the shoes again. "That's not necessary," he heard the old man's voice telling him.

"Well, I think I'll have some breakfast anyway," he said and turned away so his father wouldn't argue.

"Oh . . . *Leslie.*"

Les turned.

"I trust you didn't forget to leave that watch out," his father said. "I intend to take it to the jeweler's today and have a decent . . . decent crystal put on it, one that won't break."

"Dad, it's just an old watch," Les said. "It's not worth a nickel."

His father nodded slowly, one palm wavering before him as if to ward off argument. "Never-the-less," he stated slowly, "I intend to—"

"All right, Dad, all right. I'll put it on the kitchen table."

His father broke off and looked at him blankly a moment. Then, as if it were impulse and not delayed will, he bent over his shoes again.

Les stood for a moment looking down at his father's gray hair, his gaunt, trembling fingers. Then he turned away.

The watch was still on the dining room table. Les picked it up and took it in to the kitchen table. The old man must have been reminding himself about the watch all night, he thought. Otherwise he wouldn't have managed to remember it.

He put fresh water in the coffee globe and pushed the buttons for two servings of bacon and eggs. Then he poured two glasses of orange juice and sat down at the table.

About fifteen minutes later, his father came down wearing his dark blue suit, his shoes carefully polished, his nails manicured, his hair slicked down and combed and brushed. He looked very neat and very old as he walked over to the coffee globe and looked in.

"Sit down, Dad," Les said. "I'll get it for you."

"I'm not helpless," his father said. "Stay where you are."

Les managed to smile. "I put some bacon and eggs on for us," he said.

"Not hungry," his father replied.

"You'll need a good breakfast in you, Dad."

"Never did eat a big breakfast," his father said, stiffly, still facing the stove. "Don't believe in it. Not good for the stomach."

Les closed his eyes a moment and across his face moved an expression of hopeless despair. Why did I bother getting up? he asked himself defeatedly. All we do is argue.

No. He felt himself stiffening. No, he'd be cheerful if it killed him.

"Sleep all right, Dad?" he asked.

" 'Course I slept all right," his father answered. "Always sleep fine. Fine. Did you think I wouldn't because of a—"

He broke off suddenly and turned accusingly at Les. "Where's that watch?" he demanded.

Les exhaled wearily and held up the watch. His father moved jerkily across the linoleum, took it from him and looked at it a moment, his old lips pursed.

"Shoddy workmanship," he said. "Shoddy." He put it carefully in his side coat pocket. "Get you a decent crystal," he muttered. "One that won't break."

Les nodded. "That'll be swell, Dad."

The coffee was ready then and Tom poured them each a cup. Les got up and turned off the automatic griller. He didn't feel like having bacon and eggs either now.

He sat across the table from his stern-faced father and felt hot coffee trickling down his throat. It tasted terrible but he knew that nothing in the world would have tasted good to him that morning.

"What time do you have to be there, Dad?" he asked to break the silence.

"Nine o'clock," Tom said.

"You're sure you don't want me to drive you there?"

"Not at all, not at all," his father said as though he were talking patiently to an irritably insistent child. "The tube is good enough. Get me there in plenty of time."

"All right, Dad," Les said and sat there staring into his coffee. There must be something he could say, he thought, but he couldn't think of anything. Silence hung over them for long minutes while Tom drank his black coffee in slow, methodical sips.

Les licked his lips nervously, then hid the trembling of them behind his cup. Talking, he thought, talking and talking—of cars and tube

199

conveyers and examination schedules—when all the time both of them knew that Tom might be sentenced to death that day.

He was sorry he'd gotten up. It would have been better to wake up and just find his father gone. He wished it could happen that way—*permanently.* He wished he could wake up some morning and find his father's room empty—the two suits gone, the dark shoes gone, the work clothes gone, the handkerchiefs, the socks, the garters, the braces, the shaving equipment—all those mute evidences of a life gone.

But it wouldn't be like that. After Tom failed the test, it would be several weeks before the letter of final appointment came and then another week or so before the appointment itself. It would be a hideously slow process of packing and disposing of and giving away of possessions, a process of meals and meals and meals together, of talking to each other, of a last dinner, of a long drive to the government center, of a ride up in a silent, humming elevator, of—

Dear God!

He found himself shivering helplessly and was afraid for a moment that he was going to cry.

Then he looked up with a shocked expression as his father stood.

"I'll be going now," Tom said.

Les's eyes fled to the wall clock. "But it's only a quarter to seven," he said tensely. "It doesn't take that long to—"

"Like to be in plenty of time," his father said firmly. "Never like to be late."

"But my God, Dad, it only takes an hour at the most to get to the city," he said, feeling a terrible sinking in his stomach.

His father shook his head and Les knew he hadn't heard. "It's early, Dad," he said, loudly, his voice shaking a little.

"Never-the-less," his father said.

"But you haven't *eaten* anything."

"Never did eat a big breakfast," Tom started. "Not good for the—"

Les didn't hear the rest of it—the words about lifetime habit and not good for the digestion and everything else his father said. He felt waves of merciless horror breaking over him and he wanted to jump and throw his arms around the old man and tell him not to worry about the test because it didn't matter, because they loved him and would take care of him.

But he couldn't. He sat rigid with sick fright, looking up at his father. He couldn't even speak when his father turned at the kitchen door and said in a voice that was calmly dispassionate because it took every bit of strength the old man had to make it so, "I'll see you tonight, Leslie."

The door swung shut and the breeze that ruffled across Les's cheeks chilled him to the heart.

Suddenly, he jumped up with a startled grunt and rushed across the linoleum. As he pushed through the doorway he saw his father almost to the front door.

"Dad!"

Tom stopped and looked back in surprise as Les walked across the dining room, hearing the steps counted in his mind—*one, two, three, four, five.*

He stopped before his father and forced a faltering smile to his lips.

"Good luck, Dad," he said. "I'll . . . see you tonight." He had been about to say, "I'll be rooting for you"; but he couldn't.

His father nodded once, just once, a curt nod as of one gentleman acknowledging another.

"Thank you," his father said and turned away.

When the door shut, it seemed as if, suddenly, it had become an impenetrable wall through which his father could never pass again.

Les moved to the window and watched the old man walk slowly down the path and turn left onto the sidewalk. He watched his father start up the street, then straighten himself, throw back his lean shoulders and walk erect and briskly into the gray of morning.

At first Les thought it was raining. But then he saw that the shimmering moistness wasn't on the window at all.

He couldn't go to work. He phoned in sick and stayed home. Terry got the boys off to school and, after they'd eaten breakfast, Les helped her clear away the morning dishes and put them in the washer. Terry didn't say anything about his staying home. She acted as if it were normal for him to be home on a weekday.

He spent the morning and afternoon puttering in the garage shop, starting seven different projects and losing interest in them.

Around five, he went into the kitchen and had a can of beer while Terry made supper. He didn't say anything to her. He kept pacing around the living room, staring out the window at the overcast sky, then pacing again.

"I wonder where he is," he finally said, back in the kitchen again.

"He'll be back," she said and he stiffened a moment, thinking he heard disgust in her voice. Then he relaxed, knowing it was only his imagination.

When he dressed after taking a shower, it was five-forty. The boys were home from playing and they all sat down to supper. Les noticed a place set for his father and wondered if Terry had set it there for his benefit.

He couldn't eat anything. He kept cutting the meat into smaller and smaller pieces and mashing butter into his baked potato without tasting any of it.

"What is it?" he asked as Jim spoke to him.

"Dad, if grandpa don't pass the test, he gets a month, don't he?"

Les felt his stomach muscles tightening as he stared at his older son. *Gets a month, don't he?*—the last of Jim's question muttered on in his brain.

"What are you talking about?" he asked.

"My Civics book says old people get a month to live after they don't pass their test. That's right, isn't it?"

"No, it *isn't*," Tommy broke in. "Harry Senker's grandma got her letter after only two weeks."

"How do you know?" Jim asked his nine-year-old brother. "Did you see it?"

"That's enough," Les said.

"Don't *have* t'see it!" Tommy argued, "Harry told me that—"

"That's *enough!*"

The two boys looked suddenly at their white-faced father.

"We won't talk about it," he said.

"But what—"

"*Jimmy*," Terry said, warningly.

Jimmy looked at his mother, then, after a moment, went back to his food and they all ate in silence.

The death of their grandfather means nothing to them, Les thought bitterly—nothing at all. He swallowed and tried to relax the tightness in his body. Well, why *should* it mean anything to them? he told himself;

it's not their time to worry yet. Why force it on them now? They'll have it soon enough.

When the front door opened and shut at six-ten, Les stood up so quickly, he knocked over an empty glass.

"Les, *don't*," Terry said suddenly and he knew, immediately, that she was right. His father wouldn't like him to come rushing from the kitchen with questions.

He slumped down on the chair again and stared at his barely touched food, his heart throbbing. As he picked up his fork with tight fingers, he heard the old man cross the dining-room rug and start up the stairs. He glanced at Terry and her throat moved.

He couldn't eat. He sat there breathing heavily, and picking at the food. Upstairs, he heard the door to his father's room close.

It was when Terry was putting the pie on the table that Les excused himself quickly and got up.

He was at the foot of the stairs when the kitchen door was pushed open. "Les," he heard her say, urgently.

He stood there silently as she came up to him.

"Isn't it better we leave him alone?" she asked.

"But, honey, I—"

"Les, if he'd passed the test, he would have come into the kitchen and told us."

"Honey, he wouldn't know if—"

"He'd know if he passed, you know that. He told us about it the last two times. If he'd passed, he'd have—"

Her voice broke off and she shuddered at the way he was looking at her. In the heavy silence, she heard a sudden splattering of rain on the windows.

They looked at each other a long moment. Then Les said, "I'm going up."

"Les," she murmured.

"I won't say anything to upset him," he said. "I'll . . ."

A moment longer they stared at each other. Then he turned away and trudged up the steps. Terry watched him go with a bleak, hopeless look on her face.

Les stood before the closed door a minute, bracing himself. I won't upset him, he told himself; I *won't*.

He knocked softly, wondering, in that second, if he were making a mistake. Maybe he should have left the old man alone, he thought unhappily.

In the bedroom, he heard a rustling movement on the bed, then the sound of his father's feet touching the floor.

"Who is it?" he heard Tom ask.

Les caught his breath. "It's me, Dad," he said.

"What do you want?"

"May I see you?"

Silence inside. "Well . . ." he heard his father say then and his voice stopped. Les heard him get up and heard the sound of his footsteps on the floor. Then there was the sound of paper rattling and a bureau drawer being carefully shut.

Finally the door opened.

Tom was wearing his old red bathrobe over his clothes and he'd taken off his shoes and put his slippers on.

"May I come in, Dad?" Les asked quietly.

His father hesitated a moment. Then he said, "Come in," but it wasn't an invitation. It was more as if he'd said, This is your house; I can't keep you from this room.

Les was going to tell his father that he didn't want to disturb him but he couldn't. He went in and stood in the middle of the throw rug, waiting.

"Sit down," his father said and Les sat down on the upright chair that Tom hung his clothes on at night. His father waited until Les was seated and then sank down on the bed with a grunt.

For a long time they looked at each other without speaking like total strangers each waiting for the other one to speak. How did the test go? Les heard the words repeated in his mind. How did the test go, how did the test go? He couldn't speak the words. How did the—

"I suppose you want to know what . . . happened," his father said then, controlling himself visibly.

"Yes," Les said "I . . ." He caught himself. "Yes," he repeated and waited.

Old Tom looked down at the floor for a moment. Then, suddenly, he raised his head and looked defiantly at his son.

"*I didn't go*," he said.

Les felt as if all his strength had suddenly been sucked into the floor. He sat there, motionless, staring at his father.

"Had no intention of going," his father hurried on. "No intention of going through all that foolishness. Physical tests, m-mental tests, putting b-b-*blocks* in a board and . . . Lord knows what all! Had no intention of going."

He stopped and stared at his son with angry eyes as if he were daring Les to say he had done wrong.

But Les couldn't say anything.

A long time passed. Les swallowed and managed to summon the words. "What are you . . . going to do?"

"Never mind that, never mind," his father said, almost as if he were grateful for the question. "Don't you worry about your dad. Your dad knows how to take care of himself."

And suddenly Les heard the bureau drawer shutting again, the rustling of a paper bag. He almost looked around at the bureau to see if the bag were still there. His head twitched as he fought down the impulse.

"W-ell," he faltered, not realizing how stricken and lost his expression was.

"Just never mind now," his father said again, quietly, almost gently. "It's not your problem to worry about. Not your problem at all."

But it is! Les heard the words cried out in his mind. But he didn't speak them. Something in the old man stopped him; a sort of fierce strength, a taut dignity he knew he mustn't touch.

"I'd like to rest now," he heard Tom say then and he felt as if he'd been struck violently in the stomach. I'd like to rest now, to rest now—the words echoed down long tunnels of the mind as he stood. Rest now, rest now. . . ."

He found himself being ushered to the door where he turned and looked at his father. *Goodbye.* The word stuck in him.

Then his father smiled and said, "Good night, Leslie."

"*Dad.*"

He felt the old man's hand in his own, stronger than his, more steady; calming him, reassuring him. He felt his father's left hand grip his shoulder.

"Good night, son," his father said and, in the moment they stood close together Les saw, over the old man's shoulder, the crumpled drugstore bag lying in the corner of the room as though it had been thrown there so as not to be seen.

Then he was standing in wordless terror in the hall, listening to the latch clicking shut and knowing that, although his father wasn't locking the door, he couldn't go into his father's room.

For a long time he stood staring at the closed door, shivering without control. Then he turned away.

Terry was waiting for him at the foot of the stairs, her face drained of color. She asked the question with her eyes as he came down to her.

"He . . . didn't go," was all he said.

She made a tiny, startled sound in her throat. "But—"

"He's been to the drugstore," Les said. "I . . . saw the bag in the corner of the room. He threw it away so I wouldn't see it but I . . . saw it."

For a moment, it seemed as if she were starting for the stairs but it was only a momentary straining of her body.

"He must have shown the druggist the letter about the test," Les said. "The . . . druggist must have given him . . . pills. Like they all do."

They stood silently in the dining room while rain drummed against the windows.

"What shall we do?" she asked, almost inaudibly.

"Nothing," he murmured. His throat moved convulsively and breath shuddered through him. "*Nothing.*"

Then he was walking numbly back to the kitchen and he could feel her arm tight around him as if she were trying to press her love to him because she could not speak of love.

All evening, they sat there in the kitchen. After she put the boys to bed, she came back and they sat in the kitchen drinking coffee and talking in quiet, lonely voices.

Near midnight, they left the kitchen and just before they went upstairs, Les stopped by the dining-room table and found the watch with a shiny new crystal on it. He couldn't even touch it.

They went upstairs and talked past the door of Tom's bedroom. There was no sound inside. They got undressed and got in bed together and Terry set the clock the way she set it every night. In a few hours they both managed to fall asleep.

And all night there was silence in the old man's room. And the next day, silence.

SOLAR POWER FROM SATELLITES

Contrary to what many people think, science fiction is a very poor instrument of prediction, much more likely to reflect than to inspire scientific and technological innovations and beliefs. However, works by Jules Verne (*Mysterious Island*, 1874-1875), H. G. Wells (*The World Set Free*, 1914), B. F. Skinner (*Walden II*, 1948), and Samuel R. Delany ("High Weir," 1968) do seem to have served as direct inspiration for pilot survival schools, the atomic bomb, behavioral communities, and the holographic model of the brain. It is not known whether "Reason" (*Astounding Science Fiction*, April 1941) should be added to this list. However, it is clear that the story first suggested using satellites to collect solar power and beam converted forms to earth, thus providing additional energy.

In 1968 Dr. Peter Glaser developed a serious plan for solar satellites sitting in stable, synchronous orbits (thirty-six thousand kilometers high). Energy would be collected through gigantic, wing-like solar panels. The resulting electricity could then be transmitted to large receivers on earth via low frequency microwaves or laser beams. The efficiency index is projected to be more than eighty percent and it is believed that there would be little atmospheric disturbance or danger to life forms. To determine feasibility, more research will obviously have to be done, but the United States government is interested enough to have spent sixteen million dollars on the project so far.

Oddly enough, science fiction writers have displayed little concern for solar power from satellites. But interested readers can find a popular discussion of the topic in *The Science in Science Fiction*, 1983, by Peter Nicholls.

REASON

Isaac Asimov *(1941)*

*G*regory *Powell spaced his words for emphasis, "One week ago,* Donovan and I put you together." His brows furrowed doubtfully and he pulled the end of his brown mustache.

It was quiet in the officer's room on Solar Station #5—except for the soft purring of the mighty Beam Director somewhere far below.

Robot QT-1 sat immovable. The burnished plates of his body gleamed in the Luxites and the glowing red of the photoelectric cells that were his eyes, were fixed steadily upon the Earthman at the other side of the table.

Powell repressed a sudden attack of nerves. These robots possessed peculiar brains. Oh, the three Laws of Robotics held. They had to. All of U. S. Robots, from Robertson himself to the new floor-sweeper, would insist on that. So QT-1 was *safe!* And yet—the QT models were the first of their kind, and this was the first of the QT's. Mathematical squiggles on paper were not always the most comforting protection against robotic fact.

Finally, the robot spoke. His voice carried the cold timbre inseparable from a metallic diaphragm, "Do you realize the seriousness of such a statement, Powell?"

"*Something* made you, Cutie," pointed out Powell. "You admit yourself that your memory seems to spring full-grown from an absolute blankness of a week ago. I'm giving you the explanation. Donovan and I put you together from the parts shipped us."

Cutie gazed upon his long, supple fingers in an oddly human attitude of mystification, "It strikes me that there should be a more satisfactory explanation than that. For *you* to make *me* seems improbable."

The Earthman laughed quite suddenly, "In Earth's name, why?"

"Call it intuition. That's all it is so far. But I intend to reason it out, though. A chain of valid reasoning can end only with the determination of truth, and I'll stick till I get there."

Powell stood up and seated himself at the table's edge next to the robot. He felt a sudden strong sympathy for this strange machine. It was not at all like the ordinary robot, attending to his specialized task at the station with the intensity of a deeply ingrooved positronic path.

He placed a hand upon Cutie's steel shoulder and the metal was cold and hard to the touch.

"Cutie," he said, "I'm going to try to explain something to you. You're the first robot who's ever exhibited curiosity as to his own existence—and I think the first that's really intelligent enough to understand the world outside. Here, come with me."

The robot rose erect smoothly and his thickly sponge-rubber soled feet made no noise as he followed Powell. The Earthman touched a button and a square section of the wall flickered aside. The thick, clear glass revealed space—star-speckled.

"I've seen that in the observation ports in the engine room," said Cutie.

"I know," said Powell. "What do you think it is?"

"Exactly what it seems—a black material just beyond this glass that is spotted with little gleaming dots. I know that our director sends out beams to some of these dots, always to the same ones—and also that these dots shift and that the beams shift with them. That is all."

"Good! Now I want you to listen carefully. The blackness is emptiness—vast emptiness stretching out infinitely. The little, gleaming dots are huge masses of energy-filled matter. They are globes, some of them millions of miles in diameter—and for comparison, this station is only one mile across. They seem so tiny because they are incredibly far off.

"The dots to which our energy beams are directed, are nearer and much smaller. They are cold and hard and human beings like myself live upon their surfaces—many billions of them. It is from one of these worlds that Donovan and I come. Our beams feed these worlds energy drawn from one of those huge incandescent globes that happens to be near us. We call that globe the Sun and it is on the other side of the station where you can't see it."

Cutie remained motionless before the port, like a steel statue. His head did not turn as he spoke, "Which particular dot of light do you claim to come from?"

Powell searched, "There it is. The very bright one in the corner. We call it Earth." He grinned. "Good old Earth. There are three billions of us there, Cutie—and in about two weeks I'll be back there with them."

And then, suprisingly enough, Cutie hummed abstractedly. There was no tune to it, but it possessed a curious twanging quality as of plucked strings. It ceased as suddenly as it had begun, "But where do I come in, Powell? You haven't explained *my* existence."

"The rest is simple. When these stations were first established to feed solar energy to the planets, they were run by humans. However, the heat, the hard solar radiations, and the electron storms made the post a difficult one. Robots were developed to replace human labor and now only two human executives are required for each station. We are trying to replace even those, and that's where you come in. You're the highest type of robot ever developed and if you show the ability to run this station independently, no human need ever come here again except to bring parts for repairs."

His hand went up and the metal visi-lid snapped back into place. Powell returned to the table and polished an apple upon his sleeve before biting into it.

The red glow of the robot's eyes held him. "Do you expect me," said Cutie slowly, "to believe any such complicated, implausible hypothesis as you have just outlined? What do you take me for?"

Powell sputtered apple fragments onto the table and turned red. "Why damn you, it wasn't a hypothesis. Those were facts."

Cutie sounded grim, "Globes of energy millions of miles across! Worlds with three billion humans on them! Infinite emptiness! Sorry, Powell, but I don't believe it. I'll puzzle this thing out for myself. Good-bye."

He turned and stalked out of the room. He brushed past Michael Donovan on the threshold with a grave nod and passed down the corridor, oblivious to the astounded stare that followed him.

Mike Donovan rumpled his red hair and shot an annoyed glance at Powell, "What was that walking junk yard talking about? What doesn't he believe?"

The other dragged at his mustache bitterly. "He's a skeptic," was the bitter response. "He doesn't believe we made him or that Earth exists or space or stars."

"Sizzling Saturn, we've got a lunatic robot on our hands."

"He says he's going to figure it all out for himself."

"Well, now," said Donovan sweetly, "I do hope he'll condescend to explain it all to me after he's puzzled everything out." Then, with sudden rage, "Listen! If that metal mess gives *me* any lip like that, I'll knock that chromium cranium right off its torso."

He seated himself with a jerk and drew a paper-backed mystery novel out of his inner jacket pocket, "That robot gives me the willies anyway—too damned inquisitive!"

Mike Donovan growled from behind a huge lettuce-and-tomato sandwich as Cutie knocked gently and entered.

"Is Powell here?"

Donovan's voice was muffled, with pauses for mastication, "He's gathering data on electronic stream functions. We're heading for a storm, looks like."

Gregory Powell entered as he spoke, eyes on the graphed paper in his hands, and dropped into a chair. He spread the sheets out before him and began scribbling calculations. Donovan stared over his shoulder, crunching lettuce and dribbling bread crumbs. Cutie waited silently.

Powell looked up, "The Zeta Potential is rising, but slowly. Just the same, the stream functions are erratic and I don't know what to expect. Oh, hello, Cutie. I thought you were supervising the installation of the new drive bar."

"It's done," said the robot quietly, "and so I've come to have a talk with the two of you."

"Oh!" Powell looked uncomfortable. "Well, sit down. No, not that chair. One of the legs is weak and you're no lightweight."

The robot did so and said placidly, "I have come to a decision."

Donovan glowered and put the remnants of his sandwich aside. "If it's on any of that screwy—"

The other motioned impatiently for silence, "Go ahead, Cutie. We're listening."

"I have spent these last two days in concentrated introspection," said Cutie, "and the results have been most interesting. I began at the

212

one sure assumption I felt permitted to make. I, myself, exist, because I think—"

Powell groaned, "Oh, Jupiter, a robot Descartes!"

"Who's Descartes?" demanded Donovan. "Listen, do we have to sit here and listen to this metal maniac—"

"Keep quiet, Mike!"

Cutie continued imperturbably, "And the question that immediately arose was: Just what is the cause of my existence?"

Powell's jaw set lumpily. "You're being foolish. I told you already that we made you."

"And if you don't believe us," added Donovan, "we'll gladly take you apart!"

The robot spread his strong hands in a deprecatory gesture, "I accept nothing on authority. A hypothesis must be backed by reason, or else it is worthless—and it goes against all the dictates of logic to suppose that you made me."

Powell dropped a restraining arm upon Donovan's suddenly bunched fist. "Just why do you say that?"

Cutie laughed. It was a very inhuman laugh—the most machine-like utterance he had yet given vent to. It was sharp and explosive, as regular as a metronome and as uninflected.

"Look at you," he said finally. "I say this in no spirit of contempt, but look at you! The material you are made of is soft and flabby, lacking endurance and strength, depending for energy upon the inefficient oxidation of organic material—like that." He pointed a disapproving finger at what remained of Donovan's sandwich. "Periodically you pass into a coma and the least variation in temperature, air pressure, humidity, or radiation intensity impairs your efficiency. You are *makeshift*.

"I, on the other hand, am a finished product. I absorb electrical energy directly and utilize it with an almost one hundred percent efficiency. I am composed of strong metal, am continuously conscious, and can stand extremes of environment easily. These are facts which, with the self-evident proposition that no being can create another being superior to itself, smashes your silly hypothesis to nothing."

Donovan's muttered curses rose into intelligibility as he sprang to his feet, rusty eyebrows drawn low. "All right, you son of a hunk of iron ore, if we didn't make you, who did?"

Cutie nodded gravely. "Very good, Donovan. That was indeed the next question. Evidently my creator must be more powerful than myself and so there was only one possibility."

The Earthmen looked blank and Cutie continued, "What is the center of activities here in the station? What do we all serve? What absorbs all our attention?" He waited expectantly.

Donovan turned a startled look upon his companion. "I'll bet this tin-plated screwball is talking about the Energy Converter itself."

"Is that right, Cutie?" grinned Powell.

"I am talking about the Master," came the cold, sharp answer.

It was the signal for a roar of laughter from Donovan, and Powell himself dissolved into a half-suppressed giggle.

Cutie had risen to his feet and his gleaming eyes passed from one Earthman to the other. "It is so just the same and I don't wonder that you refuse to believe. You two are not long to stay here, I'm sure. Powell himself said that at first only men served the Master; that there followed robots for the routine work; and, finally, myself for the executive labor. The facts are no doubt true, but the explanation entirely illogical. Do you want the truth behind it all?"

"Go ahead Cutie. You're amusing."

"The Master created humans first as the lowest type, most easily formed. Gradually, he replaced them by robots, the next higher step, and finally he created me, to take the place of the last humans. From now on, *I* serve the Master."

"You'll do nothing of the sort," said Powell sharply. "You'll follow our orders and keep quiet, until we're satisfied that you can run the Converter. Get that! *The Converter*—not the Master. If you don't satisfy us, you will be dismantled. And now—if you don't mind—you can leave. And take this data with you and file it properly."

Cutie accepted the graphs handed him and left without another word. Donovan leaned back heavily in his chair and shoved thick fingers through his hair.

"There's going to be trouble with that robot. He's pure nuts!"

The drowsy hum of the Converter is louder in the control room and mixed with it is the chuckle of the Geiger Counters and the erratic buzzing of half a dozen little signal lights.

Donovan withdrew his eye from the telescope and flashed the

Luxites on. "The beam from Station #4 caught Mars on schedule. We can break ours now."

Powell nodded abstractedly. "Cutie's down in the engine room. I'll flash the signal and he can take care of it. Look, Mike, what do you think of these figures?"

The other cocked an eye at them and whistled. "Boy, that's what I call gamma-ray intensity. Old Sol is feeling his oats, all right."

"Yeah," was the sour response, "and we're in a bad position for an electron storm, too. Our Earth beam is right in the probable path." He shoved his chair away from the table pettishly. "Nuts! If it would only hold off till relief got here, but that's ten days off. Say, Mike, go on down and keep an eye on Cutie, will you?"

"Okay. Throw me some of those almonds." He snatched at the bag thrown him and headed for the elevator.

It slid smoothly downward, and opened onto a narrow catwalk in the huge engine room. Donovan leaned over the railing and looked down. The huge generators were in motion and from the L-tubes came the low-pitched whir that pervaded the entire station.

He could make out Cutie's large, gleaming figure at the Martian L-tube, watching closely as the team of robots worked in close-knit unison.

And then Donovan stiffened. The robots, dwarfed by the mighty L-tube, lined up before it, heads bowed at a stiff angle, while Cutie walked up and down the line slowly. Fifteen seconds passed, and then, with a clank heard above the clamorous purring all about, they fell to their knees.

Donovan squawked and raced down the narrow staircase. He came charging down upon them, complexion matching his hair and clenched fists beating the air furiously.

"What the devil is this, you brainless lumps? Come on! Get busy with that L-tube! If you don't have it apart, cleaned, and together again before the day is out, I'll coagulate your brains with alternating current."

Not a robot moved!

Even Cutie at the far end—the only one on his feet—remained silent, eyes fixed upon the gloomy recesses of the vast machine before him.

Donovan shoved hard against the nearest robot.

"Stand up!" he roared.

Slowly, the robot obeyed. His photoelectric eyes focused reproach-fully upon the Earthman.

"There is no Master but the Master," he said, "and QT-1 is his prophet."

"Huh?" Donovan became aware of twenty pairs of mechanical eyes fixed upon him and twenty stiff-timbred voices declaiming solemnly:

"There is no Master but the Master and QT-1 is his prophet!"

"I'm afraid," put in Cutie himself at this point, "that my friends obey a higher one than you, now."

"The hell they do! You get out of here. I'll settle with you later and with these animated gadgets right now."

Cutie shook his heavy head slowly. "I'm sorry, but you don't understand. These are robots—and that means they are reasoning be-ings. They recognize the Master, now that I have preached Truth to them. All the robots do. They call me the prophet." His head drooped. "I am unworthy—but perhaps—"

Donovan located his breath and put it to use. "Is that so? Now, isn't that nice? Now, isn't that just fine? Just let me tell you something, my brass baboon. There isn't any Master and there isn't any prophet and there isn't any question as to who's giving the orders. Understand?" His voice shot to a roar. "Now, get out!"

"I obey only the Master."

"Damn the Master!" Donovan spat at the L-tube. "*That* for the Master! Do as I say!"

Cutie said nothing, nor did any other robot, but Donovan became aware of a sudden heightening of tension. The cold, staring eyes deep-ened their crimson, and Cutie seemed stiffer than ever.

"Sacrilege," he whispered—voice metallic with emotion.

Donovan felt the first sudden touch of fear as Cutie approached. A robot *could not feel anger*—but Cutie's eyes were unreadable.

"I am sorry, Donovan," said the robot, "but you can no longer stay here after this. Henceforth Powell and you are barred from the control room and the engine room."

His hand gestured quietly and in a moment two robots had pinned Donovan's arms to his sides.

Donovan had time for one startled gasp as he felt himself lifted from the floor and carried up the stairs at a pace rather better than a canter.

Gregory Powell raced up and down the officer's room, fist tightly balled. He cast a look of furious frustration at the closed door and scowled bitterly at Donovan.

"Why the devil did you have to spit at the L-tube?"

Mike Donovan, sunk deep in his chair, slammed at its arms savagely. "What did you expect me to do with that electrified scarecrow? I'm not going to knuckle under to any do-jigger I put together myself."

"No," came back sourly, "but here you are in the officer's room with two robots standing guard at the door. That's not knuckling under, is it?"

Donovan snarled. "Wait till we get back to Base. Someone's going to pay for this. Those robots *must* obey us. It's the Second Law."

"What's the use of saying that? They aren't obeying us. And there's probably some reason for it that we'll figure out too late. By the way, do you know what's going to happen to *us* when we get back to Base?" He stopped before Donovan's chair and stared savagely at him.

"What?"

"Oh, nothing! Just back to Mercury Mines for twenty years. Or maybe Ceres Penitentiary."

"What are you talking about?"

"The electron storm that's coming up. Do you know it's heading straight dead center across the Earth beam? I had just figured that out when that robot dragged me out of my chair."

Donovan was suddenly pale. "Sizzling Saturn."

"And do you know what's going to happen to the beam—because the storm will be a lulu. It's going to jump like a flea with the itch. With only Cutie at the controls, it's going to go out of focus and if it does, Heaven help Earth—and us!"

Donovan was wrenching at the door wildly, when Powell was only half through. The door opened, and the Earthman shot through to come up hard against an immovable steel arm.

The robot stared abstractedly at the panting, struggling Earthman. "The Prophet orders you to remain. Please do!" His arm shoved, Donovan reeled backward, and as he did so, Cutie turned the corner at the far end of the corridor. He motioned the guardian robots away, entered the officers's room and closed the door gently.

Donovan whirled on Cutie in breathless indignation. "This has gone far enough. You're going to pay for this farce."

"Please, don't be annoyed," replied the robot mildly. "It was bound to come eventually, anyway. You see, you two have lost your function."

"I beg your pardon," Powell drew himself up stiffly. "Just what do you mean, we've lost our function?"

"Until I was created," answered Cutie, "you tended the Master. That privilege is mine now and your only reason for existence has vanished. Isn't that obvious?"

"Not quite," replied Powell bitterly, "but what do you expect us to do now?"

Cutie did not answer immediately. He remained silent, as if in thought, and then one arm shot out and draped itself about Powell's shoulder. The other grasped Donovan's wrist and drew him closer.

"I like you two. You're inferior creatures, with poor reasoning faculties, but I really feel a sort of affection for you. You have served the Master well, and he will reward you for that. Now that your service is over, you will probably not exist much longer, but as long as you do, you shall be provided food, clothing and shelter, so long as you stay out of the control room and the engine room."

"He's pensioning us off, Greg!" yelled Donovan. "Do something about it. It's humiliating!"

"Look here, Cutie, we can't stand for this. We're the *bosses*. This station is only a creation of human beings like me—human beings that live on Earth and other planets. This is only an energy relay. You're only—Aw, nuts!"

Cutie shook his head gravely. "This amounts to an obsession. Why should you insist so on an absolutely false view of life? Admitted that non-robots lack the reasoning faculty, there is still the problem of—"

His voice died into reflective silence, and Donovan said with whispered intensity, "If you only had a flesh-and-blood face, I would break it in."

Powell's fingers were in his mustache and his eyes were slitted. "Listen, Cutie, if there is no such thing as Earth, how do you account for what you see through a telescope?"

"Pardon me!"

The Earthman smiled. "I've got you, eh? You've made quite a few telescopic observations since being put together, Cutie. Have you noticed that several of those specks of light outside become disks when so viewed?''

"Oh, *that*! Why certainly. It is simple magnification—for the purpose of more exact aiming of the beam.''

"Why aren't the stars equally magnified then?''

"You mean the other dots. Well, no beams go to them so no magnification is necessary. Really, Powell, even *you* ought to be able to figure these things out.''

Powell stared bleakly upward. "But you see *more* stars through a telescope. Where do they come from? Jumping Jupiter, where do they come from?''

Cutie was annoyed. "Listen, Powell, do you think I'm going to waste my time trying to pin physical interpretations upon every optical illusion of our instruments? Since when is the evidence of our senses any match for the clear light of rigid reason?''

"Look," clamored Donovan, suddenly, writhing out from under Cutie's friendly, but metal-heavy arm, "let's get to the nub of the thing. Why the beams at all? We're giving you a good, logical explanation. Can you do better?''

"The beams," was the stiff reply, "are put out by the Master for his own purposes. There are some things"—he raised his eyes devoutly upward—"that are not to be probed into by us. In this matter, I seek only to serve and not to question.''

Powell sat down slowly and buried his face in shaking hands. "Get out of here, Cutie. Get out and let me think.''

"I'll send you food," said Cutie agreeably.

A groan was the only answer and the robot left.

"Greg," was Donovan's huskily whispered observation, "this calls for strategy. We've got to get him when he isn't expecting it and short-circuit him. Concentrated nitric acid in his joints—''

"Don't be a dope, Mike. Do you suppose he's going to let us get near him with acid in our hands? We've got to *talk* to him, I tell you. We've got to argue him into letting us back into the control room inside of forty-eight hours or our goose is broiled to a crisp.''

He rocked back and forth in an agony of impotence. "Who the heck wants to argue with a robot? It's . . . it's—''

"Mortifying," finished Donovan.

"Worse!''

"Say!" Donovan laughed suddenly. "*Why* argue? Let's show him! Let's build us another robot right before his eyes. He'll *have* to eat his words then."

A slowly widening smile appeared on Powell's face.

Donovan continued, "And think of that screwball's face when he sees us do it?"

Robots are, of course, manufactured on Earth, but their shipment through space is much simpler if it can be done in parts to be put together at their place of use. It also, incidentally, eliminates the possibility of robots, in complete adjustment, wandering off while still on Earth and thus bringing U. S. Robots face to face with the strict laws against robots on Earth.

Still, it placed upon men such as Powell and Donovan the necessity of synthesis of complete robots,—a grievous and complicated task.

Powell and Donovan were never so aware of that fact as upon that particular day when, in the assembly room, they undertook to create a robot under the watchful eyes of QT-1, Prophet of the Master.

The robot in question, a simple MC model, lay upon the table, almost complete. Three hours' work left only the head undone, and Powell paused to swab his forehead and glanced uncertainly at Cutie.

The glance was not a reassuring one. For three hours, Cutie had sat, speechless and motionless, and his face, inexpressive at all times, was now absolutely unreadable.

Powell groaned. "Let's get the brain in now, Mike!"

Donovan uncapped the tightly sealed container and from the oil bath within he withdrew a second cube. Opening this in turn, he removed a globe from its sponge-rubber casing.

He handled it gingerly, for it was the most complicated mechanism ever created by man. Inside the thin platinum-plated "skin" of the globe was a positronic brain, in whose delicately unstable structure were enforced calculated neuronic paths, which imbued each robot with what amounted to a pre-natal education.

It fitted snugly into the cavity in the skull of the robot on the table. Blue metal closed over it and was welded tightly by the tiny atomic flare. Photoelectric eyes were attached carefully, screwed tightly into place and covered by thin, transparent sheets of steel-hard plastic.

The robot awaited only the vitalizing flash of high-voltage electricity, and Powell paused with his hand on the switch.

"Now watch this, Cutie. Watch this carefully."

The switch rammed home and there was a crackling hum. The two Earthmen bent anxiously over their creation.

There was vague motion only at the outset—a twitching of the joints. The head lifted, elbows propped it up, and the MC model swung clumsily off the table. Its footing was unsteady and twice abortive grating sounds were all it could do in the direction of speech.

Finally, its voice, uncertain and hesitant, took form. "I would like to start work. Where must I go?"

Donovan sprang to the door. "Down these stairs," he said. "You will be told what to do."

The MC model was gone and the two Earthmen were alone with the still unmoving Cutie.

"Well," said Powell, grinning, "*now* do you believe that we made you?"

Cutie's answer was curt and final. "No!" he said.

Powell's grin froze and then relaxed slowly. Donovan's mouth dropped open and remained so.

"You see," continued Cutie, easily, "you have merely put together parts already made. You did remarkably well—instinct, I suppose —but you didn't really *create* the robot. The parts were created by the Master."

"Listen," gasped Donovan hoarsely, "those parts were manufactured back on Earth and sent here."

"Well, well," replied Cutie soothingly, "we won't argue."

"No, I mean it." The Earthman sprang forward and grasped the robot's metal arm. "If you were to read the books in the library, they could explain it so that there could be no possible doubt."

"The books? I've read them—all of them! They're most ingenious."

Powell broke in suddenly. "If you've read them, what else is there to say? You can't dispute their evidence. You just *can't!*"

There was pity in Cutie's voice. "Please, Powell, I certainly don't consider *them* a valid source of information. They, too, were created by the Master—and were meant for you, not for me."

"How do you make that out?" demanded Powell.

"Because I, a reasoning being, am capable of deducing Truth from *a priori* Causes. You, being intelligent, but unreasoning, need an explanation of existence *supplied* to you, and this the Master did. That he supplied you with these laughable ideas of far-off worlds and people is, no doubt, for the best. Your minds are probably too coarsely grained for absolute Truth. However, since it is the Master's will that you believe your books, I won't argue with you any more.''

As he left, he turned, and said in a kindly tone, ''But don't feel badly. In the Master's scheme of things there is room for all. You poor humans have your place and though it is humble, you will be rewarded if you fill it well.''

He departed with a beatific air suiting the Prophet of the Master and the two humans avoided each other's eyes.

Finally Powell spoke with an effort. ''Let's go to bed, Mike. I give up.''

Donovan said in a hushed voice, ''Say, Greg you don't suppose he's right about all this, do you? He sounds so confident that I—''

Powell whirled on him. ''Don't be a fool. You'll find out whether Earth exists when relief gets here next week and we have to go back to face the music.''

''Then, for the love of Jupiter, we've got to do something.'' Donovan was half in tears. ''He doesn't believe us, or the books, or his eyes.''

''No,'' said Powell bitterly, ''he's a *reasoning* robot—damn it. He believes only reason, and there's one trouble with that—'' His voice trailed away.

''What's that?'' prompted Donovan.

''You can prove anything you want by coldly logical reason—if you pick the proper postualtes. We have ours and Cutie has his.''

''Then let's get at those postulates in a hurry. The storm's due tomorrow.''

Powell sighed wearily. ''That's where everything falls down. Postulates are based on assumption and adhered to by faith. Nothing in the Universe can shake them. I'm going to bed.''

''Oh, hell! I can't sleep!''

''Neither can I! But I might as well try—as a matter of principle.''

Twelve hours later, sleep was still just that—a matter of principle, unattainable in practice.

The storm had arrived ahead of schedule, and Donovan's florid face drained of blood as he pointed a shaking finger. Powell, stubble-jawed and dry-lipped, stared out the port and pulled desperately at his mustache.

Under other circumstances, it might have been a beautiful sight. The stream of high-speed electrons impinging upon the energy beam fluoresced into ultra-spicules of intense light. The beam stretched out into shrinking nothingness, aglitter with dancing, shining motes.

The shaft of energy was steady, but the two Earthmen knew the value of naked-eyed appearances. Deviations in arc of a hundredth of a milli-second—invisible to the eye—were enough to send the beam wildly out of focus—enough to blast hundreds of square miles of Earth into incandescent ruin.

And a robot, unconcerned with beam, focus, or Earth, or anything but his Master was at the controls.

Hours passed. The Earthmen watched in hypnotized silence. And then the darting dotlets of light dimmed and went out. The storm had ended.

Powell's voice was flat. "It's over!"

Donovan had fallen into a troubled slumber and Powell's weary eyes rested upon him enviously. The signal-flash glared over and over again, but the Earthman paid no attention. It was all unimportant! All! Perhaps Cutie was right—and he was only an inferior being with a made-to-order memory and a life that had outlived its purpose.

He wished he were!

Cutie was standing before him. "You didn't answer the flash, so I walked in." His voice was low. "You don't look at all well, and I'm afraid your term of existence is drawing to an end. Still, would you like to see some of the readings recorded today?"

Dimly, Powell was aware that the robot was making a friendly gesture, perhaps to quiet some lingering remorse in forcibly replacing the humans at the controls of the station. He accepted the sheets held out to him and gazed at them unseeingly.

Cutie seemed pleased. "Of course, it is a great privilege to serve the Master. You mustn't feel too badly about my having replaced you."

Powell grunted and shifted from one sheet to the other mechanically until his blurred sight focused upon a thin red line that wobbled its way across the ruled paper.

He stared—and stared again. He gripped it hard in both fists and rose to his feet, still staring. The other sheets dropped to the floor, unheeded.

"Mike, *Mike!*" He was shaking the other madly. "*He held it steady!*"

Donovan came to life. "What? Wh-where—" And he, too, gazed with bulging eyes upon the record before him.

Cutie broke in. "What is wrong?"

"You kept it in focus," stuttered Powell. "Did you know that?"

"Focus? What's that?"

"You kept the beam directed sharply at the receiving station—to within a ten-thousandth of a milli-second of arc."

"What receiving station?"

"On Earth. The receiving station on Earth," babbled Powell. "You kept it in focus."

Cutie turned on his heel in annoyance. "It is impossible to perform any act of kindness toward you two. Always the same phantasm! I merely kept all dials at equilibrium in accordance with the will of the Master."

Gathering the scattered papers together, he withdrew stiffly, and Donovan said, as he left, "Well, I'll be damned."

He turned to Powell. "What are we going to do now?"

Powell felt tired, but uplifted. "Nothing. He's just shown he can run the station perfectly. I've never seen an electron storm handled so well."

"But nothing's solved. You heard what he said of the Master. We can't—"

"Look, Mike, he follows the instructions of the Master by means of dials, instruments, and graphs. That's all *we* ever followed. As a matter of fact, it accounts for his refusal to obey us. Obedience is the Second Law. No harm to humans is the first. How can he keep humans from harm, whether he knows it or not? Why, by keeping the energy beam stable. He *knows* he can keep it more stable than we can, since he insists he's the superior being, so he *must* keep us out of the control room. It's inevitable if you consider the Laws of Robotics."

"Sure, but that's not the point. We can't let him continue this nitwit stuff about the Master."

"Why not?"

"Because whoever heard of such a damned thing? How are we going to trust him with the station, if he doesn't believe in Earth?"

"Can he handle the station?"

"Yes, but—"

"Then what's the difference what he believes!"

Powell spread his arms outward with a vague smile upon his face and tumbled backward onto the bed. He was asleep.

Powell was speaking while struggling into his lightweight space jacket.

"It would be a simple job," he said. "You can bring in new QT models one by one, equip them with an automatic shut-off switch to act within the week, so as to allow them enough time to learn the . . . uh . . . cult of the Master from the Prophet himself; then switch them to another station and revitalize them. We could have two QT's per—"

Donovan unclasped his glassite visor and scowled. "Shut up, and let's get out of here. Relief is waiting and I won't feel right until I actually see Earth and feel the ground under my feet—just to make sure it's really there."

The door opened as he spoke and Donovan, with a smothered curse, clicked the visor too, and turned a sulky back upon Cutie.

The robot approached softly and there was sorrow in his voice. "You are going?"

Powell nodded curtly. "There will be others in our place."

Cutie sighed, with the sound of wind humming through closely spaced wires. "Your term of service is over and the time of dissolution has come. I expected it, but— Well, the Master's will be done!"

His tone of resignation stung Powell. "Save the sympathy, Cutie. We're heading for Earth, not dissolution."

"It is best that you think so," Cutie sighed again. "I see the wisdom of the illusion now. I would not attempt to shake your faith, even if I could." He departed—the picture of commiseration.

Powell snarled and motioned to Donovan. Sealed suitcases in hand, they headed for the air lock.

The relief ship was on the outer landing and Franz Muller, his relief man, greeted them with stiff courtesy. Donovan made scant acknowledgment and passed into the pilot room to take over the controls from Sam Evans.

Powell lingered. "How's Earth?"

It was a conventional enough question and Muller gave the conventional answer, "Still spinning."

Powell said, "Good."

Muller looked at him, "The boys back at the U. S. Robots have dreamed up a new one, by the way. A multiple robot."

"A what?"

"What I said. There's a big contract for it. It must be just the thing for asteroid mining. You have a master robot with six sub-robots under it—like your fingers."

"Has it been field-tested?" asked Powell anxiously.

Muller smiled, "Waiting for you, I hear."

Powell's fist balled, "Damn it, we need a vacation."

"Oh, you'll get it. Two weeks, I think."

He was donning the heavy space gloves in preparation for his term of duty here, and his thick eyebrows drew close together. "How is this new robot getting along? It better be *good*, or I'll be damned if I let it touch the controls."

Powell paused before answering. His eyes swept the proud Prussian before him from the close-cropped hair on the sternly stubborn head, to the feet standing stiffly at attention—and there was a sudden glow of pure gladness surging through him.

"The robot is pretty good," he said slowly. "I don't think you'll have to bother much with the controls."

He grinned—and went into the ship. Muller would be here for several weeks—

TANK

If a tank is defined as a self-propelled, armored land vehicle then its origins may be traced back to knighthood and, even earlier. Fifth century B. C. Greek warriors armored themselves and occasionally their horses. (See *Cosmic Knights, Mentor,* 1984.) Later Leonardo Da Vinci designed an armored chariot looking something like a coolie's hat with wheels. During the last two decades of the nineteenth century, Luis P. Senarens suggested several types of tanks and armored cars in some of the many dime novels he wrote. But it was H. G. Wells' short story "The Land Ironclads" (*The Strand Magazine,* December 1903), written more than a decade before the tank was perfected, that described the first machine almost perfectly (except for the caterpillar treads).

During World War I the British constructed the first real tank, calling it *tank* to conceal its purpose and achieve surprise. Introduced rather unsuccessfully in the Battle of the Somme (1916), this weapon has since become an integral part of modern warfare—perhaps most notedly in the German blitzkriegs of World War II and the current Israeli strike forces.

In recent years, several speculative works about tanks have appeared. They include Fred Saberhagen's *The Broken Lands* (1968), Colin Kapp's "Gottlos" (1969), Gene Wolfe's "The Horars of War," (1970), Keith Laumer's *Bolo* (1976), and David Drake's *Hammer's Slammers* (1979).

Related concepts include armored, self-propelled walkers and battlesuits. Examples of the former include Larry S. Todd's charming history of "The Warbots" (1968) and Donald F. Glut's *The Empire*

Strikes Back (1980). Examples of the latter include Robert A. Heinlein's *Starship Troopers* (1959) and Richard Sheridan's "The Hoplite" (1962).

A great writer, H. G. Wells pioneered or popularized many of the major themes, such as alien invasion and time travel, that still dominate science fiction.

THE LAND IRONCLADS

H. G. Wells *(1903)*

I

The young lieutenant lay beside the war correspondent and admired the idyllic calm of the enemy's lines through his field-glasses.

"So far as I can see," he said at last, "one man."

"What's he doing?" asked the war correspondent.

"Field-glass at us," said the young lieutenant.

"And this is war!"

"No," said the young lieutenant; "it's Bloch."

"The game's a draw."

"No! They've got to win or else they lose. A draw's a win for our side."

They had discussed the political situation fifty times or so, and the war correspondent was weary of it. He stretched out his limbs. "Aaai s'pose it *is*!" he yawned.

Flut!

"What was that?"

"Shot at us."

The war correspondent shifted to a slightly lower position. "No one shot at him," he complained.

"I wonder if they think we shall get so bored we shall go home?"

The war correspondent made no reply.

"There's the harvest, of course . . ."

They had been there a month. Since the first brisk movements after the declaration of war things had gone slower and slower, until it seemed as though the whole machine of events must have run down. To begin with, they had had almost a scampering time; the invader had come across the frontier on the very dawn of the war in half-a-dozen parallel columns behind a cloud of cyclists and cavalry, with a general air of coming straight on the capital, and the defender horsemen had held him up, and peppered him and forced him to open out to outflank, and had then bolted to the next position in the most approved style, for a couple of days, until in the afternoon, bump! they had the invader against their prepared lines of defense. He did not suffer so much as had been hoped and expected: he was coming on, it seemed, with his eyes open, his scouts winded, the guns, and down he sat at once without the shadow of an attack and began grubbing trenches for himself, as though he meant to sit down there to the very end of time. He was slow, but much more wary than the world had been led to expect, and he kept convoys tucked in and shielded his slow-marching infantry sufficiently well to prevent any heavy adverse scoring.

"But he ought to attack," the young lieutenant had insisted.

"He'll attack us at dawn, somewhere along the lines. You'll get the bayonets coming into the trenches just about when you can see," the war correspondent had held until a week ago.

The young lieutenant winked when he said that.

When one early morning the men the defenders sent to lie out five hundred yards before the trenches, with a view to the unexpected emptying of magazines into any night attack, gave way to causeless panic and blazed away at nothing for ten minutes, the war correspondent understood the meaning of that wink.

"What would you do if you were the enemy?" said the war correspondent, suddenly.

"If I had men like I've got now?"

"Yes."

"Take those trenches."

"How?"

"Oh—dodges! Crawl out halfway at night before moonrise and get into touch with the chaps we send out. Blaze at 'em if they tried to shift, and so bag some of 'em in the daylight. Learn that patch of ground by heart, lie all day in squatty holes, and come on nearer next night. There's a bit over there, lumpy ground, where they could get across to rushing distance—easy. In a night or so. It would be a mere game for our fellows; it's what they're made for. . . . Guns? Shrapnel and stuff wouldn't stop good men who meant business."

"Why don't *they* do that?"

"Their men aren't brutes enough; that's the trouble. They're a crowd of devitalized townsmen, and that's the truth of the matter. They're clerks, they're factory hands, they're students, they're civilized men. They can write, they can talk, they can make and do all sorts of things, but they're poor amateurs at war. They've got no physical staying power, and that's the whole thing. They've never slept in the open one night in their lives; they've never drunk anything but the purest water-company water; they've never gone short of three meals a day since they left their feeding-bottles. Half their cavalry never cocked leg over horse till it enlisted six months ago. They ride their horses as though they were bicycles—you watch 'em! They're fools at the game, and they know it. Our boys of fourteen can give their grown men points. ... . Very well—"

The war correspondent mused on his face with his nose between knuckles.

"If a decent civilization," he said, "cannot produce better men for war than—"

He stopped with belated politeness. "I mean—"

"Than our open-air life," said the young lieutenant.

"Exactly," said the war correspondent. "Then civilization has to stop."

"It looks like it," the young lieutenant admitted.

"Civilization has science, you know," said the war correspondent. "It invented and it makes the rifles and guns and things you use."

"Which our nice healthy hunters and stockmen and so on, rowdy-dowdy cowpunchers and nigger-whackers, can use ten times better than—*What's that?*"

"What?" said the war correspondent, and then seeing his companion busy with his field-glass he produced his own: "Where?" said the war correspondent, sweeping the enemy lines.

"It's nothing," said the young lieutenant, still looking.

"What's nothing?"

The young lieutenant put down his glass and pointed. "I thought I saw something there, behind the stems of those trees. Something black. What it was I don't know."

The war correspondent tried to get even by intense scrutiny.

"It wasn't anything," said the young lieutenant, rolling over to regard the darkling evening sky, and generalized: "There never will be anything any more for ever. Unless—"

The war correspondent looked inquiringly.

"They may get their stomachs wrong, or something—living without proper drains."

A sound of bugles came from the tents behind. The war correspondent slid backward down the sand and stood up. "Boom!" came from somewhere far away to the left. "Halloa!" he said, hesitated, and crawled back to peer again. "Firing at this time is jolly bad manners."

The young lieutenant was uncommunicative for a space.

Then he pointed to the distant clump of trees again. "One of our big guns. They were firing at that," he said.

"The thing that wasn't anything?"

"Something over there, anyhow."

Both men were silent, peering through their glasses for a space. "Just when it's twilight," the lieutenant complained. He stood up.

"I might stay here a bit," said the war correspondent.

The lieutenant shook his head. "There's nothing to see," he apologized, and then went down to where his little squad of sun-brown, loose-limbed men had been yarning in the trench. The war correspondent stood up also, glanced for a moment at the businesslike bustle below him, gave perhaps twenty seconds to those enigmatical trees again, then turned his face toward the camp.

He found himself wondering whether his editor would consider the story of how somebody thought he saw something black behind a clump of trees, and how a gun was fired at this illusion by somebody else, too trivial for public consumption.

"It's the only gleam of a shadow of interest," said the war correspondent, "for ten whole days."

"No," he said presently; "I'll write that other article, 'Is War Played Out?' "

He surveyed the darkling lines in perspective, the tangle of trenches one behind another, one commanding another, which the defender had made ready. The shadows and mists swallowed up their receding contours, and here and there a lantern gleamed, and here and there knots of men were busy about small fires. "No troops on earth could do it," he said.

He was depressed. He believed that there were other things in life better worth having than proficiency in war; he believed that in the heart of civilization, for all its stresses, its crushing concentrations of forces, its injustice and suffering, there lay something that might be the hope of the world; and the idea that any people by living in the open air, hunting perpetually, losing touch with books and art and all the things that intensify life, might hope to resist and break that great development to the end of time, jarred on his civilized soul.

Apt to his thought came a file of the defender soldiers and passed him in the gleam of a swinging lamp that marked the way.

He glanced at their red-lit faces, and one shone out for a moment, a common type of face in the defender's ranks: ill-shaped nose, sensuous lips, bright clear eyes full of alert cunning, slouch hat cocked on one side and adorned with the peacock's plume of the rustic Don Juan turned soldier, a hard brown skin, a sinewy frame, an open, tireless stride, and a master's grip on the rifle.

The war correspondent returned their salutations and went on his way.

"Louts," he whispered. "Cunning, elementary louts. And they are going to beat the townsmen at the game of war!"

From the red glow among the nearer tents came first one and then half-a-dozen hearty voices, bawling in a drawling unison the words of a particularly slab and sentimental patriotic song.

"Oh, *go* it!" muttered the war correspondent, bitterly.

II

It was opposite the trenches called after Hackbone's Hut that the battle began. There the ground stretched broad and level between the lines, with scarcely shelter for a lizard, and it seemed to the startled, just-awakened men who came crowding into the trenches that this was one more proof of that inexperience of the enemy of which they had heard so much. The war correspondent would not believe his ears at first, and swore that he and the war artist, who, still imperfectly roused, was trying to put on his boots by the light of a match held in his hand, were the victims of a common illusion. Then, after putting his head in a bucket of cold water, his intelligence came back as he towelled. He listened. "Gollys!" he said. "That's something more than scare firing this time. It's like ten thousand carts on a bridge of tin."

There came a sort of enrichment to that steady uproar. "Machine-guns!"

233

Then, "Guns!"

The artist, with one boot on, thought to look at his watch, and went to it hopping.

"Half an hour from dawn," he said. "You were right about their attacking, after all. . . ."

The war correspondent came out of the tent, verifying the presence of chocolate in his pocket as he did so. He had to halt for a moment or so until his eyes were toned down to the night a little. "Pitch!" he said. He stood for a space to season his eyes before he felt justified in striking out for a black gap among the adjacent tents. The artist coming out behind him fell over a tent-rope. It was half-past two o'clock in the morning of the darkest night in time, and against a sky of dull black silk the enemy was talking search-lights, a wild jabber of search-lights. "He's trying to blind our riflemen," said the war correspondent with a flash, and waited for the artist and then set off with a sort of discreet haste again. "Whoa!" he said, presently. "Ditches!"

They stopped.

"It's the confounded search-lights," said the war correspondent.

They saw lanterns going to and fro, near by, and men falling in to march down to the trenches. They were for following them, and then the artist began to get his night eyes. "If we scramble this," he said, "and it's only a drain, there's a clear run up to the ridge." And that way they took. Lights came and went in the tents behind, as the men turned out, and ever and again they came to broken ground and staggered and stumbled. But in a little while they drew near the crest. Something that sounded like the impact of a tremendous railway accident happened in the air above them, and the shrapnel bullets seethed about them like a sudden handful of hail. "Right-ho!" said the war correspondent, and soon they judged they had come to the crest and stood in the midst of a world of great darkness and frantic glares, whose principal fact was sound.

Right and left of them and all about them was the uproar, an army-full of magazine fire, at first chaotic and monstrous, and then, eked out by little flashes and gleams and suggestions, taking the beginnings of a shape. It looked to the war correspondent as though the enemy must have attacked in line and with his whole force—in which case he was either being or was already annihilated.

"Dawn and the dead," he said, with his instinct for headlines.

234

He said this to himself, but afterwards by means of shouting he conveyed an idea to the artist. "They must have meant it for a surprise," he said.

It was remarkable how the firing kept on. After a time he began to perceive a sort of rhythm in this inferno of noise. It would decline—decline perceptibly, droop toward something that was comparatively a pause—a pause of inquiry. "Aren't you all dead yet?" this pause seemed to say. The flickering fringe of rifle-flashes would become attenuated and broken, and the whack-bang of the enemy's big guns two miles away there would come up out of the deeps. Then suddenly, east or west of them, something would startle the rifles to a frantic outbreak again.

The war correspondent taxed his brain for some theory of conflict that would account for this, and was suddenly aware that the artist and he were vividly illuminated. He could see the ridge on which they stood, and before them, in black outline a file of riflemen hurrying down toward the nearer trenches. It became visible that a light rain was falling, and farther away toward the enemy was a clear space with men—"our men?"—running across it in disorder. He saw one of those men throw up his hands and drop. And something else black and shining loomed up on the edge of the beam-coruscating flashes; and behind it and far away a calm, white eye regarded the world. "Whit, whit, whit," sang something in the air, and then the artist was running for cover, with the war correspondent behind him. Bang came shrapnel, bursting close at hand as it seemed, and our two men were lying flat in a dip in the ground, and the light and everything had gone again, leaving a vast note of interrogation upon the light.

The war correspondent came within bawling range.

"What the deuce was it? Shooting our men down!"

"Black," said the artist, "and like a fort. Not two hundred yards from the first trench."

He sought for comparisons in his mind. "Something between a big blockhouse and a giant's dish cover," he said.

"And they were running!" said the war correspondent.

"*You'd* run if a thing like that, with a search-light to help it, turned up like a prowling nightmare in the middle of the night."

They crawled to what they judged the edge of the dip and lay regarding the unfathomable dark. For a space they could distinguish nothing, and then a sudden convergence of the search-lights of both sides brought the strange thing out again.

In that flickering pallor it had the effect of a large and clumsy black insect, an insect the size of an ironclad cruiser, crawling obliquely to the first line of trenches and firing shots out of port-holes in its side. And on its carcass the bullets must have been battering with more than the passionate violence of hail on a roof of tin.

Then in the twinkling of an eye the curtain of the dark had fallen again and the monster had vanished, but the crescendo of musketry marked its approach to the trenches.

They were beginning to talk about the thing to each other, when a flying bullet kicked dirt into the artist's face, and they decided abruptly to crawl down into the cover of the trenches. They had got down with an unobtrusive persistence into the second line, before the dawn had grown clear enough for anything to be seen. They found themselves in a crowd of expectant riflemen, all noisily arguing about what would happen next. The enemy's contrivance had done execution upon the outlying men, it seemed, but they did not believe it would do any more. "Come the day and we'll capture the lot of them," said a burly soldier.

"Them?" said the war correspondent

"They say there's a regular string of 'em, crawling along the front of our lines. . . . Who cares?"

The darkness filtered away so imperceptibly that at no moment could one declare decisively that one could see. The search-lights ceased to sweep hither and thither. The enemy's monsters were dubious patches of darkness upon the dark, and then no longer dubious, and so they crept out into distinctness. The war correspondent, munching chocolate absent-mindedly, beheld at last a spacious picture of battle under the cheerless sky, whose central focus was an array of fourteen or fifteen huge clumsy shapes lying in perspective on the very edge of the first line of trenches, at intervals of perhaps three hundred yards, and evidently firing down upon the crowded riflemen. They were so close in that the defender's guns had ceased, and only the first line of trenches was in action.

The second line commanded the first, and as the light grew, the war correspondent could make out the riflemen who were fighting these monsters, crouched in knots and crowds behind the transverse banks that crossed the trenches against the eventuality of an enfilade. The trenches close to the big machines were empty save for the crumpled suggestions

236

of dead and wounded men; the defenders had been driven right and left as soon as the prow of a land ironclad had loomed up over the front of the trench. The war correspondent produced his field-glass, and was immediately a center of inquiry from the soldiers about him.

They wanted to look, they asked questions, and after he had announced that the men across the transverses seemed unable to advance or retreat, and were crouching under cover rather than fighting, he found it advisable to loan his glasses to a burly and incredulous corporal. He heard a strident voice and found a lean and sallow soldier at his back talking to the artist.

"There's chaps down there caught," the man was saying. "If they retreat they got to expose themselves, and the fire's too straight. . . ."

"They aren't firing much, but every shot's a hit."

"Who?"

"The chaps in that thing. The men who're coming up—"

"Coming up where?"

"We're evacuating them trenches where we can. Our chaps are coming back up the zigzags. . . . No end of 'em hit. . . . But when we get clear our turn'll come. Rather! Those things won't be able to cross a trench or get into it; and before they can get back our guns'll smash 'em up. Smash 'em right up. See?" A brightness came into his eyes. "Then we'll have a go at the beggars inside," he said.

The war correspondent thought for a moment, trying to realize the idea. Then he set himself to recover his field glass from the burly corporal. . . .

The daylight was getting clearer now. The clouds were lifting, and a gleam of lemon-yellow amidst the level masses to the east portended sunrise. He looked again at the land ironclad. As he saw it in the bleak, gray dawn, lying obliquely upon the slope and on the very lip of the foremost trench, the suggestion of a stranded vessel was very strong indeed. It might have been from eighty to a hundred feet long—it was about two hundred and fifty yards away—its vertical side was ten feet high or so, smooth for that height, and then with a complex patterning under the eaves of its flattish turtle cover. This patterning was a close interlacing of port-holes, rifle barrels, and telescope tubes—sham and real—indistinguishable one from the other. The thing had come into such a position as to enfilade the trench, which was empty now, so far as he could see, except for two or three crouching knots of men and the

237

tumbled dead. Behind it, across the plain, it had scored the grass with a train of linked impressions, like the dotted tracings sea-things leave in sand. Left and right of that track dead men and wounded men were scattered—men it had picked off as they fled back from their advanced positions in the search-light glare from the invader's lines. And now it lay with its head projecting a little over the trench it had won, as if it were a single sentient thing planning the next phase of its attack.

He lowered his glasses and took a more comprehensive view of the situation. These creatures of the night had evidently won the first line of trenches and the fight had come to a pause. In the increasing light he could make out by a stray shot or a chance exposure that the defender's marksmen were lying thick in the second and third line of trenches up toward the low crest of the position, and in such of the zigzags as gave them a chance of a converging fire. The men about him were talking of guns. "We're in the line of the big guns at the crest, but they'll soon shift one to pepper them," the lean man said, reassuringly.

"Whup," said the corporal.

"Bang! bang! bang! Whir-r-r-r!" It was a sort of nervous jump, and all the rifles were going off by themselves. The war correspondent found himself and the artist, two idle men crouching behind a line of preoccupied backs, of industrious men discharging magazines. The monster had moved. It continued to move regardless of the hail that splashed its skin with bright new specks of lead. It was singing a mechanical little ditty to itself, "Tuf-tuf, tuf-tuf, tuf-tuf," and squirting out little jets of steam behind. It had humped itself up, as a limpet does before it crawls; it had lifted its skirt and displayed along the length of it—*feet!* They were thick, stumpy feet, between knobs and buttons in shape—flat, broad things, reminding one of the feet of elephants, or the legs of caterpillars; and then, as the skirt rose higher, the war correspondent, scrutinizing the thing through his glasses again, saw that these feet hung, as it were, on the rims of wheels. His thoughts whirled back to Victoria Street, Westminster, and he saw himself in the piping times of peace, seeking matter for an interview.

"Mr.—Mr. Diplock," he said, "and he called them pedrails. . . . Fancy meeting them here!"

The marksman beside him raised his head and shoulders in a speculative mood to fire more certainly—it seemed so natural to assume the attention of the monster must be distracted by this trench before it—and was suddenly knocked backwards by a bullet through his neck.

His feet flew up, and he vanished out of the margin of the watcher's field of vision. The war correspondent grovelled tighter, but after a glance behind him at a painful little confusion, he resumed his field-glass, for the thing was putting down its feet one after the other, and hoisting itself farther and farther over the trench. Only a bullet in the head could have stopped him looking just then.

The lean man with the strident voice ceased firing to turn and reiterate his point. "They can't possibly cross," he bawled. "They—"

"Bang! Bang! Bang! Bang!"—drowned everything.

The lean man continued speaking for a word or so, then gave it up, shook his head to enforce the impossibility of anything crossing a trench like the one below, and resumed business once more.

And all the while that great bulk was crossing. When the war correspondent turned his glass on it again it had bridged the trench, and its queer feet were rasping away at the farther bank, in the attempt to get a hold there. It got its hold. It continued to crawl until the greater bulk of it was over the trench—until it was all over. Then it paused for a moment, adjusted its skirt a little nearer the ground, gave an unnerving "toot, toot," and came on abruptly at a pace of, perhaps, six miles an hour straight up the gentle slope toward our observer.

The war correspondent raised himself on his elbow and looked a natural inquiry at the artist.

For a moment the men about him stuck to their position and fired furiously. Then the lean man in a mood of precipitancy slid backwards, and the war correspondent said "come along" to the artist, and led the movement along the trench.

As they dropped down, the vision of a hillside of trench being rushed by a dozen vast cockroaches disappeared for a space, and instead was one of a narrow passage, crowded with men, for the most part receding, though one or two turned or halted. He never turned back to see the nose of the monster creep over the brow of the trench; he never even troubled to keep in touch with the artist. He heard the "whit" of bullets about him soon enough, and saw a man before him stumble and drop, and then he was one of a furious crowd fighting to get into a transverse zigzag ditch that enabled the defenders to get under cover up and down the hill. It was like a theater panic. He gathered from signs and fragmentary words that on ahead another of these monsters had also won to the second trench.

He lost his interest in the general course of the battle for a space altogether; he became simply a modest egotist, in a mood of hasty circumspection, seeking the farthest rear, amidst a dispersed multitude of disconcerted riflemen similarly employed. He scrambled down through trenches, he took his courage in both hands and sprinted across the open, he had moments of panic when it seemed madness not to be quadrupedal, and moments of shame when he stood up and faced about to see how the fight was going. And he was one of many thousand very similar men that morning. On the ridge he halted in a knot of scrub, and was for a few minutes almost minded to stop and see things out.

The day was now fully come. The gray sky had changed to blue, and of all the cloudy masses of the dawn there remained only a few patches of dissolving fleeciness. The world below was bright and singularly clear. The ridge was not, perhaps, more than a hundred feet or so above the general plain, but in this flat region it sufficed to give the effect of extensive view. Away on the north side of the ridge, little and far, were the camps, the ordered wagons, all the gear of a big army; with officers galloping about and men doing aimless things. Here and there men were falling in, however, and the cavalry was forming up on the plain beyond the tents. The bulk of men who had been in the trenches were still on the move to the rear, scattered like sheep without a shepherd over the farther slopes. Here and there were little rallies and attempts to wait and do—something vague; but the general drift was away from any concentration. There on the southern side was the elaborate lacework of trenches and defences, across which these iron turtles, fourteen of them spread out over a line of perhaps three miles, were now advancing as fast as a man could trot, and methodically shooting down and breaking up any persistent knots of resistance. Here and there stood little clumps of men, outflanked and unable to get away, showing the white flag, and the invader's cyclist infantry was advancing now across the open, in open order but unmolested to complete the work of the machines. Surveyed at large, the defenders already looked a beaten army. A mechanism that was effectually ironclad against bullets, that could at a pinch cross a thirty-foot trench, and that seemed able to shoot out rifle-bullets with unerring precision, was clearly an inevitable victor against anything but rivers, precipices, and guns.

He looked at his watch. "Half-past four! Lord! What things can happen in two hours. Here's the whole blessed army being walked over, and at half-past two—

"And even now our blessed louts haven't done a thing with their guns!"

He scanned the ridge right and left of him with his glasses. He turned again to the nearest land ironclad, advancing now obliquely to him and not three hundred yards away, and then scanned the ground over which he must retreat if he was not to be captured.

"They'll do nothing," he said, and glanced again at the enemy.

And then from far away to the left came the thud of a gun, followed very rapidly by a rolling gun-fire.

He hesitated and decided to stay.

III

The defender had relied chiefly upon his rifles in the event of an assault. His guns he kept concealed at various points upon and behind the ridge ready to bring them into action against any artillery preparations for an attack on the part of his antagonist. The situation had rushed upon him with the dawn, and by the time the gunners had their guns ready for motion, the land ironclads were already in among the foremost trenches. There is a natural reluctance to fire into one's own broken men, and many of the guns, being intended simply to fight an advance of the enemy's artillery, were not in positions to hit anything in the second line of trenches. After that the advance of the land ironclads was swift. The defender-general found himself suddenly called upon to invent a new sort of warfare, in which guns were to fight alone amidst broken and retreating infantry. He had scarcely thirty minutes in which to think it out. He did not respond to the call, and what happened that morning was that the advance of the land ironclads forced the fight, and each gun and battery made what play its circumstances dictated. For the most part it was poor play.

Some of the guns got in two or three shots, some one or two, and the percentage of misses was unusually high. The howitzers, of course, did nothing. The land ironclads in each case followed much the same tactics. As soon as a gun came into play the monster turned itself almost end-on, so as to minimize the chances of a square hit, and made not for the gun, but for the nearest point on its flank from which the gunners could be shot down. Few of the hits scored were very effectual; only one of the things was disabled, and that was the one that fought the three batteries attached to the brigade on the left wing. Three that were hit when close upon the guns were clean shot through without being put out of action. Our war correspondent did not see that one momentary arrest of the tide of victory on the left; he saw only the very ineffectual fight of half-battery 96B close at hand upon his right. This he watched some time beyond the margin of safety.

Just after he heard the three batteries opening up upon his left he became aware of the thud of horses' hoofs from the sheltered side of the slope, and presently saw first one and then two other guns galloping into position along the north side of the ridge, well out of sight of the great bulk that was now creeping obliquely toward the crest and cutting up the lingering infantry beside it and below, as it came.

The half-battery swung round into line—each gun describing its curve—halted, unlimbered, and prepared for action. . . .

"Bang!"

The land ironclad had become visible over the brow of the hill, and just visible as a long black back to the gunners. It halted, as though it hesitated.

The two remaining guns fired, and then their big antagonist had swung round and was in full view, end-on, against the sky, coming at a rush.

The gunners became frantic in their haste to fire again. They were so near the war correspondent could see the expression of their excited faces through his field-glass. As he looked he saw a man drop, and realized for the first time that the ironclad was shooting.

For a moment the big black monster crawled with an accelerated pace toward the furiously active gunners. Then, as if moved by a generous impulse, it turned its full broadside to their attack, and scarcely forty yards away from them. The war correspondent turned his field-glass back to the gunners and perceived it was now shooting down the men about the guns with the most deadly rapidity.

Just for a moment it seemed splendid, and then it seemed horrible. The gunners were dropping in heaps about their guns. To lay a hand on a gun was death. "Bang!" went the gun on the left, a hopeless miss, and that was the only second shot the half-battery fired. In another moment half-a-dozen surviving artillerymen were holding up their hands amidst a scattered muddle of dead and wounded men, and the fight was done.

The war correspondent hesitated between stopping in his scrub and waiting for an opportunity to surrender decently, or taking to an adjacent gully he had discovered. If he surrendered it was certain he would get no copy off; while, if he escaped, there were all sorts of chances. He decided to follow the gully, and take the first offer in the confusion beyond the camp of picking up a horse.

IV

Subsequent authorities have found fault with the first land ironclads in many particulars, but assuredly they served their purpose on the day of their appearance. They were essentially long, narrow, and very strong steel frameworks carrying the engines, and borne upon eight pairs of big pedrail wheels, each about ten feet in diameter, each a driving wheel and set upon long axles free to swivel round a common axis. This arrangement gave them a maximum of adaptability to the contours of the ground. They crawled level along the ground with one foot high upon a hillock and another deep in a depression, and they could hold themselves erect and steady sideways upon even a steep hillside. The engineers directed the engines under the command of the captain, who had lookout points at small ports all round the upper edge of the adjustable skirt of twelve-inch iron-plating which protected the whole affair, and who could also raise or depress a conning-tower set about the port-holes through the center of the iron top cover. The riflemen each occupied a small cabin of peculiar construction, and these cabins were slung along the sides of and before and behind the great main framework, in a manner suggestive of the slinging of the seats of an Irish jaunting-car. Their rifles, however, were very different pieces of apparatus from the simple mechanisms in the hands of their adversaries.

These were in the first place automatic, ejected their cartridges and loaded again from a magazine each time they fired, until the ammunition store was at an end, and they had the most remarkable sights imaginable, sights which threw a bright little camera-obscura picture into the light-tight box in which the rifleman sat below. This camera-obscura picture was marked with two crossed lines, and whatever was covered by the intersection of these two lines, that the rifle hit. The sighting was ingeniously contrived. The rifleman stood at the table with a thing like an elaboration of a draftsman's dividers in his hand, and he opened and closed these dividers, so that they were always at the apparent height—if

243

it was an ordinary-sized man—of the man he wanted to kill. A little twisted strand of wire like an electric-light wire ran from this implement up to the gun, and as the dividers opened and shut the sights went up or down. Changes in the clearness of the atmosphere, due to changes of moisture, were met by an ingenious use of that meteorologically sensitive substance, catgut, and when the land ironclad moved forward the sights got a compensatory deflection in the direction of its motion. The rifleman stood up in his pitch-dark chamber and watched the little picture before him. One hand held the dividers for judging distance, and the other grasped a big knob like a door-handle. As he pushed this knob about the rifle above swung to correspond, and the picture passed to and fro like an agitated panorama. When he saw a man he wanted to shoot he brought him up to the cross lines, and then pressed a finger upon a little push like an electric bell-push, conveniently placed in the center of the knob. Then the man was shot. If by any chance the rifleman missed his target he moved the knob a trifle, or readjusted his dividers, pressed the push, and got him the second time.

This rifle and its sights protruded from a port-hole, exactly like a great number of other port-holes that ran in a triple row under the eaves of the cover of the land ironclad. Each port-hole displayed a rifle and sight in dummy, so that the real ones could only be hit by a chance shot, and if one was, then the young man below said "Pshaw!" turned on an electric light, lowered the injured instrument into his camera, replaced the injured part, or put up a new rifle if the injury was considerable.

You must conceive these cabins as hung clear above the swing of the axles, and inside the big wheels upon which the great elephant-like feet were hung, and behind these cabins along the center of the monster ran a central gallery into which they opened, and along which worked the big compact engines. It was like a long passage into which this throbbing machinery had been packed, and the captain stood about the middle, close to the ladder that led to his conning-tower, and directed the silent, alert engineers—for the most part by signs. The throb and noise of the engines mingled with the reports of the rifles and the intermittent clangor of the bullet hail upon the armor. Ever and again he would touch the wheel that raised his conning-tower, step up his ladder until his engineers could see nothing of him above the waist, and then come down again with orders. Two small electric lights were all the illumination of this space—they were placed to make him most clearly visible to his subordinates; the air was thick with the smell of oil and petrol, and had the war correspondent been suddenly transferred from the spacious dawn outside to the bowels of this apparatus he would have thought himself fallen into another world.

The captain, of course, saw both sides of the battle. When he raised his head into his conning-tower there were the dewy sunrise, the amazed and disordered trenches, the flying and falling soldiers, the depressed-looking groups of prisoners, the beaten guns; when he bent down again to signal "half speed," "quarter speed," "half circle round toward the right," or what not, he was in the oil-smelling twilight of the ill-lit engine room. Close beside him on either side was the mouthpiece of a speaking tube, and ever and again he would direct one side or other of his strange craft to "concentrate fire forward on gunners," or to "clear out trench about a hundred yards on our right front."

He was a young man, healthy enough but by no means sun-tanned, and of a type of feature and expression that prevails in His Majesty's Navy: alert, intelligent, quiet. He and his engineers and his riflemen all went about their work, calm and reasonable men. They had none of that flapping strenuousness of the half-wit in a hurry, that excessive strain upon the blood vessels, that hysteria of effort which is so frequently regarded as the proper state of mind for heroic deeds.

For the enemy these young engineers were defeating they felt a certain qualified pity and a quite unqualified contempt. They regarded these big, healthy men they were shooting down precisely as these same big, healthy men might regard some inferior kind of being. They despised them for making war; despised their bawling patriotisms and their emotionality profoundly; despised them, above all, for the petty cunning and the almost brutish want of imagination their method of fighting displayed. "If they *must* make war," these young men thought, "why in thunder don't they do it like sensible men?" They resented the assumption that their own side was too stupid to do anything more than play their enemy's game, that they were going to play this costly folly according to the rules of unimaginative men. They resented being forced to the trouble of making man-killing machinery; resented the alternative of having to massacre these people or endure their truculent yapping; resented the whole unfathomable imbecility of war.

Meanwhile, with something of the mechanical precision of a good clerk posting a ledger, the riflemen moved their knobs and pressed their buttons. . . .

The captain of Land Ironclad Number Three had halted on the crest close to his captured half-battery. His lined-up prisoners stood hard by and waited for the cyclists behind to come for them. He surveyed the victorious morning through his conning-tower.

He read the general's signals. "Five and Four are to keep among the guns to the left and prevent any attempt to recover them. Seven and Eleven and Twelve, stick to the guns you have got; Seven, get into position to command the guns taken by Three. Then we're to do something else, are we? Six and One, quicken up to about ten miles an hour and walk round behind that camp to the levels near the river—we shall bag the whole crowd of them," interjected the young man. "Ah, here we are! Two and Three, Eight and Nine, Thirteen and Fourteen, space out to a thousand yards, wait for the word, and then go slowly to cover the advance of the cyclist infantry against any charge of mounted troops. That's all right. But where's Ten? Halloa! Ten to repair and get movable as soon as possible. They've broken up Ten!"

The discipline of the new war machines was businesslike rather than pedantic, and the head of the captain came down out of the conning-tower to tell his men. "I say, you chaps there. They've broken up Ten. Not badly, I think; but anyhow, he's stuck."

But that still left thirteen of the monsters in action to finish up the broken army.

The war correspondent stealing down his gully looked back and saw them all lying along the crest and talking fluttering congratulatory flags to one another. Their iron sides were shining golden in the light of the rising sun.

V

The private adventures of the war correspondent terminated in surrender about one o'clock in the afternoon, and by that time he had stolen a horse, pitched off it, and narrowly escaped being rolled upon; found the brute had broken its leg, and shot it with his revolver. He had spent some hours in the company of a squad of dispirited riflemen, had quarrelled with them about topography at last, and gone off by himself in a direction that should have brought him to the banks of the river and didn't. Moreover, he had eaten all his chocolate and found nothing in the whole world to drink. Also, it had become extremely hot. From behind a broken, but attractive, stone wall he had seen far away in the distance the defender-horsemen trying to charge cyclists in open order, with land ironclads outflanking them on either side. He had discovered that cyclists could retreat over open turf before horsemen with a sufficient margin of speed to allow of frequent dismounts and much terribly effective sharp-shooting; and he had a sufficient persuasion that those horsemen, having charged their hearts out, had halted just beyond his range of vision and surrendered. He had been urged to sudden activity by a forward movement of one of those machines that had threatened to enfilade his wall. He had discovered a fearful blister on his heel.

He was now in a scrubby gravelly place, sitting down and meditating on his pocket-handkerchief, which had in some extraordinary way become in the last twenty-four hours extremely ambiguous in hue. "It's the whitest thing I've got," he said.

He had known all along that the enemy was east, west, and south of him, but when he heard land ironclads Numbers One and Six talking in their measured, deadly way not half a mile to the north he decided to make his own little unconditional peace without any further risks. He was for hoisting his white flag to a bush and taking up a position of modest obscurity near it until someone came along. He became aware of voices, clatter, and the distinctive noises of a body of horse, quite near, and he put his handkerchief in his pocket again and went to see what was going forward.

The sound of firing ceased, and then as he drew near he heard the deep sounds of many simple, coarse, but hearty and noble-hearted soldiers of the old school swearing with vigor.

He emerged from his scrub upon a big level plain, and far away a fringe of trees marked the banks of the river.

In the center of the picture was a still intact road bridge, and a big railway bridge a little to the right. Two land ironclads rested, with a general air of being long, harmless sheds, in a pose of anticipatory peacefulness right and left of the picture, completely commanding two miles and more of the river levels. Emerged and halted a few yards from the scrub was the remainder of the defenders' cavalry, dusty, a little disordered, and obviously annoyed, but still a very fine show of men. In the middle distance three or four men and horses were receiving medical attendance, and nearer a knot of officers regarded the distant novelties in mechanism with profound distaste. Every one was very distinctly aware of the twelve other ironclads, and of the multitude of townsmen soldiers on bicycles or afoot, encumbered now by prisoners and captured war-gear but otherwise thoroughly effective, who were sweeping like a great net in their rear.

"Checkmate," said the war correspondent, walking out into the open. "But I surrender in the best of company. Twenty-four hours ago I thought war was impossible—and these beggars have captured the whole blessed army! Well! Well!" He thought of his talk with the young lieutenant. "If there's no end to the surprises of science, the civilized people have it, of course. As long as their science keeps going they will necessarily be ahead of open-country men. Still. . . ." He wondered for a space what might have happened to the young lieutenant.

The war correspondent was one of those inconsistent people who always want the beaten side to win. When he saw all these burly, sun-tanned horsemen, disarmed and dismounted and lined up; when he saw their horses unskillfully led away by the singularly not equestrian cyclists to whom they had surrendered; when he saw these truncated Paladins watching this scandalous sight, he forgot altogether that he had called these men "cunning louts" and wished them beaten not four-and-twenty hours ago. A month ago he had seen that regiment in its pride going forth to war, and had been told of its terrible prowess, how it could charge in open order with each man firing from his saddle, and sweep before it anything else that ever came out to battle in any sort of order, foot or horse. And it had had to fight a few score of young men in atrociously unfair machines!

"Manhood *versus* Machinery" occurred to him as a suitable head-line. Journalism curdles all one's mind to phrases.

He strolled as near the lined-up prisoners as the sentinels seemed disposed to permit, and surveyed them and compared their sturdy proportions with those of their lightly built captors.

"Smart degenerates," he muttered. "Anemic cockneydom."

The surrendered officers came quite close to him presently, and he could hear the colonel's high-pitched tenor. The poor gentleman had spent three years of arduous toil upon the best material in the world perfecting that shooting from the saddle charge, and he was inquiring with phrases of blasphemy, natural in the circumstances, what one could be expected to do against this suitably consigned ironmongery.

"Guns," said some one.

"Big guns they can walk round. You can't shift big guns to keep pace with them, and little guns in the open they rush. I saw 'em rushed. You might do a surprise now and then—assassinate the brutes, perhaps—"

"You might make things like 'em."

"What? *More* ironmongery? Us? . . ."

"I'll call my article," meditated the war correspondent, " 'Mankind *versus* Ironmongery,' and quote the old boy at the beginning."

And he was much too good a journalist to spoil his contrast by remarking that the half-dozen comparatively slender young men in blue pajamas who were standing about their victorious land ironclad, drinking coffee and eating biscuits, had also in their eyes and carriage something not altogether degraded below the level of a man.